Death of a
of a
Snow
Ghost

Death
of a
Snow
Ghost

A Cabin by the Lake Mystery

Linda Norlander

LEVEL
BEST BOOKS

For Miranda, Nadia and Gus with love

Praise for A Cabin by the Lake Mysteries

Praise for *Death of a Starling*

"*Death of A Starling*, the second novel in Linda Norlander's delightful A Cabin by the Lake mystery series, offers something compelling for every reader. If you're partial to sense of place, *Starling* delivers a wonderful evocation of Minnesota's great Northwoods. Interesting characters, some quirky, some very dark, jump from the pages of every chapter. There's a bit of romance, a lot of suspense, some fine inclusion of elements of the Ojibwe culture, and a wonderfully serpentine plot that's sure to keep you guessing to the end. I can't think of a better read at a summer cabin or in front of a roaring winter fire."—William Kent Krueger, *New York Times* Best-Selling Author

Praise for *Death of a Snow Ghost*

"Trouble finds Jamie and this time it's as deep as the snow outside her door. The easiest of her worries is a deadline for a manuscript, and uncertain love adds a wrinkle. The real challenge begins when she literally drives into a unique criminal enterprise. It's cold in the Land of 10,000 Lakes, but Linda Norlander's deft storytelling reveals just how deep desire and greed run, and how compassion and understanding are the ultimate warmth."—Gabriel Valjan, author of the Company Files and Shane Cleary Mysteries series

"In *Death of a Snow Ghost*, author Linda Norlander delivers another riveting tale. The writing is as sharp as a Minnesota winter and as sympathetic as its amateur-sleuth heroine, Jamie Forest. Norlander reaches for, and achieves, a book that far surpasses the confines of its genre. The villains, as well as the heroes, are fully fleshed characters, and the narrative is tightly woven around the central theme of justice. Past and present collide as Jamie embarks upon her pursuit of a killer who targets the most vulnerable of young women. Romance and humor, thrills and chills, and a most satisfying conclusion make *Death of a Snow Ghost* a must-read book."—Lori Robbins, author of the On Pointe and Master Class mystery series

A Roadside Delivery

The car filled with the aroma of fresh-baked pumpkin pies for my first Thanksgiving in the cabin by Lake Larissa. Since my cooking skills did not include making pies, I'd ordered them from the bakery in town. Tomorrow I would thaw the twenty-two-pound turkey sitting in a box in the back seat and use the tattered Betty Crocker cookbook I'd bought at a garage sale to make a stuffing for it. I would show my skeptical Minnesota friends that even a girl from New York City could make a Norman Rockwell feast.

I was driving on the highway between town and the cabin in an area the locals called the marsh. It was a lowland filled with high weeds, cattails and skeletal tamarack. It had the air of desolation and loneliness, a wasteland before coming upon the Northwoods forest. I never liked driving the five miles across it.

As I breathed in the spicy nutmeg of the pumpkin pies, I was reminded of the Thanksgiving in New York when my mother and I came across the snow lady. I must have been about seven and we were on our way to the Macy's Thanksgiving Day Parade. A light dusting of snow covered the park as we walked by the bench where she lay. She was wrapped in an olive-green blanket with a thin layer of snow covering her.

Something about the color of the skin on her face intrigued me. I ran to her before my mother could hold me back. Close up I saw her eyes, wide open, clouded and unseeing. As my mother pulled me away, I remember crying out. "Mama, is that lady a ghost?"

"No, honey, she's just sleeping."

1

She hurried me to a bakery across from the park where she told me to stay in front. She went back to talk with the clerk, and I stood in the doorway inhaling the rich smells of pumpkin pies.

Later, when the parade was over and we were walking back by the park, the bench was empty. "Mama, I guess the snow ghost lady waked up."

Mama grabbed my arm and tugged me along. All she said was, "It's not 'waked' honey, it's 'woke.'" Mother was a stickler about grammar.

Today I noticed how a light snowfall had dusted the weeds in the ditch just like that day in the park. With a light shudder, I brought my thoughts back to the present. While I mentally ticked off the tasks to do before Thanksgiving a sudden snow squall blew across the road. The swirling snow created hypnotic patterns on the pavement. As I watched the dancing snow in front of me, I thought I caught a movement out of the corner of my eye.

"What was that?"

It looked like a ghost shrouded in a white haze. Ahead on my side of the road, it weaved in and out of my sight. The snow squall thickened, and the apparition disappeared. Did I really see a ghost?

Squeezing my eyes shut for a moment, I muttered, "Come on Jamie. You know there are no ghosts."

I slowed down, creeping forward in hopes that I had imagined the movement. I had too much to do before Thanksgiving to have to deal with someone drunk on the side of the road. For a moment, the air cleared. I saw nothing on the road or on the shoulder.

Just as I was speeding up, the ghost lurched back on the shoulder from the tall, boggy weeds of the ditch. This time I saw it was a human dressed in a white puffy jacket and white pants. I slammed on my brakes as the person in white turned and staggered onto the road. In the millisecond it took for the brakes to hold, I prayed not to hear a thump against the car.

The car skidded to a halt as my heart pounded so hard, I felt it in my eyes. Quickly unstrapping my seatbelt, I threw open the car door and dashed out. A gust of wind sent icy stinging snow into my face and a chill down my back. The ghost stood in front of the car swaying. She was no phantom, just a young woman, possibly a teenager. She grimaced in pain.

2

"My God. Did I hit you?"

She continued to sway.

Was she drunk? I stepped closer to her. "Are you alright?"

Moaning, she bent over, clutching her stomach. I saw the swell of her belly beneath the puffy jacket.

When I reached her, she gasped, *"Bebé* coming!"

I took her arm, hoping for a passing car to flag down. This part of the road had little traffic after tourist season. Still, I strained to hear a car approaching. All I heard was the sweep of wind whistling through the weeds. Guiding her back to car, I helped her into the passenger seat. "It's okay. I'll get help."

I tried my phone knowing the cell reception in the marsh was spotty. *Please have some bars.*

Nothing.

Next to me, her face reddened as she started to bear down. My knowledge of women in labor was limited to season one of *Call the Midwife.* Even so, I knew she shouldn't be pushing until I got help.

"Don't push," I pleaded. "We have to get you to the hospital."

She ignored me. *"Bebé* coming!"

What now? I shut my eyes, picturing the television midwives. I needed to look, to see if the baby's head was coming out.

"Back seat. We need to put you in the backseat so I can check for the baby."

"¡Ayudame! ¡Ayudame!"

As she cried out, I noticed her Hispanic features—the tangle of dark hair that had slipped out of a ponytail and the smooth tan of her skin. "Do you speak English?"

"¡No mucha!"

I tugged at her to get her out of the front of the car and into the back. This time I kept up a mantra from my limited knowledge of Spanish. *"Está bien."*

Shoving the box with the frozen turkey and the boxes of pies onto the floor, I eased her into the back seat. "I have to look."

She grunted with effort. I got as close to her face as possible and showed her how to blow with her lips closed like the laboring women on television did.

While she panted and blew, I pulled down the white pants and underwear. They were soaked. I didn't want to look. I wanted to be happily on my way to the cabin.

The top of a little head with dark hair shown through. "Crowning," I gasped, remembering what the midwives had called it. What did they do next? My brain stalled as I swallowed back panic. *Come on, Jamie. People have babies every day. You can do this.*

I didn't hear the car pull up behind me as I bent over to get closer to the baby. My mind was on autopilot. Catch the baby, make sure it's breathing, keep it warm. My Spanish disappeared as I repeated over and over. "It's okay, it's okay."

The head began to emerge. I nearly jumped when a deep, resonant voice asked, "Is everything all right?" I turned quickly to see a man in his late thirties with brown hair pulled back in a ponytail and a pierced ear with a diamond stud. He wore a beige wool overcoat and leather driving gloves. Both were too fancy for this part of the state.

"She's having a baby. Could you get help? No cellphone reception here." I turned back to the girl. She took a deep breath ready to push. "Hurry. Your phone should work if you drive a mile up the road. Tell them she's crowning and we're at milepost 43."

"Uh, okay." He leaned over my shoulder to look in. For a moment, the girl stared at his face. I could have sworn I heard her gasp as her eyes widened.

"Hurry!" I snapped at him. "This baby is coming!"

As I concentrated on the baby sliding out, I heard the sound of car tires. "Help is coming," I said more to myself than the girl.

"Keep it warm, Jamie. Keep the baby warm." I looked around for something. The only blanket I had was in the back of the car. In the box with the frozen turkey, however, was a brand-new white hand-embroidered tablecloth, my one extravagant purchase for the Thanksgiving dinner. As the baby emerged, I grabbed the tablecloth.

"*Bebé* okay?" The mother gasped, raising her head.

The baby was pink and warm and wet in my hands as I wrapped the tablecloth around her. She squawked and let out a cry, her face turning red with effort. "She's okay!"

"*¿Una niña?*"

"*Sí, una niña.*"

I found tears dribbling down my cheeks as I handed the baby to her. For a moment, I was reluctant to let the crying infant go as if she now belonged to me. How often does one accidentally deliver a baby?

Taking a deep breath, I laughed. "She's beautiful. Ah, *bonita.* Yes?"

"*Sí. Sí. Bonita.*" The girl looked at me, her large brown eyes shining with tears.

A gust of wind swept through the open door of the car. I needed to close it and crank up the heater.

The ambulance arrived faster than I expected. I had just covered the girl with the blanket from the back of the car when I heard the siren.

As it approached, the girl looked at me and I saw fear in how her eyes widened. "No take *bebé. Por favor.* No take *bebé.*" She started to cry.

To calm her I introduced myself. "*Mi llamo* Jamie." I pointed to myself ruing the decision I'd made years ago to study Italian rather than Spanish.

"*Mi llamo Carmela.*"

I smiled, pointing to the baby. "*¿Su nombre?*"

She frowned. "No take *bebé!*"

"No one is going to take your baby. You relax." I had no idea if she understood me, but she managed a weak smile.

Seth, one of the volunteer EMTs, ran the hardware store in town. He approached the car with the same calm manner he used on his customers who were dealing with leaky toilets and broken windows. "What have we got here?"

Relieved, I felt a little giddiness come on. "Oh, you know, your normal roadside delivery." I filled him in on what little I knew about her while his partner, a clerk from the hospital tended to the new mom and baby. "She says her name is Carmela and she seems very afraid that someone is going to take her baby."

"We'll get her to the hospital and they can sort things out." As they eased her out of the backseat of the car, he turned to me with a grin. "Nice work—for a mob lady, that is."

Since arriving in the Northwoods of Minnesota, my New York accent had pegged me as one of the Sopranos. I laughed at him. "You'd be surprised what they teach you in Mafia school."

As the ambulance drove away, I felt something drain from me. Suddenly, my legs were shaky, and my head was too heavy for my body. I stretched my arms over my head, letting my breath out slowly, "All right. Back to your boring life."

I wondered about the man with the diamond earring and silently thanked him for making the call. I drove home with the sweet smell of new baby mingling with the spice of pumpkin pie wondering who Carmela was, why she was alone on that road, and why she was so afraid. It struck me that she might have been running away. But from what?

"Not your concern, Jamie." My voice had a hoarse quality to it as I spoke to the empty passenger seat. Since moving to the cabin and living alone, I found I was talking a lot to either my dog or the empty air.

When I arrived home, Bronte, my rescue dog greeted me with so much enthusiasm she almost knocked me over as I maneuvered into the kitchen with the frozen turkey and pies. She sniffed at the box and looked at me with a puzzled expression.

"I know. I know. You smell something besides pumpkin pie, don't you?"

Once settled, I resisted calling the hospital for an update until I'd poured myself a beer. I toasted the newborn and punched in the number of the hospital.

Norma, the head nurse answered. "Ah, Jamie. I hear you're the new Jackpine County midwife. How are you doing?"

I laughed. She was on my Thanksgiving guest list because her kids were all in Minneapolis and she had to work the Thanksgiving evening shift. "I'm happily toasting the new baby. How are mom and baby doing?"

Norma hesitated. I assumed it was because she wasn't allowed to give out patient information. "We've been requested not to give out any information on the 'Mary's Place' girls."

"Mary's Place? What's that?"

A buzzer rang in the background. "Oops. Gotta go. I'll explain at Thanksgiving. Oh, and you didn't hear it from me, but the two of them are fine. Baby is a little small but doing well."

After she hung up, I googled "Mary's Place, Killdeer, Minnesota" but found nothing. "Curious." A spiderlike tingling crawled up the back of my neck. Why was a young woman in labor wandering out on the bog? Was she running away from something, or to something?

Bronte stared up at me. I patted her head. "So strange. Here I was musing about the sleeping lady who was probably dead, and I ended up holding a new life. Who knew?"

That night, a dream came to me. I cradled a newborn baby holding it close to my body knowing that somewhere in the shadows a man stood reaching for her.

Mary's Place

On Wednesday I busied myself with Thanksgiving preparations. The instructions on the turkey suggested thawing in the refrigerator, but it was still rock-solid frozen. I finally called Jilly, my friend who works for the *Killdeer Times* for help.

"It's not going to thaw in time. What should I do?"

Jilly laughed. "You've never wrestled a twenty-pound frozen turkey before, have you?"

"Well, to be honest, my dad and I used to celebrate Thanksgiving by going to this wonderful Thai restaurant in Queens." I pictured the small café filled with the aroma of curry and added, "My only experience with a turkey is the one I married and eventually divorced."

Jilly gave me instructions on safe thawing that didn't involve my plan of plunging the bird into hot water. "Put it out on the counter and wrap it with newspapers so it stays chilled while it thaws. If it's not thawed by tonight, put it in cold water and change the water often."

We talked about my dinner party and what the guests were bringing. "I'm doing the turkey, dressing, potatoes and gravy. They're contributing the rest."

Jilly sounded amused. "Hope we don't have a snowstorm, or you might be stuck eating it all yourself. By the way, I thought your roadside delivery would be a great story for the *Times*, but Jeanine, my sulky editor said it would be old news by next week when we do the post-Thanksgiving edition. Besides, the new mom is from Mary's Place and they don't like publicity."

"What do you know about Mary's Place?"

"Not much. A young couple moved into the old Torgerson house on the edge of town this fall. You know the one near the beginning of the Lady Slipper trail?"

She was referring to a two-story house with a sagging porch. "That house looked like it needed some work."

"No kidding. It's one of the properties owned by M.C. Bevins."

"You mean the guy who owns the trucking company?"

"And half the town."

I remembered him from a county board meeting. He was a big, gruff-looking man in his late fifties. He was promoting the mining operation at the same time our Lady Slipper Trail Group was trying to convince the board members of the dangers to our lakes.

"What is this Mary's Place?" It sounded a little like a convent or something.

"It's a shelter of some sort. They have three or four pregnant girls there. They say the girls come from detention centers near the Mexican border." She put her hand over the phone and said something to someone in the office. When she came back, she apologized. "Oh. Sorry. I have to deal with a delivery problem." She chuckled. "A paper delivery, not a baby delivery."

After the call, I wondered again why Carmela was on that lonely stretch of highway. Maybe she was disoriented and trying to get back home or to her family. Since I needed to drive into town for another tablecloth, I decided I'd stop by the hospital with a gift for the baby.

Bronte brought the smell of fresh air with her when she trotted through the door. I'd never noticed air quality until I moved to Lake Larissa. In New York summer or winter we always had exhaust and garbage mingled in with the odors of fried food. Before closing the door, I took a deep breath, savoring the crispness and scent of pine. "Ah wilderness."

After hefting the frozen turkey onto the counter and wrapping it up in layers of the *Killdeer Times*, I pulled on my woolen hat and jacket. Before I walked out the door, I squatted down and scratched Bronte behind the ears. "Now, remember, girl, that bird is not for you. Don't you dare think otherwise." Bronte licked my hand as if she understood.

Was it really a good idea to leave the Thanksgiving turkey with a dog who liked nothing better than to chew on dead chipmunks?

The sky was a brilliant blue in the slanted lighting of the winter sun. When I drove through the marsh, I noted exactly where I'd stopped to avoid the snow ghost. Multiple car tracks crisscrossed the shoulder of the road. I thought about Carmela and the joy on her face as she held her baby and for a moment, I also remembered the look of fear when the stranger in the expensive coat stopped to help.

Killdeer bustled with shoppers picking up groceries and supplies for the holiday. Even the parking lot in front of North Country Gifts was full. A bell jingled when I opened the door and I was bathed in the warmth of the shop and the mingled smells of cinnamon and vanilla. Several people browsed the aisles looking at the usual gift shop crafts, soaps, and artwork. In a corner with the children's section, I found exactly what I wanted. It was a small, stuffed teddy bear wearing a heart necklace.

Along with the teddy bear, I picked out another embroidered tablecloth, cringing at how much this would set my tight budget back. The embroidery around the edges of the cream-colored linen cloth was done in a multicolor geometric pattern. Studying it, I admired the intricacy of the stitching as I waited in line at the counter.

Brad, the owner of the shop and husband to my friend Rob raised his eyebrows at me when I reached him. The two of them were guests for my dinner tomorrow. "I hear you've been on some deliveries."

"No secrets in this town."

A brief frown crossed his face. "No kidding about that."

He and Rob as the first married gay couple in Killdeer had endured a lot a few years ago when they announced their plan to wed. The furor died down quickly however because they were both so well-liked. Still, every once in a while, the shop had been vandalized. The last time, when someone spray painted "fags not welcome" on the store window, a group from one of the churches known for its conservative views showed up unannounced with buckets and cleaning supplies and washed it off.

As a line formed behind me, I quickly gave Brad my credit card, keeping my fingers crossed that I hadn't maxed it out. "I hear you're bringing something special."

His eyes sparkled. "It's a surprise. Rob said his grandmother used to make it. We'll see if I can pull it off."

While Rob was full-blooded Ojibwe, Brad was blond-haired and blue-eyed. I loved the idea of something native and local to go with the turkey and fixings. I wished him luck. "Can't wait."

Outside, the sun's glare obscured my vision and I accidentally bumped into a man walking toward the store. My package went flying. "Oops, sorry." We both bent down to pick it up. When I shaded my eyes and looked at him the first thing I noticed was the diamond stud earring.

"You're the person who called the ambulance yesterday, aren't you?"

He studied me for a moment before handing me the package. A smile formed, revealing a dimple on his chin. "Oh, sure." He extended his hand. "Nice to meet you under different circumstances. I'm Rex Jordan."

I shook his hand. "Jamie Forest."

He wore dark glasses that matched his face shape. He reminded me of the Wall Street brokers I used to see hurrying down the street in Manhattan holding their smartphones and talking as if the rest of the world didn't exist.

We stood for a moment in silence until I realized I was staring. Clearing my throat, I lifted my package, "A gift for the new baby."

His smile widened revealing perfect white teeth. "I hear they are doing fine."

"Uh, thanks for calling the ambulance."

He nodded. "Good timing, I guess."

I wanted to know what someone dressed like an ad in *GQ* was doing in Killdeer. The politeness my father taught me, told me to hold my tongue. Instead, I opened the bag to make sure the teddy bear hadn't gotten wet.

He pointed to it. "I hope it's okay."

"I think the bear will survive."

Rex wrinkled his brow for a moment as if trying to figure out if I was serious. His expression smoothed and he laughed. "They're tough—those teddys."

Again, we were both silent. I really needed to get to the hospital and back to the cabin to make sure Bronte hadn't eaten the turkey. "Well, I should be going."

As I stepped away, he called. "Wait. Would you like to grab a cup of coffee?"

I hesitated only a moment. How could I turn down a man in a Norwegian Wool coat and Ray-Ban glasses? "Sure. I could use some coffee."

We walked a few storefronts down the street to Swenson's Bakery. Like the gift shop, the bakery was thick with the scents of cinnamon and sweet spices. The owner, wearing a crisp white apron, took our order at the counter. "I hear you're the new midwife in town." While she talked to me, she kept an admiring gaze on Rex.

"I don't plan to make a career of it." I watched her watching him. Rex was worth an admiring gaze. No doubt about that.

Before I could pay, Rex handed her a twenty. "My treat."

We sat at a little table by the window. I observed a couple of women looking at us from across the street. I guessed they were wondering about Rex. So was I.

"Um," I found myself stumbling for words as we settled into the chair. "What brings you to Killdeer?"

"Business."

"Oh?"

He set his coffee cup down. "I'm an immigration lawyer. I've been doing some pro bono work with a non-profit to help the girls at Mary's Place."

I remembered Carmela's expression when she saw him. Maybe it wasn't fear like I'd first thought. "Oh. I thought Carmela might have recognized you."

"Could be, although I've barely met the girls—got into town yesterday."

"I hear they come from detention camps. Is that true?"

He lowered his voice. "It's complicated."

"Do you have any idea why Carmela was out on the highway yesterday?"

"The girls at Mary's Place have had significant trauma in their lives. Maybe the pain of labor caused her to run. I'm not sure we'll ever know." He stirred a lump of sugar into his coffee. "Did she say anything to you about me?"

I chuckled. "Ah, she was kind of busy at the time."

He nodded. "Sometimes the girls are afraid of me at first. They don't have much reason to trust people."

I thought about that lonely stretch of highway. "Were you looking for her?"

He held his hands up. "Actually, no. I'm embarrassed to say, I was lost. Took a wrong turn, I guess."

"Oh." There were very few wrong turns to take in Killdeer, but I didn't pursue it.

The door opened and a woman walked in talking loudly. "Did you hear about that girl having her baby in the back of someone's car? They say she's one of those illegals. They just want to have their brats here so they can stay." Her companion shushed her pointing to our table.

I recognized the woman with the braying voice. Last summer when we were working with another environmental group to halt the development of mining in the county, she was one of the loudest voices in support of the mining company at a community meeting.

I whispered, "She thinks anyone who isn't like her should go back to 'where they came.' Including the Native Americans…and me."

Rex raised his eyebrows pushing his chair back. "You see what I mean about things being complicated?" He glanced at his watch. "Unfortunately, I have to be on my way." He stood, offering me his hand. "Nice meeting you, Jamie Forest. Maybe we can do this again sometime."

Before we parted, we exchanged business cards. He read mine and smiled. "Freelance editor, eh? How's business?"

I laughed even though the reality wasn't very funny. "It's good enough to keep my dog fed."

Rex's card showed that his office was in El Paso, Texas. Probably a good place to practice immigration law.

"You're a long way from home."

His phone rang before he could answer. "Sorry, I've got to get this."

The braying woman stared at me as we walked out. I tried to imagine what was going through her head, but decided she wasn't worth the effort.

It was almost noon when I walked up to the nurse's station at the hospital.

I didn't know the nurse on duty. Norma was off today working on what she called her mother's special Thanksgiving dish. Since Norma was full-blooded Ojibwe, I assumed it would be an old family native recipe. The nurse at the station glanced up at me from her place in front of the computer screen.

"Hi, I'm here to see Carmela and her new baby."

I braced myself to argue with her if she said Carmela wasn't allowed visitors. "Sure." She pointed down the hall. "Room 102. Baby is with her."

The window drapes were pulled against the glare of the sunlight. Carmela sat up in bed cradling her baby and singing softly to her. She glanced up with a startled expression. As soon as she recognized me her face broke into a big smile. She pointed to the baby sleeping in her arms. *"Su nombre es Bonita Amy."*

I stood by her resisting the temptation to touch the little head. "Her name?"

"Si. Si. Bonita Amy." She pointed at me her smile widening, *"Amy."*

"Oh my god. You mean Jamie? My name?"

"Si."

I had to wipe away the tear that slipped down my cheek. I hardly deserved to have a baby named after me. "Thank you. It's an honor." I handed her the little teddy bear. "For Bonita Amy."

She lifted the baby to me with a nod. I held her as she made newborn grunting noises. "Beautiful baby."

When the nurse came in, I found I was reluctant to give her back. She felt so warm in my arms. "Sorry to interrupt but we need to do some lab work and have the doctor check you out."

Once again, I saw the look of fear. I remembered what Rex had said about the trauma she probably had gone through. As I handed the baby back, I assured her. "I'll come back to visit. Okay?"

She nodded. "Pleeze help me."

Reaching in my bag, I took out one of my cards. "You can call me anytime."

Outside, the temperature had dropped. A chill gust of wind cut through me as I hurried to the car. The weather was changing.

Thanksgiving

Once home, I found Bronte parked by the kitchen counter staring longingly at the thawing turkey. I laughed off the sense of chill I'd felt in the hospital parking lot. Everything would be all right. Besides, I had a text on my phone from Jim saying he hoped to make it for dinner tomorrow.

Jim Monroe was a State Trooper currently stationed in Minneapolis, five hours away. We'd met last summer. He claimed to have been taken in by my New York accent and 'East Coast tree-hugger mentality.' I claimed I only wanted him for his money and his muscular thighs. Our relationship and time in bed had been interrupted this fall because his young son was being treated for leukemia in the Twin Cities.

"Good news, girl. Jim is coming tomorrow." I clicked off the phone, opened the door and shooed Bronte out. "You need a break from bird-watching."

On Thanksgiving morning, I was up before the sun. According to Betty Crocker's cookbook, I needed to get the turkey stuffed and in the oven to roast for six to seven hours. Dinner was planned for three in the afternoon, and I wanted the big bird to be roasting by eight.

Jilly had warned me that I had to take the gizzards and neck out of the cavity of the turkey. What she failed to tell me was how difficult it was to try to pull them out when the turkey was still icy on the inside. I wrestled with it, cursing aloud until Bronte pawed at my leg with a worried whine.

"It's okay, girl," I grunted, finally getting the neck out. I stared at it and the giblets in their little paper pack. "Yuck. I think I'll become a vegetarian." To make matters worse, the phone pinged with a text from Jim.

Sorry. Roads icy. Called into work. Can't make the party.

The sad-face emoji did not make me feel any better. I resisted texting my disappointment. Instead, I took a photo of the uncooked turkey. **See what u r missing?**

By late morning the cabin filled with the aroma of roasting turkey. I sat at the table peeling potatoes and thinking about Carmela and the baby with my name. She seemed so afraid someone would take the baby. I'd never had a child, but for a brief moment, I'd felt that bond when I held Bonita Amy. Now that the baby was born, would she be returned to a wretched detention center? Would she be deported? As far as I knew, because she was born here, Bonita was officially an American citizen, but I wasn't sure of Carmela's status.

Maybe after Thanksgiving, I would contact Rex and find out what he knew. From the little I'd read, immigration laws and refugee status were complex issues made more complicated by people who wanted to "keep America for the Americans."

When I looked out the window after the last potato was peeled, fluffy snowflakes drifted down from the sky. By the time the guests arrived, the yard would be covered in white, a perfect setting.

The snow stopped before any of the guests came, but the sky remained a slate gray. The weather app on my phone predicted more snow later in the afternoon. I built a fire in the fireplace and watched as the logs sparked and crackled. "The Hallmark Channel couldn't do much better than this, could they?" I patted Bronte as she lay in front of the fire licking little ice balls off her paws.

Clarence Engstrom and Joe Pelletier arrived first. Clarence was the octogenarian town lawyer and Joe was his aide-de-camp. Cold winter air followed them in.

"Smells delightful," Clarence declared. Joe, in his usual manner, simply nodded.

"No girlfriend?" I asked him. His expression darkened as he shook his head.

"Had a little tiff, I'm told," Clarence whispered as if Joe couldn't hear him.

16

Joe handed me a covered bowl. "Cranberries from Clarence's house-keeper."

"Couldn't have Thanksgiving without cranberries," Clarence winked. "Of course, I can't stand them. Never could."

Soon after they settled in front of the fireplace with mugs of hot apple cider, Rob and Brad arrived. Rob had built my new kitchen cabinets last summer and was my go-to handyman for anything that went wrong in the cabin. He stood in the doorway in a red checkered flannel shirt looking like a Native American version of Paul Bunyan. Brad, much shorter, looked like he'd just walked out of a high-end men's clothing store in his creased slacks, crisp shirt, and little bowtie. How the two of them found each other was still a mystery to me.

"I brought corn, blueberry, and wild rice salad. Rob assures me it tastes just like his grandmother's." Brad set a bowl covered in plastic wrap on the counter. "I haven't sampled it yet."

"Looks tasty."

I heated the water for the potatoes while the four of them chatted in the living room. Norma arrived as the water started to bubble. "Smells heavenly in here." She carried her casserole dish to the oven. "This needs to be warmed. Do you have room for it?"

To my dismay, an odor of burnt meat wafted into the kitchen when she opened the oven door. "Looks like your drumsticks are well-done."

I stared at the deep brown almost charred look of the turkey drumsticks. "Oh damn. Now what do I do? The thermometer says the turkey isn't done, yet." Where was Betty Crocker when I needed her?

Norma tut-tutted, grabbed some aluminum foil, and wrapped up the legs and the wings. "That should do it."

"They didn't teach me about roasting birds in my poetry MFA program, I'm afraid. Glad I have a nurse around to bandage the bird."

Norma smiled. "My suggestion? Next year roast it in a plastic roasting bag. Works for me every time."

Travis Booker, my last guest arrived just before the turkey came out of the oven. He was still dressed in his State Trooper uniform. With a sheepish shrug, he contributed a box of potato chips to the feast. "Sorry. No time to cook."

I doubted Travis had cooked more than a microwave dinner in his life. Clarence called over his shoulder, "Bet you fried those chips yourself."

"Yup. Then I took them to the Old Dutch Potato Chip factory to have them packaged."

Aside from turkey drumsticks and wings that were too dry and chewy, the bird came out okay, but it wouldn't make the cover of *Bon Appetit* anytime soon. We sat at the table with its new tablecloth and toasted each other.

"To friends." I clinked my glass against Joe's.

Clarence pointed to Norma's casserole. "I haven't had a green bean casserole since my wife died."

I tasted it. "Native American recipe?"

Everyone at the table laughed. Norma explained. "It's the famous cream of mushroom soup, green bean and fried onion ring casserole. Been in the family since the fifties."

"Even my mother used to make it on the reservation." Rob winked.

I looked at my guests and thought about Thanksgiving last year in New York. My dad had died, my husband had found someone new and I was being evicted from my apartment. I spent the holiday with a plate of macaroni and cheese and a bottle of wine wondering what to do with my life. I woke up the next morning with a massive hangover, an upset stomach, and a resolve to make a change.

Conversation at the table quickly turned to my baby delivery experience. With a touch of embarrassment, I told them about Bonita Amy's name. "She couldn't quite pronounce Jamie."

"Poor girl." Norma helped herself to more mashed potatoes. "I wonder what will happen to her?"

"I know she's terrified that someone will try to take her baby." I thought about her desperate words asking me to help. "I hope Rex can sort it out for her."

Travis looked up from his plate with a puzzled expression. "Who's Rex?"

I told them about how he called for the ambulance and how we had coffee yesterday. "He told me he's an immigration lawyer. He should be able to help her."

I looked at the faces at the table and felt a sinking feeling. Could she be helped? With resolve, I said, "How about we have a toast to the new baby and wish her well." I raised my wine glass.

Later, when I served the pumpkin pie, Rob commented, "This is the best pie I think I've ever tasted."

I laughed, looking at Travis. "I made them all myself and brought them into town to the bakery to have them boxed."

It started snowing again as we were finishing dessert and drinking coffee. Norma glanced outside. "I should go. Sorry to eat and run, but I'm doing the twelve-hour night shift. Need to be there by seven and I don't want to end up in a snowdrift."

Everyone else agreed that while it was a wonderful party, the snow was sending them scurrying. Only Travis lingered.

I knew he liked me, but I had made it clear earlier in the fall that I was committed to Jim. Still, I enjoyed his company. We sat on the floor in front of the fireplace with Bronte happily chewing a rawhide toy between us.

"So." He stared at the fire. "You've added baby delivery to your skills."

"If only I could charge, I might be able to afford to pay the electric bill next month."

"That bad?"

My financial woes were not a secret. When I'd moved to the cabin last spring, I'd had this naïve New Yorkers notion that as long as I owned the cabin I could live on very little. I didn't account for unglamorous things like a new furnace, a tank of propane to keep it going, and a new septic system. My bank account was in the "eking by" stage. What little regular income I had came from a small annuity of my father's and contract editing work.

"Well, let's say I won't starve quite yet." I scratched Bronte behind the ears. "And I won't have to turn my dog into labra-noodle soup."

With the bustle of the meal, I hadn't paid much attention to how much alcohol Travis had consumed, but as he gazed at me, I saw a bleariness in his eyes. It was time to pump him full of coffee and send him on his way.

He grinned at me. "Why don't you marry me, and you can spend your days blissfully writing poetry?" Spend came out *shpend*.

"Travis, I'm cutting you off." I picked up his empty wine glass and walked into the kitchen. "Time for you to go home."

I brewed another pot of coffee and when I took a mug back to him, his head rested against the couch as he snored softly. It looked like I would have an overnight guest—on the couch, not the bed.

After I finished the dishes and cleaned up, I roused him. "You can stay on the couch if you like. It's snowing outside."

"Huh?"

I pointed out the window. The front porch light illuminated the snow as it poured out of the sky. He groaned and crawled up onto the couch. I covered him with a blanket and headed off to bed.

As I lay in bed with Bronte beside me, I wondered where I was going with Jim, with this cabin, with my life. As if to answer, my phone rang. Caller ID said Killdeer Memorial Hospital.

"Jamie, it's Norma." Her voice was calm, but I sensed tension underneath. "We've been swamped in the ER. When I had a chance to check on Carmela, she wasn't there. I wondered, since I saw your business card on her table if she'd called you?"

"No. I haven't spoken with her today. What about the baby? Is she there?"

"That's the thing. The baby is still here in the bassinet by the bed."

"Carmela wouldn't leave her baby. I'm sure of that."

I heard a sigh from Norma. "I'll keep looking."

Outside the wind had picked up, throwing icy snow against the window of the bedroom. Carmela wouldn't go anywhere without Bonita Amy, would she?

Black Crow Pond

After Norma's call, I couldn't sleep. Where had Carmela gone? She'd asked me for help, and I hadn't done anything. Maybe I should have tried to track down Rex. Maybe I should have made a report to the sheriff. As I thought about it, though, I wondered what I would say to the sheriff. Carmela is scared someone is after her baby? No, I really had nothing to report.

With these thoughts roiling in my head, I tossed around, unable to settle down. Bronte gave up, jumped off the bed, and went into the living room to join Travis.

I finally drifted off to sleep by imagining myself on the rock by the lake basking in the warmth of the sun lulled by the slap of the waves against the shore. I awoke to the weak light of dawn and the sound of Travis swearing in the kitchen. When I heard a crashing noise, I knew it was time to slip out of the warmth of the comforter and rescue the dishes.

Travis stood by the coffee maker, hair disheveled, holding a package of whole coffee beans. "How the hell do you make coffee with these?" He did not look happy.

I took the bag from him. "You sit, I'll make the coffee."

After the coffee brewed and he ate a bowl of cereal, he asked if I minded if he took a shower. "I have a change of clothes in the car."

Bronte followed him out to his banged-up Ford Focus. I'd never quite understood why a man who drove powerful vehicles in his job as a state trooper, settled for an old car with rust eating away at the wheel wells.

Outside the day was gray and foggy with the temperature just above freezing. The melting snow dripped off the branches of the evergreen trees. I gazed longingly at my rock in front of the cabin. It was too cold, though, to go sit unless I wanted to bundle up. Right now, I simply wanted some quiet.

While I ate a piece of toast, Travis showered. Perhaps I'd made an error in judgment inviting him to Thanksgiving. I didn't want to give him the wrong impression. Yet, when I'd made the plans, Jim was supposed to join us. As that thought swirled through my head, Bronte thumped her tail at the sound of a vehicle approaching.

"Who could that be?"

She loped to the back door, wiggling and yipping. Before I could let her out, Jim swung the door open.

"Oh, my god. I wasn't expecting you." I ran to him.

He received me with a big hug. "I was hoping you might have some leftover turkey."

He smelled fresh like the outdoors. I looked up at him, appreciating the deep brown of his eyes and the crookedness of his smile.

Right on cue, Travis walked into the kitchen toweling his hair. "Hey."

Jim let go of me and peered at him. "Travis." His tone was flat.

I suddenly became tongue-tied as I watched the two of them. It reminded me of a ritual I'd once watched on a nature show—two bucks asserting their masculinity. Jim was over six feet tall with strong Native American features and Travis was shorter and stockier with a day's growth of blond stubble. Who would win the doe?

One of the romance authors who contracted with me for editing couldn't have written a cheesier scene. Instead of trying to explain why I had a man in my shower, I started to giggle. It was the worst kind of giggle—a cross between a star-struck teenage girl and the evil Joker of the Batman series.

"Excuse me," I gasped. "Help yourself to coffee. I'm going to get dressed." I hiccupped my way to the bedroom wondering what kind of madness had overtaken me. Bronte, confused by my outburst, followed me.

"Listen," I said to my dog, "if you smell testosterone, ignore it."

Ten minutes later, with my short dark hair combed and my teeth brushed, I walked back into the kitchen. Jim and Travis were seated at the table engaged in an intense conversation. To my disappointment, it wasn't over me—the doe. It was about a police incident outside of Killdeer.

"I'm driving my pickup so I didn't have a scanner. But I saw several of the sheriff's cars headed toward the south end of Black Crow Pond."

Travis rolled his eyes. "Probably some dumb drunken snowmobiler going through the ice. Seems we lose a citizen or two every couple of years to drowning."

I slipped into the chair next to Jim. "What's going on?"

He pointed to his phone. "Just checking to see if the sheriff needs help. Something is going on just outside of town."

I leaned over to look at the screen on his phone. A text popped up. **Unidentified woman found in pond. No help needed.**

My hands turned instantly cold. "What woman?" I couldn't keep the shake out of my voice.

Both Travis and Jim stared at me.

"Did he say who it was?" My voice rose as I pictured Carmela's empty hospital room.

Jim shrugged and pointed to the text. "That's all I know."

Without saying another word, I ran to the bedroom for my phone. With shaking fingers, I tapped in the number to the hospital. The phone rang twelve times with no answer. I ended the call fighting back tears.

"What is it?" Jim walked into the bedroom and put his arm around me.

"She asked for help and I didn't do anything."

"What are you talking about?"

In a jumble of words, I told him about Norma's call last night and about how Carmela's last words to me were a cry for help.

"Call the hospital again. They're probably still swamped. Check to see if Carmela is there. Travis and I will see if we can track down more information."

When I finally got through to the hospital the person who answered was out of breath. "Killdeer Memorial." I didn't recognize the voice.

"I'm checking to see if you found Carmela in room 102? The new mom with her baby?" I realized as I spoke that I didn't even know her last name.

"I'm sorry, I don't see a Carmela on the census. She must have been discharged. Room 102 is empty. I have to go now." Abruptly she hung up.

I stared at the phone.

Out in the kitchen, Travis was talking with someone on the phone. He looked up at me with a worried expression. "My deputy friend says the woman they found must have fallen through the thin ice. She has dark hair and looks Hispanic."

My legs suddenly weakened under me.

The Snow Ghost Lady

"We have to find out." I paced in the kitchen while Travis and Jim stared at me. "It might be Carmela. I need to know."

"Don't jump to conclusions," Travis said in a reassuring voice that only succeeded in irritating me.

"I need to know." I snapped. "She asked me for help." Without thinking, without putting some kind of plan together I grabbed my jacket and my keys. "I'm going there."

"Wait. You know they won't let you through."

I glared at him. "You guys are state troopers, you get permission."

With a sigh, Jim stood up. "How about if the three of us go together?" He looked at Travis. "If we don't, I think Jamie will make enough of a racket to get her arrested."

I rode in Jim's pickup as he followed Travis down the snowy driveway. The truck bounced in the potholes, splashing up a combination of slush and mud.

"You really need to get this road fixed or you'll get stuck if we have a big storm."

I barely heard him. He'd taken on a soothing tone that rubbed me the wrong way. I felt like he was using his Trooper voice to calm a hysterical driver. I opened my mouth to tell him to quit trying to placate me, but at that moment, a deer darted out in front of Travis's car. He braked and swerved, missing the deer but running off the edge of the drive into the soft snow and leaf-covered dirt. Jim barely missed hitting Travis.

Jim continued to use his calm voice, but I heard the pressure behind it.

"I'll make sure he's okay. You stay in the truck."

I wanted to leap out of the truck and push Travis's car back onto the drive so we could get going. I took a deep breath and repeated, "Calm down. Calm down." If Carmela was the person they'd found in the pond, it wouldn't make much difference what time I got there. As one of my writers once said, "Dead is dead."

Both Jim and Travis knew how to get his car unstuck. They inspected the wheel that was mired in the soft earth, discussed possible ways to get it out, and finally decided on the old-fashioned, "you push and I'll rock the car back and forth" method. At this point, I joined Jim, pushing as Travis repeated putting the car in drive and then in reverse. We created enough rocking momentum for the car to move ahead and finally catch onto packed gravel.

The pushing effort left me winded and drained. I turned to Jim. "I'm sorry. I know I overreacted, but I need to know if Carmela is okay."

He nodded and gave me a quick hug before we got back in the pickup to follow Travis. As he drove, I noticed how he gripped the steering wheel. I wondered if he was having second thoughts about spending time with a wigged-out New York transplant.

When we reached Black Crow Pond, two sheriff's cars and an ambulance blocked the access road to the pond. Several people stood around looking cold and tired. Jim motioned me to stand back as he and Travis walked over to one of the deputies. I watched them with increasing apprehension. If it was Carmela in the water, what about Bonita Amy? If it was Carmela, why was she out on the pond?

I surveyed the area around the pond. It was behind a residential area. Our Lady Slipper Trail skirted the edge of it though it wasn't visible behind the pine trees and aspens bordering the water. Mary's Place was somewhere in this neighborhood. Maybe Carmela went for a walk and became disoriented in the snow. But why would she be out when she should have been in the hospital?

All these questions caused my temples to throb as Jim and Travis continued to talk with the deputy. Finally, the deputy nodded, and Jim walked back to me.

"They've got her out of the water. Greg says we can go down and take a quick look. They're waiting for the coroner before moving her. They'll have to do an autopsy in Duluth." He studied me and must have noted my distress. "You don't have to do this. Someone else can do the identification."

I thought about the young mother happily cradling her baby. "No, I'll do it."

Travis was already at the scene when Jim led me down the muddied path to the pond. The snow had been trampled into a mush of dirt and leaves and weeds. A tarp had been spread near the shore of the weedy pond. On it was a figure covered by an olive-colored blanket. Beyond the tarp, I could see the place where the ice had broken leaving a gaping hole. I closed my eyes and shivered.

Jim leaned close and whispered, "You sure you want to do this?"

I nodded although all of a sudden, I wasn't so sure. Swallowing back a hint of nausea, I walked over to the tarp and squatted down. Gently I pulled the blanket away and held my breath.

Her face, despite the darker complexion, was a ghostly blue-white, almost the color of the snow surrounding the tarp. Wet tufts of dark brown hair were plastered to her forehead. Her eyes were open, but it was if they had been covered with a film. I felt like I was seven again looking at the snow ghost lady in the park. I took in a sharp breath of air that smelled of rotting leaves and wet snow.

I pictured Carmela dressed all in white as the snow engulfed her the day I'd found her by the side of the road. As I peered at the unseeing eyes, I felt for a moment like I couldn't breathe, like my lungs had suddenly seized up.

Taking a deep breath, I gently put the blanket back, covering her face, and stood up. My voice came out in a whisper. "It's not her. It's not Carmela." My relief was sprinkled with guilt. I was happy it wasn't Carmela but deeply saddened by the loss of this young woman.

Travis stepped to me. "Are you sure?"

"It's someone else. But she looks Hispanic like Carmela." The world blurred as my eyes filled with tears.

The raw wind whipped at my cheeks and I started to shake hard enough that my teeth chattered.

"Let's get you out of here."

As we walked up the mushy, slippery path, I heard a commotion near the sheriff's vehicles. Rex Jordan stood speaking to Greg the deputy. "It might be one of my clients." He pointed at the pond. "I need to know."

"Sir, we can't let you go down there."

I hurried over to them. "Greg, I know this man. He's a lawyer." Turning to Rex, I took a deep breath. "It's not Carmela. I didn't recognize the girl."

"Was it Rita?"

Confused, I shook my head. "I don't know Rita."

"She's one of the girls from Mary's Place. She just had a baby two weeks ago. I was trying to get her papers ready..." His voice trailed off.

I looked at Jim. "Maybe he can identify her."

While the deputy accompanied Rex to the pond, I explained to Jim about Rex. "I met him on Wednesday. He works for some organization that helps people with asylum."

"Oh?" I couldn't read Jim's expression.

It took only a few minutes before Rex came back. He looked grim. "I don't get it. Why was Rita out on the pond? This doesn't make sense. We were working things out for her."

"You know her?"

"This doesn't make any sense."

He turned away from me to talk with the deputy. "I have to tell them at the house."

They walked to the sheriff's car together and I couldn't hear their conversation. By now I was truly cold. Instead of putting on boots like a seasoned Minnesotan, I had slipped on my Nikes. My feet were soaked and turning numb.

Jim took my arm and walked me to the truck. "You don't need frostbite. Let's get some hot coffee."

My phone rang as I buckled into the seat belt. "Jamie, it's Norma. I'm calling to apologize. The shift was so crazy but we found your friend right after I called you. She'd gotten turned around taking a walk in the hallway."

I closed my eyes unable to reply, as the image of Rita so white and so dead on the tarp cycled in my brain.

"Jamie? Are you there?"

"Uh…sorry. Um thanks for telling me."

"One more thing, they discharged her this morning back to that home."

I thanked her and ended the call, still feeling numb.

Jim and I sat in the warmth of the Loonfeather Café drinking coffee. I found the smell of fried food to be comforting even though I had no appetite. "What will happen?"

Jim dipped his French fry into ketchup. "They'll do an autopsy. It will tell them whether she drowned…" His voice dropped off.

I leaned toward him. "What? You know something else."

Jim concentrated on pulling apart a piece of a glazed donut. He cleared his throat but said nothing.

"Jim? What is it?"

He rubbed his forehead before looking at me. "I shouldn't be saying anything, but it looked to me like she had blood matted in her hair. It might have happened when she fell…or…" He didn't finish the sentence.

In my panic, I hadn't noticed any blood. "You mean someone might have hit her?"

He shrugged, clearly uncomfortable. "Let's let the coroner decide."

I wanted to push him more, but he was right. The autopsy might say more.

As I warmed up with my coffee, I thought about Carmela. "Can we make one stop before we go home?"

Mary's Place was on the edge of town at the end of a neglected city street. Other than the light that shown from the window in front, it looked abandoned. The walk from the street had been shoveled in a haphazard manner as if the person doing the shoveling had been in a hurry. A new dark-colored SUV sat in front. Behind it was the sheriff's vehicle. Greg, in the driver's seat, stopped tapping at his phone long enough to give us a little wave.

"Can you stay in the truck? I'll only be a minute. I want to see if Carmela is here."

Jim pointed to Greg. "I'll have a little conversation with him. Maybe he has some insight on this place."

The snow crunched under my feet as I walked up the wooden porch steps. The steps creaked in a way that indicated the boards were rotting. A wooden swing swayed in the cold breeze, its white paint peeling. Behind me, I heard Jim's voice greeting Greg.

While they talked, I knocked on the door straining to hear sounds inside. If Carmela was there, or Rita's baby, maybe I would hear their cries. At first, I heard nothing, not the soft padding of footsteps to answer the door, not the low murmur of voices. I raised my hand to knock again when I heard a piercing cry. "Nooooo…"

No one came to the door.

The Shelter for Women

Without thinking, I shoved the door open. Immediately, I noted the smell in the house. Mildew, bleach, and a flowery deodorizer.

"Hello?" The carpet in the hallway was wet with melting snow tracked in from outside. Immediately to my right was a staircase covered with the same carpet. At one time it might have been an off-white, but now it was worn down to a dirty gray. I followed the hallway to the sound of voices once again calling out, "Hello?"

They were gathered in the kitchen, Rex, a slightly overweight young woman with frizzy red hair, and a man with a military buzz cut and a minister's collar.

"Excuse me. I knocked but no one answered."

Rex raised his eyebrows in surprise. "Jamie?"

Now everyone turned to stare. "I...I wanted to check to see if Carmela was here."

The woman with the frizzy hair turned to me with a scowl. She had a pitted complexion from untreated acne. As my eyes adjusted to the dim light in the kitchen, I saw she was young. Not much older than Carmela. A scar ran from her mouth over her cheek to almost her ear. It looked like she'd been cut at one time with a razor.

"Who are you?" She spoke in a soft, twangy accent.

Rex motioned to me. "She's the one who helped Carmela."

As they stared at me, I felt like I had barged in on a very private meeting. None of the three appeared to be happy to see me.

The man standing next to Rex stepped forward and offered me his hand. "Thank you so much for what you did for Carmela." He had the beginnings of a dark shadow on his cheeks, as if he hadn't shaved in several days. He looked to be at least ten years older than the redheaded girl. "I'm Brewster Conway." He smiled. "The girls call me Padre even though I'm not Roman Catholic. This is my wife Kiley."

Kiley cleared her throat. "Um, glad to meet you."

Clearly, she wasn't glad to meet me. For a moment, silence filled the room. Though the floors and counters were clean, the kitchen badly needed an update. The linoleum floor was worn almost down to the wooden underflooring in places. The countertops were done in a chipped deep orange and the refrigerator was an ugly avocado green. When it clicked on, the sound was loud enough to be startling.

I broke the silence. "I'm so sorry to hear about Rita. I understand she lived here."

Brewster bowed his head. "We're in shock. God rest her soul."

They hardly appeared to be in shock, but what did I know about how people reacted to bad news. I'd had bad things happen to me but never like this.

With my jacket still on in this dingy kitchen, I quickly grew too warm. Rather than be polite and ask more about Rita, I plunged ahead. "Is Carmela here? Is she okay?"

As if to answer, I heard the sound of a baby crying upstairs.

"Is that Rita's baby?"

Kiley stiffened as if I'd slapped her. What was wrong with this place?

Rex answered. "Rita's baby is with a foster family until an adoption can be arranged."

"Oh."

Brewster's voice turned pious. "She performed a brave and loving act when she gave the baby up."

The words sounded rehearsed. I almost asked if that's why she was out on the pond. Perhaps she was having second thoughts. Perhaps she was depressed. But it was none of my business and the tension in the room suggested I keep my questions to myself.

"Is Carmela here? Can I see her?"

Kiley shoved her hands into the pockets of her blue jeans. "She's resting. We shouldn't bother her."

"Even if I can just peek in on her? You know, make sure she's okay?"

Kiley looked at Brewster who nodded. "Sure. Go on up with Kiley. But don't stay too long. She's exhausted from her ordeal."

I was tempted to ask why she wasn't still in the hospital, but I refrained. On the way to the stairs, I unzipped my jacket trying to cool off. No one had offered to take it. No one had offered a chance to sit and talk about Rita or the unusual circumstances of Bonita Amy's birth. Everyone had simply stood around the kitchen table like they'd been caught doing something illegal. I wondered what it was.

"You must feel awful about Rita. Do you know why she was out on the pond?"

At the bottom of the stairs, Kiley stopped and peered at me. In the dim light of the hallway her face was shadowed, but I saw something, perhaps fear, perhaps anger. "Rita was only with us for a short while. I don't know anything about her."

She turned and walked quickly up the stairs before I could reply.

A hallway divided the upstairs into three small bedrooms and a bathroom. All the doors were closed, and Kiley put her finger to her lips. "They're resting."

The upstairs was so quiet I wondered who she was talking about.

At the far end of the hallway, she knocked on the door. "Carmela," she whispered. "You have a visitor."

Carmela opened the door a crack. "*¿Quién es?*"

I stepped close to the doorway. "Hello, Carmela. I wanted to make sure you and Bonita Amy were okay."

A smile broke out on her face. "Amy!" She opened the door.

Kiley immediately stepped between us. "Sorry, you need your rest."

"Can I at least say hello to the baby?" I bit back the urge to shove her out of my way. Instead, I slipped by her and into the room. I'm not sure what I expected, but the room was barren except for a thin, worn oriental carpet, a dresser, a bassinet, and a single bed. Bonita Amy slept peacefully in the bassinette the teddy bear nestled by her. Carmela gazed tenderly at her baby. "She sleep."

At the door, Kiley cleared her throat and said in a louder voice. "Mom and baby need their rest."

I pulled Carmela into a hug. She whispered in my ear, "Pleez help. I keep *bebé*."

"I'll come back to see you tomorrow, okay?"

Carmela glanced quickly at Kiley and nodded.

Kiley cleared her throat again.

Outside the room after Kiley pulled the door shut, I asked her, "What is this place? Who lives here?"

"Shhh. It's quiet time."

She walked ahead of me. Once down the stairs she turned and in a low voice said one word. "Ice."

"What?"

Before she could respond, someone knocked at the front door. Rex answered it. Jim stood in the doorway. "Sorry, I'm wondering if Jamie is ready to go yet."

"I'm coming."

Once outside, I took in the sharpness of the cold air. When I looked back, I saw Rex and Brewster watching us through the open door. I waved at them and they waved back.

After I climbed into Jim's truck, I let out a deep breath. "There's something wrong about that place."

He started the truck, not looking at me. "It's a strange set-up, that's for sure."

I guessed he knew more than what he was saying. I decided that when we returned to the cabin, I'd fix some leftovers and we could eat in front of the fireplace. Once we were comfortable, I'd pump him about what he knew.

My plan might have worked out except as I was putting sliced turkey in the microwave, Jim's phone rang. He walked into the bedroom and spoke in low tones. When the call was done, he came back in the kitchen and put his arms around me. "So sorry, my little mobster, but I'm being called back to work. Another storm is coming in and they're short because of the holiday."

"You're leaving?" I pictured him beside me in bed and fought to keep my voice from rising to a squeak. "You just got here. Can't it wait until tomorrow?"

He shook his head. I wasn't sure when I studied him whether he appeared to be saddened or relieved. I knew this wasn't the time for a blow up, but I wanted to yell at him and insist he choose me before his work. Instead, I found a tear rolling down my cheek followed by another. "When do you have to go?"

He held me. "Well, maybe I could stay the night if I get up early enough to get back." He wiped the tear. "If you promise not to cry."

Bronte barked and wagged her tail. Since when did my dog understand English?

We had our turkey and salad and stuffing along with a bottle of red wine. In front of the crackling fire, he finally told me what he knew about Mary's Place.

"Greg says it's a place for pregnant women who crossed the border illegally."

I remembered Kiley's cryptic reply to my question. "You mean it's one of those contracted detention places that ICE uses?"

Jim shrugged. "It hardly seems like a lock-up, does it? He thought it was owned by a non-profit church organization."

"Well, it sure is shabby. What else did he say?"

Bronte flopped down beside me with a contented burp. I'd broken all rules about good pet care and given her a little bit of turkey skin.

"Not much. The girl who drowned was seeking asylum from the Mexican cartels according to Rex. She'd just signed papers to give the baby up for adoption. The baby was in foster care somewhere in Southern Minnesota until the adoptive parents could pick him up."

Something wasn't right with this picture. "Maybe she was having second thoughts? Was this a suicide?" I remembered what Jim had said about blood on the side of her head. "Maybe someone hit her?"

"I ran that by Greg when you were in the house. He thought the blood was probably from falling before she went through the ice."

"Oh? What if someone wanted to hurt her? Maybe a cartel person got to her?"

Jim turned to me with a half-smile. "Oh, Jamie the poet, I think you are reading into things. I'm guessing it was an accident. If Rita came from a warm climate, she probably didn't know anything about thin ice."

"Maybe."

We made love that night under the thick down comforter while another inch of light fluffy snow fell. Somehow, though, it wasn't the same as before. We did all the right things and yet it was like someone pushed automatic pilot. Maybe we were simply both tired. Maybe the trauma of the day and the long drive for Jim. Maybe...

I wasn't content in the afterglow. Rita's sightless eyes haunted me and Carmela's plea rang out—*pleez, pleez*. Was someone trying to take Bonita Amy from her? While I watched the slow cadence of Jim's breathing, I resolved to find a way to have a long conversation with Carmela. Maybe Rex could help me.

The Fender Bender

J im left at five in the morning. While he showered, I fumbled around brewing coffee more asleep than awake. I should have scrambled eggs for him and sent him away with a turkey sandwich for lunch. Life is filled with "shoulds" and the best I could do at that ungodly hour was hand him a thermos and wish him Godspeed.

Outside, the sky had cleared and light from the nearly full moon sparkled off the new snow. Bronte trotted after him and tried to jump into the pickup. Jim tugged her back to me. "No dogs allowed."

I watched as his truck bumped down the snowy drive and wondered how many more times this scene would be repeated. My rational side said he needed to be in Minneapolis with his son and his job. My other side said, "But what about me?" I shivered and went back to bed. Bronte happily licked my nose before snuggling into Jim's half of the bed.

Later in the morning, with the sun achingly bright and the wind biting through all the layers of clothes I wore, I walked the half mile to Larissa Lodge to pick up my mail. Crammed into the box was another manuscript. My editing business was flourishing thanks to Florice Annabelle LeMay, a romance writer who'd finally sold a novel. She was part of a writer's group and recommended me whenever possible. Although I'd never met Florice, I knew that her friends liked the old-fashioned blue pencil on printed manuscript type of editing. I'd tried over the past nine months to convince Florice to email her work and use track changes. She and her group steadfastly clung to paper versions.

When I opened the package and pulled out the manuscript, I immediately groaned. Four hundred pages with the title *Survivor of the Darkening Sand: Part One of the Watersmeade Trilogy* by Coral Peterson writing as C. P. Dowling.

"Oh no." My words were loud enough that Bronte raised her head in concern. I had grown fairly adept at helping Florice and her fellow romance authors but had no experience with fantasy other than reading Tolkien, J.K. Rowling, and watching the first season of *Game of Thrones*.

"Please tell me this is a romance." I picked up the first page as Bronte shook the snow she'd accumulated all over the floor. Since it started with a sword fight amongst a rival gang of "Midgers" under the double moons of Erasmus, I doubted this would be a bodice ripper.

"Hark," I muttered, "winter is coming." For the next half hour, I toyed with a bowl of cereal and stared at the manuscript. This manuscript would keep me in electricity for the next month or two. I needed to do my best.

While I contemplated the manuscript, my thoughts kept going back to my seven-year-old self and the snow lady. I wondered what had happened to her. Was she dead, like I thought or only sleeping? Mother had never spoken of it again and I hadn't dared ask her if she knew the answer. Even then, Mother was exhibiting signs of the brain disease that slowly took her life. It was rare, but every so often she'd fly into a rage. I lived in fear of triggering her.

As the snow slowly wafted out of the sky, I needed to shake these thoughts and get to work on the manuscript. My first step was to read through the book and see if I could make sense of it. I decided to put it off until later this afternoon when the sky darkened and the cabin was surrounded by night. Perhaps it would put me in the mood for "Midgers," whatever the hell they were.

My main task of the day was to drive to Mary's Place and check on Carmela like I'd promised. First, I went online and looked up any information I could find on ICE and pregnant asylum seekers. An old article in the *Washington Post* described the increase in the past several years of pregnant detainees. More women were attempting to cross the border to avoid violence in their own countries. Many were victims of rape and abuse both in their homeland

and on the trek to the United States.

I wondered about Carmela. Had she been raped? I cursed my inability to speak Spanish. Perhaps Rex or the Conways knew her history.

Several human rights organizations had filed complaints about the poor living conditions of these women while incarcerated. An activist noted, "They escape the violence and abuse only to find it here."

One of the articles said some of the women were taken to places in other states for care. Still, it seemed odd to me that ICE would house them in a small community in Northern Minnesota. For one thing, Killdeer Memorial Hospital was ill-equipped to deal with a complicated pregnancy even though they were one of the few small-town hospitals that still did normal deliveries.

I'd had a conversation with Norma last fall while we spread woodchips on the Lady Slipper Trail about the challenges of keeping a small hospital afloat. "The work is hard, doctors don't stay and the hospital barely makes enough to keep going."

Coming from New York City with all its hospitals and medical facilities, I'd never thought about it.

"We're lucky," she'd said. "Our community is big enough to keep Memorial open. But there's talk about closing it to obstetrics. Not enough babies being born to keep up with all the training."

In the bottom of my bag, I found the card Rex had given me. It said he was legal counsel for "Viaje Seguro" with the tagline, "Dedicated to Safe Journeys." The card had a web address. The website featured a photo of smiling children with Hispanic features. The page included a mission statement about assuring the health and happiness of women and children at risk. The wording was generic enough that they could have been an organization for low-income families in the United States or an international organization. With its Spanish name, I assumed it was focused and Mexico and Central America. They claimed to be a 501c3 non-profit.

I'd once fact-checked an investigative article on the world of non-profits. Some were absolute shining examples of goodwill and good practices like the Gates Foundation and Doctors Without Borders. On the other end were rich people using the law for tax purposes and self-promotion like the defunct Trump Foundation. Where was Viaje Seguro on the spectrum?

"What do you think, Bronte? Is this a Gates or a Trump organization?"

Bronte pricked up her ears to my voice. The longer I lived in the cabin by myself, the more conversations I had with my dog. She never argued with me, never told me what a bad person I was, or complained about my cooking. I appreciated that she wasn't like Andrew, my ex-husband in any way except they were both sloppy eaters.

I closed down the laptop. Time to check up on Carmela and ask the Conways about Viaje Seguro. Adapting to the Minnesota hospitality that dictated you don't show up a someone's house empty-handed, I packaged up the leftover banana bread from Thanksgiving along with the sugar cookies Clarence's housekeeper Lorraine had sent with him.

By afternoon the weather had turned winter raw. Although the temperatures soared into the high thirties, a wet wind off the lake seeped through my down jacket. Before getting into the cold car, I looked over the lake. We'd had enough days below freezing to form a layer of ice. Rob, Travis, Jim, and even Jilly had all separately warned me about the lake.

Jilly had been the most direct, her voice rising with emotion. "Don't walk on it until you see the old duffers haul their fish houses out. Even then, don't go out on it until you're sure none of them have sunk into the lake. Larissa eats people and sometimes doesn't spit them out."

I wondered why Jilly had been so adamant until Rob told me her brother drowned in a snowmobile accident at age eighteen. Right now, the lake was a vast field of white with the thin layer of snow that had fallen. The image of Rita with her dead eyes flashed by me. I intended to not set foot on the lake—ever.

Downtown Killdeer hummed with post-Thanksgiving shoppers. I stopped behind a car loading up a Christmas tree from the lot located across from the hospital. I rolled down my window to smell the fresh-cut trees and listen to "Jingle Bells" playing on tinny outdoor speakers.

Growing up in an apartment in New York City, we never had a tree. Too expensive to buy and too expensive to have delivered. Instead, we put a few lights on a poinsettia plant and called it good. I had a memory of Mother, before she got so sick, putting up a very small potted evergreen. She said this time of the year she needed something living from the forest. As the brain disease progressed though, she stopped knowing when it was Christmas. Eventually, Dad and I settled on the poinsettia.

This year I resolved to have a tree. I planned to have a Hallmark moment of trekking out into my woods to find the perfect evergreen. Bronte would dance by my side as I wielded the axe.

My reverie ended abruptly with a jarring bang and the sound of crunched metal. "What?"

A red SUV had just backed out of the tree lot into the passenger side of my car. A woman about my age stepped out of her vehicle with a puzzled expression.

"I didn't see you. I'm so sorry." She spoke in a high quivery voice as I rounded my car to inspect the large dent in the door.

I tried the door and to my relief, it opened. Still, another expense. Merry Christmas to me. I took out my phone to call the sheriff knowing I would have to file a report for insurance. "I'll call the police so we can get a report."

"Wait!" The woman's eyes widened. "Please don't call. We'll pay for it."

If this had been New York, I would have ignored her and made the call. You never know who you can trust. Here in Killdeer, it was a different story. No fender bender went unnoticed.

The lot attendant walked up. "Oh, that's quite a dent. Gonna cost a bit to fix it. You need any help, come and get me." He walked away while I took a photo of the dent.

"If you can show me your driver's license, I'll take a quick picture of it in case my insurance needs the information."

"No," she bit her lip. "I…uh, forgot it. You know with the baby and all."

The woman shifted from one foot to another. To my surprise, she started to giggle. "I wasn't paying attention."

I wondered if she was high. "Are you all right?"

"It's just that I'm so excited with the new baby."

Here we were, blocking the entrance to the tree lot and this woman shuffled like she was on the dance floor. She must have noted my confusion.

"My baby. We finally got a baby."

Who *gets* a baby?

"I'm a mom. I always wanted to be a mom."

"Oh, well congratulations then." I hoped my smile appeared sincere even though I wondered about her sanity.

She reached in her purse and I was sure she was going to show me photos. Someone tapped at their horn. Another Minnesotan thing—unlike New York City where drivers used their horns more than their brakes, people were so polite here.

Instead of photos, she handed me a business card. "Here, it's my mother's card. She'll take care of everything. Tell her I said so."

"And you are?"

"Lacey. I'm Lacey the new mom! And I have to go. The baby needs me."

The card read, "Sheryl Bevins, Property Management and Interior Designs." Related to M.C. Bevins?

Lacey turned back to her SUV.

"Wait." I wasn't at all sure I could trust this woman. "What is your name again?"

"Lacey Graham."

"Is your dad M.C. Bevins?"

She giggled again. "Yes. He's a granddad now. I'm so excited!"

Just in case, I snapped a photo of her car and the automobile license.

"Mom will take care of everything. Really, I need to go."

I walked over to the Christmas tree lot and beckoned to the attendant. "Was that woman really M.C. Bevins' daughter?"

He nodded. "Yup that's his kid."

Behind me, a driver politely honked. Time to go.

The Women of Mary's Place

M ary's Place looked as dilapidated as ever when I parked in front of it. The SUV I assumed belonged to Rex was gone replaced by a white van with Texas plates.

"You're far from home," I noted.

Gathering my food offerings, I approached the house. Curtains covering the front window were pulled shut and if the walk hadn't been shoveled, I'd have said the place was abandoned. It took several seconds of pounding on the door before Kiley answered.

"Yes?" She studied me as if she'd never seen me before.

"I'm here to see Carmela and I brought everyone cookies."

"Oh." She didn't move.

Brewster's voice called out from the kitchen. "Who is it dear?"

When Kiley turned to answer I took the opportunity to squeeze my way in. One thing about New Yorkers, we can be pushy.

"I brought cookies and banana bread." I raised my voice. "I thought everyone could use a treat."

Brewster stood in the dingy light of the hallway wearing a Minnesota Vikings sweatshirt and blue jeans. His hair needed trimming and he still hadn't shaved. He looked like he would be more comfortable in a dive bar than in a church.

I held up the package wrapped in aluminum foil. "I'm told it's the best banana bread this side of the Mississippi."

Several expressions crossed his face before he smiled and said, "Welcome."

"I told Carmela I'd be back today."

43

"Amy," Carmela's voice came from the kitchen. "You come!"

I walked by Brewster and into the kitchen. Carmela and two other women sat at the table talking softly. One peeled potatoes while another chopped peppers and onions. Carmela sat at the head of the table patting Bonita Amy against her shoulder.

Brewster followed me in. When he spoke, I noted one of the women at the table seemed to shrink back. "Well, nice to have a treat."

I wasn't sure he meant it, but I grabbed an empty chair, took off my coat, and unwrapped the cookies and the banana bread before he could change his mind. Kiley hovered in the doorway looking back and forth between Brewster and the table. There was something childlike about the way she regarded the cookies.

"Come," I motioned to her. "Join us."

"Sit with them." Brewster pointed to us. "I have some paperwork to do."

He turned and walked toward the front of the house. Once he was gone, Carmela introduced me to the other women. Elena sat next to me. She looked to be the oldest, but not much over twenty-one or twenty-two with a rounded face and lively brown eyes.

She smiled, patting her large belly. "You help my baby, too?"

I laughed. "No thank you. One delivery is enough."

"Yoli," Carmela indicated the woman on the other side of the table, who stared at her lap, not making eye contact. Her blue eyes contrasted with her brown hair and tan skin. To me, she looked like she couldn't have been more than fifteen.

"Hello." I smiled noting the slow way she peeled the potatoes. She struck me as someone moving in a trance. She did not answer my greeting.

Both Elena and Yoli had large bellies. I assumed they were in late pregnancy.

Slicing several pieces of banana bread, I passed them around. "I'm so sorry about Rita."

Yoli stiffened when I said the name. The other two stared down at the table. Had I crossed some invisible line by mentioning her?

Elena cleared her throat, motioned to the banana bread, and said, *"Gracias."*

They ate the bread like they'd never had such a treat.

"You like it?"

Yoli glanced at Elena who said, "*Es bien, ¿no?*"

I turned to Kiley who fidgeted at the table opposite Carmela. "Do you speak Spanish? I'd like to ask a few questions."

Kiley's answered in her soft drawl. "No, ma'am, I don't. We don't like to bother the women for their stories. For some, it's too painful."

"How do you know when they're in labor or having problems?"

"We know." She took another cookie and fell silent.

Bonita Amy broke the silence of the room with a miniature sounding burp and a grunting noise indicating she had filled her diapers. Carmela laughed. "*¡Aye, mi hija!*" She stood up. "*Perdóneme.*"

I stood to follow her upstairs when Kiley grabbed my arm. "She'll be fine."

It was clear to me that she didn't want me alone with Carmela. When I sat down again, Elena accidentally brushed a cookie onto the floor. We both bent down to pick it up. In a hardly audible whisper she said, "I speak English. This place is bad. Can you get us out?"

At that moment Brewster entered the kitchen clapping his hands. "Rest time, senoritas. We want those babies to be healthy."

Everyone got up from the table and began putting the peeled potatoes and the sliced peppers on the counter. As quickly as I could, I reached into my bag and took out one of my cards. When Elena filed by me, I slipped a card into her hand.

"Nice to meet you all."

As they headed down the hall to the staircase, I moved closer to Brewster. "What is the story of Mary's Place?"

"This is a house of peace for these women who have suffered so much. I think of it as a safe haven." His voice was solemn.

"How do they come to you?"

"The church finds them. We operate through an organization called Viaje Seguro. Our mission is to make sure their journey is safe, and they are well cared for."

It sounded like a canned elevator speech to me.

Upstairs, Bonita Amy issued a lusty cry. I smiled. "She seems pretty healthy considering she was born in the backseat of my car. What will happen to her?"

"Viaje Seguro will make sure she's cared for." Brewster touched my elbow and nudged me toward the front door.

"Carmela seems to think someone is trying to take her baby."

Brewster paused with a concerned expression. "They hear rumors of babies being taken at the border. I'm sure that's what she's talking about."

"What about Rita's baby?"

Brewster pushed a little harder. "Viaje Seguro is taking care of it. They have a good foster home while they find an adoptive family."

The way he said it made me think of a pet adoption service. I half expected he'd assure me the baby had shots and was appropriately chipped.

I stopped at the door and planted my feet. "I'd really like to help out here. It seems you have an important mission in keeping these women safe. Perhaps I could come in and work with them on their English. It would help them after their babies are born."

Brewster frowned. "I'm not sure. Viaje Seguro handles all of that. I'm simply God's servant."

"Oh, that's okay," I interrupted. "I'm sure Rex would be okay with it."

It's a good thing my nose wasn't made of wood because it might have grown an inch or two.

He cleared his throat. Before he could turn me down, I had my hand on the door handle. As I opened it, I smiled at him. "How about if I come on Monday morning? I wouldn't want to interfere with their afternoon rest time."

I walked out before he could say anything else. Once in the car, I sat for a moment while it warmed up. "Jamie, what has gotten into you?"

The answer involved a drowned woman, three other vulnerable women, and a baby. Something was strange in this place. It was like a detention center without the chain-link fences and barbed wire. Was Carmela trying to escape when I found her in the snowy bog? What about Rita? Was she also trying to escape?

When I arrived home, Bronte danced and woofed like I'd been gone for weeks. "Really, girl, I was only gone long enough to dent my car and push my way into a place where I wasn't welcome."

As I stood in the kitchen appreciating the coziness and warmth of the cabin, I couldn't shake the shadow of Mary's Place. I pictured the women, deep into their pregnancy sitting around the table in silence and desperation. But why?

Sheryl Bevins

y four-thirty in the afternoon it was dark. I stood outside with Bronte watching wisps of clouds obscure the stars. In the summer, years ago before mother became so sick, she would take me out by the lake and point to the constellations. I sensed her awe at the beauty of the heavens, but the vastness scared me. Growing up, I found relief in the crowds and the noise of New York City. Now, I craved the quiet and the space. Still, the openness of the sky sent me shivering inside.

After heating Thanksgiving leftovers, I started on the manuscript. First I quickly paged through it to find that C.P. Dowling had divided *Survivor of the Darkening Sand* into chapters varying from twenty to sixty pages. I looked for white spaces to break up the dense text and found very little. Even her quotes were concealed in long paragraphs. I needed to do some research on the genre to find out if this was an accepted style.

"Give me a steamy romance—even a bad one. At least I know the rules." I climbed up into the loft that held all the things I still hadn't unpacked. Digging through a box of books, I found my crusty, browning paperback copies of *The Lord of the Rings,* the first of the Harry Potter series, and a novel by Ursula Le Guin. Maybe I could get a better sense of how fantasy should read.

In the bottom of the box, I pulled out a half-used sketchbook. Squinting in the poor lighting of the loft, I opened the cover and let out a long breath of air. It contained my mother's pencil drawings. So little of Mother's life had remained after Dad put her in a nursing home. Somehow this piece of her work had gotten mixed in with my books.

I brought the books and the sketch pad down to the kitchen table. The first drawing was of the view from our Manhattan apartment. The skyline, so familiar to me, included the Chrysler Building with its Art Deco style and towering spire. The drawing was smudged with erasures and as I studied it, I sensed a franticness about it—like she'd wanted to get it done before something happened. Sadness overwhelmed me.

I set the sketchbook aside as Bronte padded over to me with a questioning look in her soft brown eyes. "Sorry, girl, I can't think about my mother right now. Too many things to do."

After a cup of tea, I turned back to C.P. Dowling and the quest for water. Ten pages into the manuscript, I fought to keep my eyes open. The story started with a short skirmish between the Midgers, defenders of Watersmeade, and the Ticks who were the invaders. The Midgers were small humans and the Ticks were scorpion-like creatures in search of water. C.P. Dowling must have spent hours coming up with the names for the Midgers. At least she didn't call them Dopey, Sleepy, and Doc. By page seven I was so overwhelmed with names like Nigu, Golix, and Noisiv that I created an Excel spreadsheet to keep them straight.

Bronte sighed contentedly at my feet as I stared at the printed pages and willed myself to stay awake. "I have to do this," I told my dog. "Or else we won't have electricity next month."

My phone pinged with a text about the time the head Midger was marching inside the castle to report to Queen Alusra about beating back the Ticks.

Grabbing the phone, I stretched the tension out of my shoulders. It was from Jim.

Back safely. How's it going?

Is that the best he could do? I tapped, **Dent in car. Mary's Place Weird. Think I hate fantasy novels. Going to drink myself into oblivion.**

A few moments later Jim called. "What are you talking about?"

I explained the dent in the car door. "A woman named Lacey backed into the passenger side of the car coming out of the Christmas tree lot. She told me she was distracted because she was so excited about her baby and her mother, Sheryl Bevins would pay for it."

"Bevins? You mean of Bevins Transport?"

"Probably. She gave me her mother's business card. Sheryl Bevins does property management and interior design. She even has a website."

"Did you report the accident? Your insurance will need it."

I felt a little heat crawl up my neck knowing I should have. "Uh, no. Lacey asked me not to. Besides, it's not a huge dent. I mean, I can still get in the car."

Jim laughed. "Oh, my New York Yankee. You know nothing of how expensive bodywork can be."

Growing up on public transportation without a car, he was right. "I'm supposed to give Sheryl the bill."

"Ha! Good luck with that. If she's from Bevins Transport, it will cost you more in time and aggravation than going through your insurance." He chuckled. "Of course, your insurance company will use it as an excuse to raise your rates."

"You're depressing me now. Can't you say something cheery?" I kept my tone light, but underneath I felt a creeping anger with him. I was tired of watching the back of his pickup leaving the driveway and tired of the broken promises about when he'd be back.

Jim ignored my remark. "Toby is your best bet for bodywork. He might not be the brightest and friendliest guy in town but he's pretty honest and fairly good at what he does."

Great. Pretty honest and fairly good. What an endorsement. Toby and I were well acquainted after several tire replacements last summer when someone had slashed my tires. "I'll go see Toby next week, I guess."

I heard staticky chatter on his end of the line. He must have been calling from his cruiser. Nice he could block out thirty seconds or so for me. I gripped the phone ready to say something I would probably regret when his voice came through. "Sorry, I've got to go. I'll call tomorrow. Maybe I can take a few days off next week." He hung up before I could reply.

Bronte slapped her tail on the floor gazing at me with her soft eyes. "Looks like you can have his side of the bed for the time being." I patted her on the head and took a long deep breath. For a second, I thought about Rex, the lawyer with the expensive coat. Could he fill that spot?

"Shame on you, Jamie." Bronte pricked up her ears at the sound of my voice. "I didn't mean you, girl."

As if my thoughts had traveled with authority through some kind of cyberspace, my phone rang with an unknown name. When I answered, Rex identified himself. "Jamie, just wondering if you've recovered from your unexpected delivery." His voice was upbeat and cheerful.

"I believe I'll survive, but nice of you to check in."

"Since I'm still in town, would you like to have dinner tomorrow night? I hear they serve a good steak at the Loonfeather."

The thought of a steak didn't tempt me, but the thought of some company did.

We talked a little about the lack of eating choices in town and decided on the time to meet. Just before he closed out the call he added, "I'll be curious to know what you think about Mary's Place. We're very proud of it."

I bit back the urge to say, really? It looked like a dump to me. Instead I thanked him for the invitation and told him I'd see him tomorrow.

When I set the phone down, I felt a slight tingling in the back of my neck. Just a hint of an insect crawling up my spine. Instead of dwelling on it, I went back to the Midgers and Queen Alusra and waded through another ten pages.

"It's a quest for water." Bronte responded by asking to go outside. As I walked to the door, I pointed to her water dish. "See, Watersmeade has the only non-contaminated well within thousands of hectares and the oracles are predicting that winter is coming without rain or snow."

It reminded me of the some of the dire predictions regarding the Earth if something wasn't done about climate change. My very small part in the environmental drama revolved around Racine Mining's quest to take copper and nickel out of the ground in Jackpine County without having a good plan on how to keep waste out of the groundwater. Currently license approval was teetering since one of their biggest secret supporters was tangled in a legal mess that included my property.

I loved Lake Larissa and the pristine wilderness surrounding it and was one of those "tree huggers" trying to keep the area from suffering pollution like other parts of the country. Because I was vocal enough, I wasn't necessarily popular with everyone in Jackpine County including M.C. Bevins. Racine promised jobs and economic security.

Those thoughts brought me back to the Bevins. Was M.C. associated with Mary's Place since he owned the house? If so, what did he know about the organization?

When I opened the door to let Bronte back in, I noted a distant hum of a snowmobile. I hoped it wasn't tearing up the Lady Slipper Trail. I also hoped it wasn't out on the lake. Even as a New Yorker with no experience on a wilderness lake, I knew the ice was still probably too thin. I thought about Jilly and how she lost her brother to the lake and quietly closed the door.

Before turning back to the Midgers and the Ticks, I took out the card Lacey had given me. It was time to talk with Jilly the person who knew everything that happened in town. I'd once said to her, "If you don't know about it, it didn't happen." Her mouth had twitched into a smile, but I'd caught a glimpse of seriousness in her eyes.

When she didn't answer the phone, I left a message. "Hey Jilly, it's Jamie. I have a question about someone named Lacey who says her mother is Sheryl Bevins. Call me."

Fourteen more pages into *Survivor of the Darkening Sand*, I now had some of the plotline. The Ticks were controlled by the evil overlord Aga Pumpert. He'd polluted his own water supply by indiscriminate mining and now wanted to take Watersmeade for his own. Queen Alusra protected not only the water source but the magic "Rock of Purification" that kept the water safe.

"Well." I set the pages down. "All we need now is a hero or heroine who is an orphan but in truth is of the royal race to become reluctantly involved."

The phone saved me from telling Bronte more of the story as she snoozed by my feet.

"It's Jilly, just got your message. What kind of trouble are you in now?" She made it sound like I was always in some kind of a mess.

I told her about Lacey and the dent in my door and wondered if her mother Sheryl would be good for the repair.

Jilly paused before she answered. "That's a complicated question."

"Really? Seems like it's a pretty straight up question. Either she will or she won't."

"Her husband M.C. is known as quite a tightwad and he holds the key to the cash box. Or so they say."

"But according to her card, she has her own business."

"Hah! What is it this time? Amway? Tupperware? Mary Kay?"

Now I was confused. "What do you mean?"

Jilly explained that home parties selling household goods was a long-established way for someone to make a little money. "Sheryl has been known for years as the queen of the home party."

Home parties were nothing I'd ever experienced in New York. "You mean she has a party at her house and sells stuff?" I pictured a dining room table laden with cookies, cake, laundry soap, and cosmetics.

"Mostly the parties are at someone else's house, but yes."

"Her card says she does property management and interior design."

"She probably collects the rent on all of the Bevins's properties in town. As for interior design, if you like everything to be done in brocade and gold fringe, she'll do it." Jilly laughed. "Sorry, I don't mean to be so catty, but Sheryl and I have had our run-ins over the years."

I pushed the card around on the table. "Okay. Changing the subject just a bit, what do you know about Lacey and her new baby? Maybe I can use the information to sweet talk Sheryl into paying for the dent in my car."

Outside, the snowmobile buzz grew louder. I strained my ears wondering if it was on the lake. I hoped not.

Although I couldn't see her, I felt Jilly was nodding. "Oh Lacey, what a sad tale. Fifteen years ago, her out-of-town boyfriend was driving drunk and rolled the car. She broke her back and had a serious head injury. She was in a coma for several days. Neither of them were buckled up."

Maybe the head injury explained Lacey's odd behavior. "Classic story."

"No kidding. Last I heard a number of years ago, Lacey was married and living in Texas. They were trying to have a baby. According to the girls at LuAnn's Cut and Curl, they were doing the whole fertility thing. M.C. and Sheryl were rumored to be paying for it."

"They must have been successful."

"Much as I don't like Sheryl, I'm glad for her. I know she really wanted a grandchild."

Bronte sauntered over to me and nudged my leg. It was time for her supper. "I have to go. My dog is calling."

"Same here except it's my lazy kids."

After I ended the call, I thought about the heartbreak of wanting a child and not being able to have one. My college roommate, Madison who was diabetic tried for several years to have a baby. She and her husband did all the fertility and in vitro things and finally gave up. The last I'd talked with her they were looking into adoption.

I pushed Mary's Place and babies out of my head. "Not mine to ponder right now. I have to find out where Queen Alusra has hidden the magic stone."

Still the spidery feeling stayed with me. Outside, the sound of the snowmobile receded, and the wind picked up.

Rex and Viaje Seguro

Settled underneath a thick comforter, I listened to the rattle of the windows as the wind whipped the cabin. I was thankful my grandmother who built the cabin understood winter in northern Minnesota. She'd insulated the walls and the ceiling. With advice from Rob, I had more insulation put between the rafters. Even with the work done, I felt the cold seeping like a spiteful spirit through the walls. At one point after midnight I got up and checked the outdoor thermometer. It registered five below zero.

"Brrr," I hurried back to the warmth of the bed wishing I had a human next to me, not a snoring dog.

By morning, the wind had died down and the sun shown a pale yellow through a haze of light clouds. The temperature hovered around zero. A mist rose from the open part of the lake that was fed by an underground spring. Soon it would ice over. Jim had pointed to it a couple of weeks ago as the lake slowly froze. "That's a dangerous spot. Even in the coldest part of the winter, the ice is brittle where the spring feeds the lake." I shuddered thinking about Rita plunging through the frigid waters to her death in Black Crow Pond.

Bronte did her business and quickly begged to come in. I thought about the depths of winter in New York and the dogs that wore fashionable coats. As Bronte brought the chill in with her, I felt a touch of guilt. "Would you like a down vest, girl?"

Dogs around here were treated like dogs. No vests, no bejeweled collars, and no paid dog walkers.

I spent the day with the "Darkening Sand." I was almost through the first third of the initial read. Resting my eyes for a moment, I set the manuscript down and explained to Bronte. "You see, Levy the orphan has lived on this island all her life and now her wise uncle who sounds a lot like Dumbledore is sending her to Queen Alusra. All she wants is to stay on her land and grow orchids, but she is to be the savior of the planet by using her inherent magical powers to awaken the purifying stone and bring the water back to the desert."

Bronte yawned but offered no opinion. I found that despite the author using every fantasy cliché except a magic wand, the story was getting to me. Perhaps because it was so cold outside and Levy's quest was through the heat and sand of the desert. Or perhaps by becoming engaged with the story I didn't have to think about Rita dying in the icy waters of the pond.

By late afternoon the temperature had risen to ten above zero. I hurried out to my frozen Subaru aware that I'd let the time slip by. I was to meet Rex in a half hour in town. Once I'd scraped all the ice off the windshield and cranked up the defrost, I shivered behind the wheel letting it warm up a bit. Jim had warned me that after one winter here the first thing I'd want to do is build a garage. At the time, in the midst of the heat of summer, it seemed like a frivolous expense. My teeth chattered as I hugged myself. Jim was right. I wondered where I'd get the money.

When I opened the door to the Loonfeather I was greeted by warmth, a cacophony of voices, and the aroma of fried foods. Rex had not arrived yet, so I took a table for two in the dining room and ordered a glass of red wine.

The roars from the bar indicated the patrons were watching football. Talking about sports was a safe icebreaker and I'd learned last summer to pay attention to baseball. Now it was football and I missed my dad explaining to me why those big men in helmets were running into each other.

Fifteen minutes later, Rex still had not come. I checked my phone but had no message from him. Rather than wait, I called him and got his voicemail. After that, I tried texting with no response.

At a half an hour I decided to order a salad and eat by myself. As the server set down the salad the bar erupted in a roar of cheers followed by clapping hands. Something good must have happened in the game. As I dug into the salad a voice called from the dining room entryway.

"Hey, Jamie." I looked up to see Travis. He wore a maroon and gold sweatshirt with the University of Minnesota Gophers logo on it. "Dining alone?"

Without asking he settled into the chair across from me. "Jim not here?"

I shook my head. "Working."

"Oh."

Did I want to confess to being stood up by a good-looking lawyer? Why not? "I was supposed to meet Rex Jordan here. He wanted to talk with me about Mary's Place."

The server came around, tapped Travis on the shoulder, and winked. "The usual?"

"You have them trained, don't you?"

He shrugged. "What can I say? I need to enjoy it in case I win that election and have to move back to Cascade."

"You're a shoo-in, you know." Travis grew up in Cascade, the county adjacent to Jackpine, and was running for sheriff in a special election.

When his beer came, the server also brought me another glass of wine. He pointed at it, "You have them trained too." He must have read the confusion on my face. "Didn't order it?"

"No."

"But I did." Rex strode up to the table. He wore a cable knit sweater over gray woolen slacks. Every time I saw him, I was reminded of slick advertisements for men's clothing.

Travis stood up and yielded the chair to him while I introduced them. "Rex this is Travis Booker. He's a friend and soon-to-be sheriff of Cascade County. He was keeping me company..." I let my voice trail off in hopes that Rex picked up how irritated I'd become.

They shook hands and Travis waved as he walked out. "Back to the game."

Rex watched him leave with an amused expression. "Seems like a nice guy."

And you would know, how? I worked to keep the annoyance out of my voice as I pointed at my half-eaten salad. "I was hungry. Do you want to order?"

He shook his head. "Sorry for being late. I was detained."

At this point, I could have made a huffy statement about replying to phone and text messages, but the expression on his face caused me to stop mid-huff. His brow was knit, and he kept making fists and then relaxing his hands as if to warm them up.

"What is it?" I asked.

He cleared his throat. "It looks like we are going to have to close Mary's Place. The Feds are very unhappy about the girl who died and about a baby being born in a stranger's car."

I considered it for a moment. It seemed to me, from what I'd read about how people seeking asylum were treated that this was a swift reaction. I told Rex what I was thinking. "I'm surprised they reacted so quickly. The reports I've seen give me a sense that the Feds don't care much about the women. They're more focused on sending them back across the border."

Rex took a deep breath. "Let's just say Viaje Seguro relies on goodwill. We don't want to jeopardize the other sites."

"What will happen to Carmela and the others?"

Rex pushed a lock of his thick brown hair away from his forehead. It was a gesture that reminded me of a teenager trying to be cool. "We have to find somewhere else. We'll look at other Viaje Seguro sites, of course."

"Did they say how long you have?"

"They want the girls moved by the end of the week."

Another roar rose from the bar. For a moment I thought about Travis raising his beer glass surrounded by people laughing and clapping. If only life was a spectator sport and we were always on the side of the winning team.

I told Rex about how I'd offered to tutor the women in English. He shook his head. "Don't bother. They'll be busy getting ready for the transfer."

Something in his voice didn't ring true. Perhaps it was the forcefulness when he said, "Don't bother." I let it go but decided I'd at least stop in tomorrow.

"Do they know they're being moved?"

Rex shrugged. "I'm not sure. I don't manage the program, I just advise. I wish I could do more. The girls have been through so much."

No kidding.

His phone rang and he excused himself. When he came back, he put some cash on the table for my wine and said, "I'm so sorry. I need to leave." Without further explanation, he hurried out. I watched him as that annoying tickle crawled up the back of my neck. It struck me that something was seriously off about Rex and about the Mary's Place situation.

"Jamie, leave it alone. This is none of your business." But the image of Rita's cold, wet body and Carmela's fearful face kept cycling through my head.

"Excuse me?" The server stood in front of me. "Did you say something?"

"Sorry, mumbling to myself."

She glanced at the doorway. "Nice looking guy. He was in here the other day with M.C. and Sheryl."

"Bevins?"

Someone called to her from another table. "Oops, gotta go. Did you want another?" She pointed at the nearly empty wine glass.

In fact, I did want another and maybe another after that one. I smiled at her with a shake of my head. "Unfortunately, I'm my designated driver."

I finished my wine, paid the bill, and stood to leave when Travis walked back into the dining room. He did not have the joyful smile that would accompany a winning team. The Vikings must have lost.

"Jamie, can I talk with you outside?" He slipped on a down jacket with frayed cuffs, a definite contrast to Rex's look.

We walked through the hum of the people at the bar. They were watching the post-game with quiet intensity. It felt like a dark cloud had descended on the barroom. How could people get so wrapped up in a game played by men who made millions of dollars to smash each other around? I might have asked Travis that question except he wore a serious expression as we walked out the door.

Outside the snow was cold enough to squeak under my hiking boots. The slight wind stung my cheeks. I wrapped my scarf a little tighter around my neck.

Travis pulled me close, out of the breeze. "Listen, it was too noisy in there to talk. I wanted you to know they've done the autopsy on Rita."

"She drowned, didn't she?"

"That's the thing. They found water in her lungs. But they also found a big gash on the side of her head."

A car crawled by throwing up a plume of vapor from its exhaust.

"What are you saying?"

"My sources are calling this a suspicious death." He paused. "Although I get the sense the sheriff doesn't want to expend a lot of resources for it. He thinks she got the gash when she fell through the ice."

"I'm not a detective, but wouldn't you wonder about it?"

Travis pressed his lips together in a grim expression. "I'll keep pressing my sources. I don't want you to get mixed up in it."

I should have thanked him for his concern. I should have said I'd stay away from Mary's Place and mind my own business. But I was once in a position where there was no one to speak for me, and I didn't want this to be buried.

"Travis, there is a wonderful little baby with my name. Well, sort my name. I'm already involved. Maybe not with Rita but with Carmela and the other women at Mary's Place." I told him what Rex had said about closing the place and relocating the women. "Carmela is terrified someone will take her baby. It's not right."

He shook his head. "Something is way off here. But let the experts handle it. Please?"

I didn't respond. Instead, I turned to the car and walked away.

On the way home, I wondered what I would or could do. Maybe a little research first. Where did these women come from and why would anyone want to murder one of them? Why was Carmela on the road? Was she trying to protect her baby from being taken?

Too many questions. On the way home with the heater warming my feet, I tried to put it together. Nothing quite fit.

Please Help Them

I sat on the rug in front of the fireplace, savoring the warmth with Bronte settled beside me. With the darkness of the evening, the temperature was dropping below zero. Outside I heard a shimmering of dead leaves being swept across the snow with the evening wind.

On my laptop, I'd pulled up several articles about asylum and the conditions for people seeking it. The stories were heartbreaking of young women fleeing the violence of home or of young women who were raped and abused on their journey to the border. What I didn't find in all the reading was much about what happened after they had babies.

"Do they get sent back with their babies? Aren't those children citizens by birth?"

Bronte nuzzled me, pushing at the laptop as if to say, stop now. You're going to drive yourself crazy.

I was about to close the computer when I found one very small, short article about a couple who adopted a baby whose mother was only fourteen years old. While the article didn't go into detail, it did mention that a non-profit organization in the United States had facilitated the adoption. Did Viaje Seguro provide that kind of service?

My phone pinged with a text from Jim.

Free at last. See you tomorrow!

I typed back. **I'll throw another log on the fire**

Maybe Jim could help me sort through my questions.

That night I dreamed about a baby locked in the backseat of my car. It was frigid outside, and I was trying to get the door of the car open. My hands were so cold they were like claws. Every time I tugged at the door the handle came off in my hand. When I stepped away holding the handle, my foot slid into an icy slush. The dream kept cycling through this scenario again and again until I woke up. In my sleep, I'd pulled the comforter askew and one foot was exposed to the cold air in the bedroom.

Bronte lifted her head as I resettled the covers. "Go back to sleep, girl." She nuzzled her head into the pillow beside me and closed her eyes. I thought about Jim's warmth and the smell of his skin next to me and wondered again if we could last together. Perhaps I was too much of an East coast Yankee for him.

Last summer when we'd finally gotten together, we'd talked about our heritage. He grew up here in the Northwoods surrounded by the tall pines and the call of the loon. His Native American heritage showed in a special sense of the earth around him. I'd grown up in New York City hardly aware that part of me was Native. Sometimes I experienced a whisper of the Ojibwe blood I'd inherited from my mother, but it was hard to explain exactly what that whisper said. A feeling that I'd been here before perhaps when I walked in my woods stepping through the leaf and needle covered ground.

As my thoughts wandered, I pictured Carmela, emerging from the snow squall. Where did she come from? Was this wintry land up north foreign to her? I suspected she was from Central America or Mexico where the earth was dry and warm. What was it like for her to be thrown into a land she didn't know where people spoke a language she didn't understand? Would she be sent back? And what about Bonita Amy?

"Too much." I threw off the covers, slipped on my thick robe and down booties. Time for a cup of hot tea.

The temperature in the kitchen was fifty-eight degrees. Despite my resolve to be tough and impervious to the cold, I plugged in the little space heater I kept in the kitchen to warm my feet.

While the mint tea steeped, I opened the laptop and stared at the screensaver. I wanted to find out what happened to babies born here if the mothers were deported. These babies were often called "anchor babies" by a conservative movement working to deny them US citizenship even though it was guaranteed in the Constitution. I found that if the parent or parents were in the United States illegally, they could not necessarily stay because their child was a citizen.

The screen wavered in front of me and I realized I was too tired to continue the search. Bronte sauntered out to the kitchen with a big yawn. "You know, just because I can't sleep doesn't mean you have to get up."

She shook herself and walked to the door. When I opened it, I was blasted with a cold wind. "Sure you want to go out?"

I flipped on the backdoor light and let her out, noting how the trees creaked in the frigid air. Bronte made it off the step before she quickly squatted, did her business, and trotted back in. Tomorrow I'd have to figure out a way to get her further from the door.

Before I closed the door, I thought I heard a whisper of voices calling from the lake. I stepped out for a moment and peered into the darkness. As my eyes adjusted to the faint twinkling of the stars, I saw nothing but a white expanse. I squinted, a shudder running through me. The whisper had a malevolent edge to it.

"Imagination, Jamie."

In the short time I stood outside, my nose had already numbed from the cold. Jim and Rob had warned me of the dangers of the weather.

"People die of hypothermia every winter. Just like they die of heart attacks when they try to shovel snow after getting no exercise except pushing the buttons on the television remote." Rob had laughed. "You'd think they would learn."

I quickly stepped inside and shut the door. Time to crawl back under the covers and hopefully dream of something more peaceful than a baby stuck in the cold backseat of my car.

The morning dawned clear and crisp. When I looked out the window over the lake, I saw only the white field of snow. I shook off the haunting whisper from last night. The lake appeared white and pristine, not ominous.

Jim texted as I finished my first cup of coffee. **Leaving Mpls. See U @ 5.**

I texted back a smiling emoji. The symbol didn't capture the thrill that ran through me as I thought about his warm body next to mine. I patted Bronte on the head. "Girl, you're going to be sleeping on the floor tonight."

My first order of business was to put on my warm clothes and take the dented Subaru to Toby for an estimate. I planned to check on Mary's Place and then take the estimate to Sheryl. I wasn't looking forward to talking with her after what Jilly told me about the Bevins's tightwad reputation.

The car started reluctantly with a cranky "arrrr" sound when I turned the key. Jim had suggested a couple of weeks ago that I get an engine heater for it. "You'll be stuck here if it goes lower than fifteen below unless you can plug the car in."

I'd shrugged him off, mainly because I didn't have the money to buy one. "See," I said to the cold car, "We don't need a fancy heater. You're a Subaru. Don't you live on love or something?" At least that's what the ads said.

The air shimmered and the slanted sun sparkled on the white layer of snow as I drove into town. It reminded me of walking through Central Park after a snowfall and before the snow melted into crusty slushy ice. For a moment, I wished I was back there with the air filled with excitement as the snowflakes poured out of the sky. When Mother was still well, we used to go down to the plaza in front of our apartment building, tilt our heads to the sky and let the snowflakes bathe our faces. The last time we did it, she had suddenly stopped with a faraway look as if something was calling to her. She grabbed my hand and tugged me back inside and muttered, "Not safe. Not safe." Less than a year later, Dad had to put her in a care home as her mind slipped deeper and deeper into darkness.

Thoughts of her brought me back to the snow lady on the park bench. The image of those unseeing eyes, like Rita's, emphasized the plight of the women at Mary's Place. Perhaps it was time to talk with Sheriff Fowler about Rita and the other women. What would I say? Sheriff, I have this uncomfortable spider-like feeling something is wrong.

"Jamie, I'm guessing he would show you to the door at that point," I uttered above the roar of the heater.

Toby, dressed in thick coveralls, came out and inspected the dent in the door. He spoke mainly in grunts as he wiped away the road spray to get a better look at the damage. "Might be able to hammer it out but it'll need new paint." He scowled as he talked. "These foreign cars, you know, hard to get parts." He scratched his head. "Might have to replace the door instead."

I pictured my bank account falling below zero. "What if I don't get it fixed."

He shrugged. "Rust from the road salt will take it pretty quick."

I sighed when he handed me the estimate. "That's a lot for a little dent."

He growled. "You could try one of them dealers in Duluth."

Great, a two-hour drive? I hoped Sheryl would pay because my insurance deductible was more than the estimate.

Before taking the estimate to Sheryl, I drove to Mary's Place. I parked behind the white van again.

The front drapes of the house were pulled shut like last time. As I knocked, I heard voices. No one came to the door. I knocked again and when no one answered, I let myself in.

"Hello!" I used what I thought was a cheery "I'm so clueless" voice. "I brought some donuts!"

Brewster stepped into the hallway from the kitchen. He wore a heavy hooded sweatshirt and denim jeans. Once again he was unshaven—hardly a ministerial look. "What?" He peered at me. "What are you doing here?"

I kept up my slightly high-pitched tone. "I thought I'd bring some donuts for your residents. It'll keep up their energy while I work with them on English."

He snatched the bakery box from me. "No lessons. We're very busy right now."

"Oh? I could come back in an hour if that would work."

Kiley slipped into the hallway and stood beside him. It was hard to tell if she had an expression of annoyance or fear. Her red hair was frizzier than ever. "You need to go," she whispered. "They're resting."

"Oh, okay. I'll just stop upstairs and say, 'hello.'"

"No!" The force in Brewster's voice caused me to step back. He noted my reaction and said in a calmer voice. "We're in the middle of our chores. This isn't a good time."

Upstairs a baby started to cry. From the top of the stairs, I heard Carmela's voice. "Amy?"

Brewster stepped forward and grabbed my arm. "You need to go."

"But..."

His hand held my arm so tight I thought he would squeeze the blood out of it as he propelled me to the door. Kiley followed behind him and as he opened the door, she bumped into me with a whisper. "They're taking them back. Please help them."

Next thing I knew, I was standing on the porch as the door slammed behind me.

I took out my phone and called Rex. The call went immediately to voicemail. Something was terribly off here and I wasn't sure where to turn next.

As if to respond to my distress, my phone rang. The caller ID made no sense to me.

Elena

Backlit in orange was the name Brewster Conway. Why would he call me when he'd just thrown me out the door?

I turned to the front door as I answered. "Brewster?"

The answer came in a heavily accented whisper. I recognized Elena's voice. "Amy? *Por favor.* They take us back across border. Can you help?"

I walked down the sidewalk with the phone pressed to my ear. She was whispering so quietly I could barely hear her. "You're not supposed to have the phone, are you?"

"No time. Carmela, she have *hermano* in Vancouver. Can you find him?"

My brain felt like I couldn't get it out of park. "What?"

"*El hermano de Carmela* he live in Vancouver. Can you find him?"

She pronounced the name "Vancover." I stiffened as a voice in my head said, *Jamie don't make promises you can't keep.*

"You must hurry. They take baby soon." Her voice rose.

"Who will take the baby?"

In the background, I heard voices. One of them belonged to Brewster. "Where the hell did I put the goddamn phone." He didn't sound very ministerial.

"I go now. His name Alfonso Serrano. You find quick."

The phone went dead. I stood staring at the dilapidated house not knowing what to do next. Should I go back in and demand to know what was going on? I saw a ruffling of the curtain in the upstairs window. For just a second, Carmela peeked out. Then she was gone.

Once in the car, I sat watching the house. My phone rang again. Quickly

I answered it expecting to see Brewster's name again. It was "unknown."

"Jamie, it's Rex. You called?"

I hesitated, not knowing if I could trust him with his expensive clothes and expensive cologne. But what choice did I have?

"Um…I just got thrown out of Mary's Place. I stopped by with donuts and they weren't happy to see me. One of the residents thought they were being taken back to where they came from."

I expected some kind of denial or some kind of reassuring words. Instead, Rex laughed. It sounded like a genuine amused sound. "Oh, dear. I fear that Brewster has gotten it all mixed up and passed it on to the girls. Yes, they are being moved, but not back to the border. We have another Viaje Seguro house in southern Minnesota near Mankato. Maybe he told them it was the border between Minnesota and Iowa."

I took a deep breath of relief. "Whew. I'm so relieved. Maybe you should talk to them."

"I'm in Duluth, but I'll be heading back that way later today. I'll call Brewster and get it straight." He cleared his throat and he took a more serious tone. "I think you should go home. I'm guessing your presence is stirring things up. Let me handle it."

I stared at the phone feeling like a child who has been dismissed. "Well…"

"We'll talk tomorrow after I get things straightened out. Take care." He ended the call.

Toby's damage estimate sat on the seat beside me. I decided to leave Mary's Place to Rex for the time being and see Sheryl. Maybe M.C. would be at home and I could ask him if he knew anything about Viaje Seguro.

The Estimate

The Bevins place was on the other side of Black Crow Pond from where they'd found Rita. A long, paved driveway led up to a new two-story brick house with a three-car garage. White smoke snaked out of the chimney running up the side of the house and the air smelled of burning wood. Large pines surrounded the property on three sides. In the back, a cleared area sloped down to the pond.

Two workmen unloaded a van, carrying boxes into one of the bays of the garage. One of them called to the other, "She wants these stacked in the back."

"What the hell are they? These boxes are heavy."

"Don't know. Don't care as long as she pays us."

Gray clouds rolled in covering the weak sunlight. I waved to them as I walked to the front door. A gust of wind whistled through the trees. Even though the setting for the house appeared to be idyllic with the woods and the pines, it felt cold and dark.

When I rang the doorbell, a small dog yipped in only the way a small dog can—high and hysterical. I heard a voice trying to hush the dog as it approached the door. Sheryl answered wearing a turtleneck sweater and a down vest. She held a small white fluff of a dog who continued to bark.

"Yes?" She gazed at me with a puzzled expression. She smelled of a sweet perfume and baby lotion.

"Hi. I'm Jamie Forest. Your daughter Lacey backed into my car the other day and I have an estimate for the damage." I held up Toby's scrawled piece of paper. I expected her to invite me in. Instead she continued to stare at me.

"Oh? I don't think she backed into anyone."

"Excuse me? She was coming out of the Christmas tree lot on Pine Street. She said she was so excited about being a mom that she didn't see me."

I dug into my bag and pulled out the business card Lacey had given me. "That's you, right?"

She patted the dog who regarded me with more intelligence than its master. Sheryl slowly shook her head. "Yes, but Lacey didn't say anything to me."

By now it was getting cold standing on the porch. "Could I come in and get this straightened out? Otherwise I need to call the police."

She puckered her lips as if to say, "shoo" before she shrugged and stood aside to let me in. "Oh. Come in I suppose."

I did not feel welcome as I stepped inside.

After talking with Jilly, I expected to see a house decorated in a French bordello style—or at least what I thought might be a French bordello style. Instead the walls were painted in light pastels with thick oriental area rugs over polished hardwood floors.

I slipped off my boots at the door and walked into the front room. A fire glowed in the fireplace. The room was decorated for Christmas including the eight-foot Norway pine I'd seen strapped to the SUV when Lacey dented my car. The room might have been a set for a Christmas Hallmark Channel movie. On the fireplace mantel amid a garland of tinsel stood a silver-framed wedding photo. Lacey smiled into the camera in a dreamy sort of way. The groom stood beside her, a thin man with dark hair, a browned face, and Hispanic features wearing a cowboy hat.

Sheryl planted herself at the door of the front room still holding the dog. It wiggled trying to get down.

I pointed to the dog. "She must smell my dog."

"Oh?" Sheryl's voice had a nasal flatness to it. I felt like I was being stared down.

We might have stood this way for many more minutes except M.C. walked into the room wearing jeans and a flannel shirt.

"We have a guest?"

I turned to him and held out my hand. "Hi. I'm Jamie Forest. Your daughter gave me Sheryl's card after she backed into my car. She said someone would take care of the damages."

His grip was firm, too firm—like he wanted me to experience his strength. When he let go, my hand felt a little numb. I showed him Toby's estimate.

M.C. hardly glanced at it. Instead, he fixed his gaze on Sheryl. "Did Lacey run into her car?"

The little dog, sensing the tension in the room, whined. Sheryl appeared to shrink back at the sound of his voice. "Uh…she didn't say anything to me."

I handed him the paper with the estimate on it. He squinted as if he needed reading glasses before he turned to me with a glare. "What kind of a scam are you running?"

I took a step back. "What do you mean?"

"Lacey doesn't drive. She hasn't got a license."

It came back to me how reluctant she was to show me her license. I pointed to the wedding photo. "Is that your daughter?"

M.C. scowled at me. "Yes?"

"Well, whether she has a license or not, she hit my car coming out of the Christmas tree lot." Heat rose up my neck into my cheeks. "Are you saying I made this up? I'm sure the Christmas tree lot attendant will vouch for me." I reached into my bag for my phone and pulled up the photo I'd taken of Lacey's car. "Does this car belong to you?"

M.C. glanced at it and then over at Sheryl.

"Maybe we need to get the sheriff involved." I made a move to call.

Next to him, Sheryl shook her head. Her voice was high and tremulous. "Please don't. Lacey has enough to deal with. She doesn't need to be questioned by the police."

Upstairs I heard the cry of a baby. Sheryl glanced at M.C. "Lacey needs me." She half ran, half stumbled out of the room.

M.C. folded his arms and watched her go without saying anything.

Anger roiled inside me as I stood in the perfectly decorated living room. Taking a deep breath, I tried to remove some of the tension from the room.

"I...uh understand you are a new grandfather. Congratulations."

M.C. didn't acknowledge my remark as he glanced at the staircase. "Lacey didn't say anything about hitting anyone. I need to check it out."

"Mr. Bevins, I assure you your daughter backed into my car. I hardly dented it myself. Perhaps it would be best if I called the sheriff and filed a report." The New Yorker in me seeped out. These Minnesotans could be so polite and so obtuse. My jaw hurt from clenching it.

The crying from upstairs reached a crescendo and stopped. Mother and grandmother must have finally calmed the baby.

He reread the estimate. "It's a little high." Again, I sensed he thought Toby and I were in collusion. I opened my mouth to defend it when the baby started crying again.

M.C.'s face darkened. "Where's that damn son-in-law?"

I waited for him to say more but he simply stood in the doorway with a tense expression. Somewhere in the back, the little dog yipped.

As if he'd been pulled out of deep thoughts, he handed the estimate back to me. "I'll take this under consideration—maybe give Toby a call. But I'm not paying for any of it until I get all the facts."

Reaching in my bag, I handed him my card. "This is how you can reach me when you've gotten 'all the facts.'" His dismissive attitude annoyed me.

He followed me to the door. As I slipped on my boots, I turned to him. "By the way, do you own the house they call Mary's Place?"

I expected either a "yes" or "no" answer. I didn't expect the expression that crossed his face. He moved a little closer to me, his voice barely above a whisper. "Why would you ask me that?"

I smelled the alcohol on his breath. M.C. Bevins had been drinking before I arrived.

I backed up nearly stumbling on the welcome mat. "I heard it was one of your properties."

He pointed up the stairs. "Any questions about that place, you ask my wife. It's her responsibility."

The door shut with a click of the lock as I stood there both confused and astounded. Was I nuts, or were they? Even outside I heard the muffled cries of a baby. I wished the poor creature good luck living in that household.

Jim's Dilemma

On the way home, I tried to sort through the events of the day. I'd been thrown out of Mary's Place, Rex had assured me the residents would be safe and Bevins claimed he had nothing to do with Mary's Place. On top of that, Sheryl who handled the properties appeared to be afraid of M.C. Did any of this make sense?

"Concentrate on Jim," I murmured as I bumped down my driveway. "Enjoy the little time you have together."

The parking area by the cabin was empty. Jim had not arrived yet. It was already late afternoon and the weak sun was slipping behind the wall of clouds. When I stepped out of the car, a large fluffy snowflake landed on my nose. Like a child, I stuck out my tongue as another fell from the sky. Before I made it to the back door, more snowflakes cascaded down.

Bronte greeted me with her usual affection. I patted her, scratched behind her ears, and then shooed her out the door. As I watched her trotting through the snow, the winter called to me. I remembered as a kid running to the plaza from our high rise in New York and joining the other cooped up kids from the building. Time to put Mary's Place aside and enjoy the snow.

I pulled on the clunky sorrel boots Jim had insisted I buy. Zipping up the used down jacket I'd found at the Killdeer thrift store, I grabbed a pair of mittens and a hat. As I walked out the door, I wondered if I looked as much like the Michelin Man as I felt with all these clothes on.

The snow created a gentle veil of white in the waning daylight. Five inches covered the ground and judging by the snow on the Subaru it was accumulating fast.

"Let's check out the lake," I called to Bronte. I wanted to stand near the shore and listen to it. Rob had once described to me how the lake talked in the winter as it iced over. "It's a groaning sound. My mother used to tell me the lake was like a bear, grunting and burrowing in for the winter."

The lake appeared to be completely iced over now. Snow covered the sand and it was hard to tell where the beach ended and the lake began. I walked tentatively toward the water. I did not want to break through. Bronte bounced beside me holding a white aspen stick.

I closed my eyes and concentrated on listening. I thought I heard a faint crackling noise—like a bear pushing its way through the forest into the den. I imagined the ice forming a tight seal over the water. Behind me, tires crunched on the snow in the driveway. Jim had arrived.

Bronte nudged me, pawing at the stick she'd just dropped at my feet. I grabbed it and ran with it up the slope while Bronte chased me.

Jim stood by his truck holding a gym bag and a thermos. He laughed. "You're better at fetch than your dog."

I nearly knocked him over. Gathering me into his embrace he whispered, "Got any coffee?"

His breath smelled of mint and his unshaven face scratched the skin of my cheek.

"You're so romantic." We kissed long enough that Bronte began to whine.

"I'm stiffening up out here." He meant it in more than one way.

Once inside, I was amazed at how short a time it took to shed all the layers of clothing I'd put on. We left a trail into the bedroom. Bronte tried to follow us in only to have the door shut on her.

Later, after showering together, I heated the remaining leftovers from Thanksgiving. Jim toasted me with a beer and a grin. "Nice to stop by every once in a while."

Outside the snow continued to sprinkle from the sky in fluffy flakes. Inside, the cabin filled with the aroma of turkey and the crackling sound of the logs in the fireplace. Bronte nuzzled into Jim's lap and gazed at him with her soft brown adoring eyes.

"Don't you dare feed her from the table." I put a plate of food in front of him.

"Wouldn't think of it." He gently pushed Bronte away and dug into the food.

"Don't they feed you in that big city?"

"Not like this."

I sat kitty-corner from him with my food and clinked my beer glass with his. "Skol, as we say in the Mafia."

"You've clearly been in Minnesota too long. I think the Mafiosos say something like, 'May you not sleep with the fishes.'"

I would have laughed except the image of Rita flashed in my head. I gripped the beer glass a little harder and shook off the picture of Rita's ghostly pale flesh and dead eyes. What was wrong with me?

As I ate my food, I noted for the first time a gauntness about Jim. Stress lines etched their way around his mouth, and he had dark circles under his eyes.

I took a bite of mashed potato and leaned closer to him. "You look worn out."

He shrugged. "Holiday season. Lots of hours."

I didn't believe him. Something deeper than long hours was haunting him. "After you have the last piece of pumpkin pie, let's talk."

Once the dishes were cleared and soaking in the sink, we settled in front of the fire with mugs of coffee.

"You're getting good at building these," Jim pointed to the crackling logs.

"I'm trying to get my Woods Woman merit badge."

He smiled and pulled me closer. It was so cozy with his arm around me and my dog settled at my feet. Jim stared at the fire and again I saw the worry lines on his face.

"What is it?" I ran my finger down his cheek.

He shifted away from me and cleared his throat. "Jamie, it's..." His voice trailed off. you.

Watching how intently he stared at the fire, I knew. *I knew.* Just as I had known when Andrew my ex-husband had fidgeted in front of me with distress written on his face. Just as I had known that Andrew was going to say.

I pushed him away with a sputter. "I've heard this before when Andrew was happily screwing someone else."

Jim wrinkled his brow. "What are you talking about?" A smile slowly formed. "Did you think I was trying to break up with you?"

I sat up straight. "Isn't that what this is all about?"

He laughed, a genuine chest-deep laugh. "Oh god. I am a bad communicator."

"What are you trying to say?"

He pulled me closer. "The commander wants to send me to a six-week training program in forensics." He took a deep breath. "In Washington D.C."

A dozen thoughts swept through my head. "What about Jake and his treatments?"

"That's the thing. He's doing well. So far it looks like he's in remission. But..."

I'd read enough about Jake's kind of leukemia to know that remission could be a fragile thing. "You're worried about how he'll do."

"More worried about how Marie will do."

I'd never met her, but Jim had told me that Marie, Jake's mother was "skittish" and was prone to drinking too much. Their brief affair had ended over six years ago before Jake was born. She'd moved to Minneapolis with another man without telling Jim she was pregnant.

I shifted so I could look directly at him. "What do you want to do?"

Jim, the strong, handsome trooper who always held himself in control, blinked hard, his eyes reddening. "That's it, I don't know. I want to be here. I want to be with Jake."

I restrained myself from jumping in. I wanted to shake him and tell him that if he wanted to be here, he should be. I waited.

"The thing is, it's a promotion—more money, more responsibility, and less pulling people over for speeding."

"But you wouldn't be stationed here, would you?"

He slowly shook his head, his hand squeezing my shoulder with enough power that it hurt.

This might have been one of the most important moments in my recent life—the moment of either commitment from him or not, except my phone rang—Caller ID unknown. I should have let it go to voicemail. I should have turned the damn phone off before we settled in front of the fire. Instead, I answered it.

"This is Jamie."

"Oh, Jamie. Rex here. I wanted you to know that I'm at Mary's Place and I think I've got everyone settled down. Brewster sends his apologies for rushing you out. He felt like things were getting out of hand."

I thought about how the minister had manhandled me and tended to agree. "What's next? Can I come tomorrow?"

Rex hesitated. "That's the thing, we think it best if you don't come. Having someone new unsettles the girls."

"But...I thought they enjoyed having me come. You know, now that I have a baby named after me."

Rex laughed, but to me, it sounded forced. "Why don't I check in with you in a couple of days. The transfer won't happen until the end of the week while we get the beds in our Mankato house ready."

Again, I sensed something in his voice, but I wasn't sure what I was hearing. Besides, he couldn't stop me if I showed up at Mary's Place. Could he?

"Okay. Thanks for the update."

After I ended the call, I filled Jim in on all that I knew—which was very little. He listened with all the appropriate "uh huhs" but I sensed his disinterest.

When I was done, he squeezed my hand. "How about if you turn your detective badge in for the night and take a little vacation."

The vacation occurred in the bedroom with Bronte settled patiently outside the door waiting for us to let her in.

Missing Yoli

Despite the warmth and comfort of Jim next to me, I slept badly. My dreams took me through a maze of tunnels where I could never reach the daylight. In the tunnel I found Rex holding out an abandoned baby. When I tried to reach for it, the baby slipped into a deep pool of icy water. I woke up with a gasp. In his sleep, Jim reached out and touched my shoulder. His hand was warm against my clammy skin.

The next morning the skies cleared, and sunlight sparkled off the new-fallen snow. Of course, growing up in New York, I'd seen snow, but never anything like this. It was eye-achingly white and soft like down feathers. Since Jim didn't need to be back in Minneapolis until tomorrow, he suggested he teach me a lesson in cross country skiing.

"If you want to appreciate winters here, you need to know how to ski."

"I know how to ski," I grumbled, too tired to think about leaving the warmth of the cabin. "You put the skis on, push your way through the snow, freeze your ears and then you fall down."

"Pretty close," he laughed. "Now, let's get you outfitted."

My bank account could barely cover electricity let alone skis. I shook my head. "Unless you can find a garage sale with skis for less than five dollars, I guess you'll have to go on your own."

In the morning light, the gauntness and tiredness had faded from Jim's face. Instead, his eyes were alight with amusement. "No worry. My treat. I know where to get a deal on everything you need."

Still grumbling, I pulled on long underwear, a cotton turtleneck, a sweater, and a thick windbreaker. Outside the air was clean and crisp and as I breathed it in, my dark mood lightened. Jim drove me into town to the sporting goods store. Within an hour, I had a pair of used skis, poles, and brand-new ski boots.

"We'll get you waxed up back at the cabin and break trail through your woods to the Lady Slipper Trail. Rob might have it all groomed by the time we get there."

Rob was the trail's official volunteer groomer. I'd heard rumors that he pulled bedsprings behind a snowmobile to pack the trail. I liked the idea of low tech. When I mentioned it to Jim on the way back to the cabin, he laughed. "I hate to tell you this, but he has an actual trail groomer. Sorry to burst your bubble."

Jim brought his skis in from the pickup along with a fishing tackle box full of wax and waxing paraphernalia. I learned quickly that Jim was an artist when it came to waxing skis. He tested the snow temperature and selected the right kick wax after making sure the skis already had a good undercoat to hold the wax.

"See," he held up a green wax. "I'll put this on the middle third of your skis so you get a good kick."

I appreciated his enthusiasm but grew bored as he used the iron to melt the wax on before buffing it with a cork to a perfection. "It'll be spring before we get outside."

"Do I detect a little whine in your voice?"

"Yes. In fact, I think I'll go back to bed. Wake me when you're done."

He set the wax and the iron down, walked over to me, and pulled me into a bear hug. "You'll be happy I did this."

Bronte wagged her tail, her butt wiggling with excitement as he set the skis outside and put on his boots. "I used to race in high school. Our team got as far as the state tournament my senior year. We came in second behind a big suburban school with money to invest in good equipment."

I laughed. "I'll let you come in first—this time."

Jim shooed Bronte back into the cabin. "Sorry, chum, dogs mess up the track. I'll throw some sticks for you later."

We headed into the woods behind the cabin with Jim breaking trail for me. After fifty yards I called to him. "Stop. I need a rest break." Between struggling to stay upright, pushing through the fresh snow, and slipping backwards, I was completely out of breath.

Jim skied back to me, his cheeks rosy and his eyes bright.

"You can go ahead if you want. I think I'll call an Uber from here."

"Ah, a little mobster wimp, huh?"

With his encouragement, we made it the quarter of a mile to the trail. The snow was packed and tracked. Jim pointed to it. "This will be much easier. You'll see." He showed me how to create a rhythm with my poles and my stride. I was surprised at how much I liked the freshness of the outdoors and the quiet of the skis sliding in the track. When we stopped for water, I gazed through the snow-covered pines at an eagle soaring high in the sky. It was eerily quiet in the woods without a wisp of breeze.

For those moments, the quiet and the human presence of a man I loved, I felt at peace. We skied for another twenty minutes before I called for a halt. "If we go any farther, I won't get back. My thighs feel like jelly already."

Jim hesitated. "You sure?"

"Listen, I can head back and you can go on if you'd like."

We agreed that he would ski for another half hour before turning around. I'd slog my way back to the cabin and fix lunch. As I skied back alone, I found I enjoyed the quiet and the seclusion. Working hard to keep my legs going, I hardly thought about Mary's Place or Jim's difficult decision. I simply took in the slight kiss of the breeze through the trees and the sprinkle of snow as it fell off the branches of the evergreens.

"Maybe this is heaven."

Once inside the warmth of the cabin, I started to shiver. My long underwear was soaked from the exertion. I peeled off my clothes and stood in the steamy shower. Had hot water ever felt so good?

By the time Jim returned, I had a pot of turkey noodle soup simmering on the stove. He walked in bringing the fresh air with him.

"Go," I pointed to the bathroom. "Shower yourself off and I'll feed you."

After lunch, we lounged in front of the fireplace. Jim told me more about his high school days as a runner and cross-country skier. "I was tall enough to play basketball, but the game never interested me. I wanted to be outdoors."

It was time to ask the hard question. "If you take this promotion, you'll spend a lot of time at a desk, won't you? Is that what you want?" I tried to keep my voice neutral, but I knew as soon as the words were out, it sounded like a plea.

Jim shifted, sitting up straighter. He said quietly, "I don't know."

I felt cut off from his thoughts. The New Yorker in me wanted to demand an answer, wanted to confront him and say, "What about me?"

I was the daughter of my father, however. Dad was always thoughtful in how he handled high emotion and conflict. Perhaps it was his staid Yankee upbringing or perhaps it was because he had learned this was the best way to handle Mother's volatility due to her brain illness.

Despite the urge to say something, I stayed quiet waiting for his reply. It didn't come. Instead, he pushed himself up, patted Bronte on the head, and said, "I promised I'd throw some sticks for your dog."

While he was outside, my phone rang with Brewster's call ID. "Hello?"

The reply came in a heavily accented whisper. "Amy?"

"Elena?"

"You come soon? They take Yoli away."

"No. Rex said they're moving you to a different house. It's okay."

"No *la migra* come for Yoli!" Her whispering voice rose. "No Rex. No Rex here. Found phone. They come soon. They want baby."

Brewster's voice came through in the background. "I've lost the damn phone again. Kiley, have you seen it?"

I heard a little gasp and banging noises before Brewster's voice demanded. "Who are you talking to?"

"Hello?" I found I was shouting.

Brewster demanded. "Who is this?"

"It's Jamie. Is Elena all right?"

"She's fine," he growled.

"She thinks immigration people took Yoli away."

Brewster groaned. "She misunderstood. Dammit, this is getting out of hand."

In the background someone cried out in Spanish and Bonita began to wail.

"They're all fine. Leave it alone, okay?" Just before he ended the call, I heard him mutter, "They don't pay me enough for this shit."

He didn't sound particularly like a man of God.

I immediately called Rex. Instead of getting him or his voicemail, I received a "call failed" message. The same thing happened when I texted him. Where was he?

Jim came in as I paced in the kitchen staring at the phone. "What's up?"

Bronte trotted over to me and shook herself off before going to her water dish.

I pointed to the phone. "I just got a call from Elena at Mary's Place. She seems to think that ICE took Yoli away. She sounded panicked. When Brewster came on the phone he said she'd misunderstood." I looked up at Jim. "They think I can help them, but I don't know what to do."

At this point, Jim took on my father's calming demeanor. "Let's talk about it. My guess is that they misunderstood just like Brewster said."

"But it doesn't seem right to me. Maybe we should go there."

"It seems to me you said something yesterday about getting thrown out."

For the next hour, we talked about the situation. Jim was of the opinion that I should "butt out." By evening, he had me convinced. "Call Brewster tomorrow and I'm guessing you'll find it's all calm and sorted out."

I sat in front of the fire mulling everything over while Jim did the dishes. Andrew, my ex, had never gotten his hands soapy with dishwater. He claimed it dried his skin, which might harm his chances of landing an acting role. Even when I was passionately in love with him, I knew it was bullshit.

"Hey, what's this?" Jim called from the kitchen, holding up the sketch pad I'd set beside the Watersmeade manuscript. "Have you taken up drawing?"

He brought it over and sat down beside me, studying the first sketch. I felt an odd reaction. I wanted to snatch it from him and declare, "That's mine!" I gently tugged it away. "It was my mother's. I found it in a box of books."

Jim peered at me with a quizzical expression. "Sorry, I didn't mean to pry."

I held onto it for a few moments and gave it back to him. "My relationship with her was…uh…complicated."

"By the look on your face, it sounds like it was painful. Was she hard to get along with?"

The fire crackled and hissed as it ate at the dried bark of a birch log. I watched as sparks rose up the chimney. "Remember I told you she died when I was sixteen."

"Bad time to lose a parent, I guess." He leaned closer to me.

"I really lost her long before she died." I told him about the progressive brain disease that took her mind and then her body. "I was twelve the last time she lived with us."

Jim opened the sketchbook once again and examined the skyline. "I'm not much of a judge of drawing, but this seems to have something special."

I shrugged. "I think she had a lot of talent…"

"But?"

Here was where I could tell him about the cold fear that resided in the pit of my stomach. The fear that maybe I had inherited whatever it was that took her. Jim deserved to know, but I couldn't get the words out. I tried to keep my tone light. "But, we'll never know. Most of her artwork is gone. I think Dad sold some of it to pay for her care." I pointed to a framed painting by the fireplace. "That was hers."

Jim walked over and studied it. "Something haunting about it."

I poked the fire hoping my silence would keep him from asking more questions. He must have read me because he changed the subject.

"A big snowstorm is coming. My weather app tells me it's moving across the Dakotas and should hit Minnesota by tomorrow afternoon. I'll need to leave early to stay ahead of it."

I kissed him. "How about if you hang around and we can be snowed in together."

"Hmmm."

We made love in a slow easy way that night. It was a sweet time but also a little unsettling. Nestled under the covers with the man I loved, I should have savored the afterglow but somehow my unease about Mother's sketchbook and the unanswered questions about Mary's Place were knotted together in my brain. I vowed that as soon as he left tomorrow, I would drive to town and check out Mary's Place for myself.

The Empty House

I sat with Jim in the predawn as he finished a bowl of oatmeal. "Good stuff. Did you make it from scratch?" He kept his voice light, but I felt the tension between us. He needed to decide about his future and I needed to open up to him. This morning was not the time for either.

Pointing to the empty packet on the counter, I smiled. "If you call putting it in the microwave making it from scratch, then yes."

Bronte sensed the distance between us as she watched with an anxious wag of her tail.

Jim studied his phone. "Weather report doesn't look good, but I should miss the onset of the snow."

I fought back the urge to shout, *Stay. Just stay with me. We can talk through all of this.*

He looked around the cabin with a worried expression. "You have enough wood in case the electricity goes out?"

"I'm good. I even have an extra book of matches."

"You know to call the snowplow guy at Larissa Lodge if the snow gets too high on your drive?"

I pointed to my phone. "I've got him on speed dial."

"And stay off the lake until you see those old duffers bring out the ice houses?"

"Yes, Dad. And I won't stay up after curfew—promise."

He laughed but his brow was still knit. I knew that this checklist was a way of avoiding the big questions.

Once he was ready to go, he held me a long time. "You know how important you are to me."

We kissed and he was gone. Once again, I watched his taillights disappear down the road.

Bronte stood at my side. I stroked her smooth fur. "I really need to find someone who will stick around, don't you think?"

When daylight finally arrived, it came on gray and dreary. In the short time I'd lived on the lake, I'd learned more about weather patterns than I ever did in eighth grade science. I knew about high and low fronts and how my body responded to changes in barometric pressure. I had a slight headache signaling the drop. A storm of some sort was on its way. More than that, I felt the annoying tingle at the nape of my neck that told me something wasn't right.

Before driving to check in on the residents of Mary's Place, I opened my laptop in search of Alfonso Serrano, the whispered name from Elena. She'd said he was Carmela's brother. I found several but none of them fit the description. Next I tried Facebook and again drew a blank. I knew in this day and age my search capabilities were very primitive. If I could talk with Carmela and get more specific information, it would help.

Before I closed down the laptop, I sent a quick email to a couple of New York editor contacts asking if they would be interested in an article about being the "Unintentional Midwife." I thought the story of Bonita Amy's birth and maybe the circumstances around it would be of interest.

If I got a nibble, I might be able to sell an article for enough money to last me through February. I was learning very quickly the life of living month-to-month. For a moment, I sat back and wondered if I would be exploiting the plight of these women for my own financial gain. Was my desire to help them purely for monetary gain?

The phone pulled me out of my thoughts. It was Travis checking up on me. "Storm is coming this way. Are you ready?"

I laughed. "You and Jim are like a couple of mother hens. I have extra matches and at least three cans of tomato soup. I'll be fine."

Travis sounded serious when he replied. "I think you might want to stock up. I'd help you but I'm in Cascade for the next several days."

"How's the campaign going?" I needed to change the topic. I didn't want Travis fussing over me.

"My campaign team is hard at work."

A group of high school students volunteered, knocking on doors and leaving flyers. Since no one was running against him, I doubted he needed them, but I was happy to see them involved.

The sky was still a heavy gray when I bumped down the ruts Jim had made in the snow. If we got more than four inches of snow, I'd need to get plowed out. While Jim's pickup did fine, my Subaru was low enough to the ground to scrape its bottom in several places.

I stopped at Larissa Lodge to make sure Lars the snowplow driver would do my driveway. I found him out by his truck smoking a cigarette. He looked to be about seventy with a grizzled beard and ruddy face.

"Sure, I'll do 'er. I always wait until it's done blowing, you know. No sense plowing to have it drift in again."

I took a twenty out of my billfold and handed it to him.

"No need to pay me, you know. Larissa Lodge has always kept this road open—in case." Still, he took the money and shoved it in his pocket.

When I first moved here last spring, Rob had coached me. "If you stay through the winter, Lars needs to be your next best friend. Otherwise, you'll be snowed in for the duration."

The highway into Killdeer was clear and dry. As I passed the spot where Bonita Amy was born, I frowned. All the tracks we'd made were long gone and the bog looked its usual lonely self. In all the excitement of her birth and the discovery of Rita's body and the oddness of Mary's Place, I hadn't thought much about why Carmela had been out on this particular road. I'd found her in such a deserted area. No houses, little traffic, and at least five miles from town.

"I need to talk to her. Maybe Elena can interpret." I glanced over at the passenger seat as if Bronte was sitting beside me. Once again, I was talking to myself. "Lady, you are getting weird."

In town, I found the grocery store to be storm preparation busy. People were stocking up on everything including toilet paper. You'd think we were expecting a hurricane. I thought through what I would need if the electricity went out and bought more flashlight batteries, kerosene for the lamps stored in the shed and charcoal for grilling outside, and several gallons of water. If I had no electricity, I knew my furnace wouldn't work and I knew I couldn't pump water from the well.

Rob had suggested I get a small generator, just in case, but I didn't have the money. I wondered, as I filled my cart whether that was a bad decision. When I reached the cashier, I hoped she wouldn't tell me I didn't have the funds in my account.

I slipped through, calculating how soon I would get a check from C.P. Dowling for *The Darkening Sand.*

If I moved back to New York City, I knew I could piece together enough work to afford a closet-sized apartment in a dicey part of town. At least I had that to fall back on.

While the town was abuzz with shoppers stocking up for the great storm, the street in front of Mary's Place was quiet. As I parked in front of the house, it occurred to me that it was too quiet. If they were getting ready to move the women, wouldn't they have some type of transport vehicle in front? Where was the white van with its Texas plates?

The only movement outside was a squirrel racing up the oak tree in front. I looked around noting for the first time how isolated this house was from the rest of the street. An undeveloped piece of land stretched on one side all the way to the parking area of the Lady Slipper Trail. On the other was a weedy vacant lot containing the remains of an old foundation.

As I walked up to the porch, light snowflakes began to fall. I didn't have much time before I needed to get back on the road. My knock echoed through the house. I knocked again. "Hello? It's Jamie. I came with some treats for everyone."

Silence. Not even the sound of footsteps on the wooden floor.

"Hello?" This time I knocked so hard I scraped my knuckles. "Ouch."

When no one answered, I tried the door. It was unlocked. Not a surprise. People around here didn't lock their doors much. I'd once tried to leave the cabin unlocked and found that years of city living wouldn't let me.

I opened the door, still calling. "Hi. It's Jamie."

Again, silence.

The house smelled cold, like someone had turned the thermostat way down. Not good for pregnant women and babies. I walked the hallway to the kitchen. The table was bare and the counters had an abandoned look.

"Hello?"

This time I thought I heard a sound overhead. Like the creak of a footstep. At the bottom of the staircase, I called up. "It's Jamie with treats. Is anyone home?"

I had this irrational thought that maybe they'd all taken a little jaunt to the clinic or to the store. If they'd already vacated the place, wouldn't they have locked the door?

Slowly I walked up the steps, stopping to announce myself several times. The doors to the upstairs bedrooms were all closed. I tried the first one and it opened to a room like Carmela's. Basic with a bed and a dresser and nothing else. The bed was stripped down to a mattress. Maybe this had been Rita's room.

I tried the room next to it. Again, the same thing, a vacant room, and a stripped bed. The Mary Sunshine in me said, "Maybe they took a trip to the laundromat." The Jamie Forest replied, "This is bad."

I hurried to the end of the hall where Carmela had been with Bonita Amy. When I opened the door, I was sure I heard something from the one bedroom I hadn't checked. Instead of looking inside Carmela's room, I stepped back to the other bedroom and opened the door.

It too was empty. Except, it didn't feel empty. I walked in. "It's Jamie. Is anyone here."

That's when I heard the little sob coming from a closed door near the bed. I walked over to it and pulled on the door. It was locked.

"Is anyone inside?"

"*Por favor.* Help me!"

"Elena, are you in there?"

"They lock me up. Say they come back soon."

I tugged at the locked door. "I…I can't get it open." I shoved back the panic that was tightening my chest. If they locked her in, something was very amiss. Something bigger than anything I had imagined.

"Key. Do you know where they keep a key?"

Elena sobbed. "No."

Settle down, Jamie, and think. I studied the door. It appeared to be locked with an old-fashioned skeleton key. Where would I find one? If worse came to worse, I could make a dash for the hardware store and buy one. But I sensed time was of the essence.

I closed my eyes and pictured what I knew of the house. Had I seen a key hanging somewhere or in a door somewhere?

"Elena, it's all right. I'm going to look for a key."

"Hurry!"

I checked all the upstairs rooms. When I opened the door to Carmela's room, I saw how empty it was. The bed was stripped and the cradle for Bonita Amy stood empty.

I ran down the stairs so fast I missed a step, stumbled, and twisted my ankle. "Damn. I don't' have time for this." I sat on the bottom step, rubbing my ankle.

Time to call for help. I reached in my pocket and realized I'd left my phone locked in the glove compartment of the car.

When I stood up, I found I could put weight on my foot even though an ache shot up my leg.

"Deal with that later," I muttered half hopping, half limping to the kitchen. Outside the snow was still coming down in slow, gentle flakes.

When I reached the kitchen, I looked around, wincing every time I moved. Where would they keep a skeleton key?

In my grandmother's old Victorian in Massachusetts, I remembered she kept a ring of keys in the pantry. I stumbled to the pantry door, noting the shelves were nearly empty. Right by the opening was a hook with a ring of keys.

As I grabbed them, I heard the sound of an approaching vehicle. "No!" Forgetting the pain in my ankle, I rushed to the stairs.

The Guest

Upstairs I fumbled with the keyring aware of the growing sound of an approaching vehicle. "I have the key. It'll be okay."

In my haste, I dropped the key ring. When it clanged to the floor, I heard Elena's sharp intake of breath.

"It's okay, Elena. Just a little clumsy." She couldn't see how my hands shook as I slipped the key into the lock. I had to wiggle it to get it to unlatch. It seemed like it took hours before the lock caught and I opened the door.

Outside, a car door slammed.

"We have to get you out of here."

Elena was huddled on the floor of an empty closet wearing only a nightgown, robe, and slippers. I helped her up. She swayed as she tried to regain her balance. By the looks of it, she was nearing her due date.

Downstairs, the front door creaked open. A man spoke in a loud voice, "He said she's upstairs. Tried to run away or something so he locked her in the closet. I've got the key."

Another voice replied, "Whose car is that outside? Do you think someone else is here?"

Elena cringed next to me. I looked around. Our choices were to hide, try to run, or negotiate with them. Elena was in no shape to run, and I was sure we'd be discovered if we tried to hide—especially because my car had given us away. They'd definitely be searching for us.

I whispered to her. "We're going to walk down the steps like nothing happened and I'm going to tell them I'm taking you to the clinic." I put my arm around her waist and guided her to the stairs.

Two men stood at the bottom gaping up at us. I recognized both of them as the ones who had been unloading boxes into Bevins's garage. The fatter one had reddened cheeks as if the effort of walking into the house had winded him. I hoped I could use that as an advantage. At least they were local guys, not the Feds. I took that as a good sign.

I called out, "I'm taking her to the clinic. I think she's in labor." I kept a good grip on Elena as we walked down the stairs. "If you can hold the door for me, I'd appreciate it."

They both stood, mouths open.

"We're supposed to take her. That's what he said."

I wanted to know who "he" was, but this wasn't the time for questions. I thought about my neighbor in Queens who was loud and assertive and a bully. I channeled her persona. Stamping my foot hard enough that the skinny guy jumped I shouted, "He sent me to take her to the clinic. Now please move unless you want to deliver this baby!"

Skinny guy moved immediately. Big guy stood planted. "He said to bring her. He didn't say nothing about no clinic."

I patted my pocket. "You want me to call and really piss him off? Or do you want to move?"

An uncertain look crossed his face and I took the opportunity to nudge Elena. We pushed by him while he fumbled for his phone. I bumped him and the phone went clattering to the floor.

Without looking back I hurried Elena to my car nearly carrying her as she slipped on the snowy sidewalk. Without waiting for her to buckle up, I started the car and pulled out, skidding on the road that now had a slick layer of snow.

"We're going to my place until we can get this figured out."

Elena whispered. "*Gracias, Amy.*"

I drove on autopilot. At the turn to the highway, a pickup truck ahead of me spun its wheels on a patch of ice. "Hurry," I said through clenched teeth forgetting that Elena could hear me.

Elena caught her breath.

I tried to put on a reassuring smile. "It's okay."

The truck finally got traction and I was able to pull out onto the highway right behind it.

Once on the road, I kept a steady grip on the wheel. The road was still dry even though snowflakes were coming down. I glanced at Elena huddled in the passenger seat. "Carmela and the others. Do you know where they went?"

Elena stared straight ahead as if in a daze. "*Sí.* Yoli go to hospital for baby. The reverend and missus they take Carmela and baby." She paused. "Is not good."

"What do you mean?"

She continued to stare out the windshield. "The padre is no man of God." She lapsed into silence.

As we neared the marsh, the snow continued to come down in large fluffy flakes. I looked ahead to see the birthplace of Bonita Amy and my numbed brain finally kicked in. A storm was coming, Elena was close to her delivery date and I was taking her back to my cabin. If we got snowed in, I could be in a position to deliver another baby.

My shoulders tensed so hard, I felt it down my spine. "I'm a poetry major, not a midwife," I muttered, pulling over to the side of the road.

Elena's eyes widened. "*¿Como?¿Que pasa?*"

Before I did a U-turn, I pointed to the snow. "My cabin could get snowed in. You need to be in town."

She grabbed at the wheel. "No! No! They take me!"

In a gentle motion, I took her hand off the wheel. "It's okay. I have a friend in town where you can stay. They won't find you there."

I prayed Clarence would be open to having a guest. "You'll be fine. My friend is a lawyer. Maybe he can help you." Taking out my phone to call him, I noted with dismay that we were in a no-bar zone.

Where was Rex during this whole mess?

As we drove back into town, we met a white van. I sped up, hoping it wasn't the two men sent to get Elena from the locked closet.

A Safe Haven

Clarence lived close to the hospital in a beautiful old Victorian house complete with a wraparound porch. When we pulled up in the front of the house Joe was shoveling the walkway to the porch.

"Stay here while I talk with Clarence. I'll come back for you." I left the car running to keep Elena warm.

Joe stopped shoveling and regarded me with his usual stoic expression. "What's up?"

I pointed to Elena. "We need some help. I'm hoping Clarence is willing to have an overnight guest."

Joe walked with me to the door as I explained how I'd found Elena locked in a closet. "Something very bad is going on, but I don't know what it is."

Clarence greeted us at the door. He wore a woolen V-neck sweater over a crisp white shirt with a red bow tie. "To what do I owe the pleasure?"

"I'm sorry to intrude, but I need help." I pointed to the car and quickly recounted what I knew about Elena. When I finished, I added, "I found her locked in a closet at Mary's Place. Who would do that?"

"Is she undocumented?" Clarence peered at the car.

"I don't know, but I think so. I do know she's scared." The fluffy snowflakes were already coating the sidewalk Joe had just shoveled.

Clarence hesitated, scratching his chin. He wrinkled his brow and for a moment I thought he'd turn us away. Then I saw the little glint of mischief in his eyes. "Well, bring her in and let's see what we can do."

Joe helped me bring Elena into the house. Her eyes were big, and she trembled as we walked in the door. Clarence held out his hand, "*Buenos dias, senorita."*

"I didn't know you spoke Spanish."

Clarence ushered us into the living room. "I am a man of very few talents, but I have a smattering of Spanish." He smiled. "Not much cause to speak it in Killdeer, of course."

Clarence settled Elena in an upholstered chair speaking to her in slow Spanish. I picked up a few words from my four years of Italian and my halting conversations with the owner of the local bodega in Queens, but not enough to understand what they were talking about. At times Elena's words spilled out so fast, Clarence had to slow her down. I watched the tension lines on her face as she spoke.

After fifteen minutes or so, Clarence turned to me. "Seems this is quite a complicated situation. I think the young lady should stay here for the night while we try to sort it out. I'm going to call Lorraine, my neighbor, and see if we can get some clothes for our guest. Meanwhile, I think she could use a good nap."

He told this to Elena in Spanish. She nodded and replied in English. "I understand *inglés* but not speak good."

Clarence directed me upstairs to one of the spare bedrooms. "Lorraine has clean sheets in the closet. Why don't you make up the bed and we'll let our mother-to-be have a rest."

I'd never been in the upstairs of Clarence's house. A thick oriental runner covered the polished wood flooring. Compared to Mary's Place this was a five-star accommodation. The spare room contained matching oak furniture including a vanity and a four-poster bed. On the vanity was an old photo of Clarence and his wife. He stood tall and dignified with an amused expression on his face. His wife, with her short-bobbed hair, stared straight into the camera with an expression that seemed to say, "Don't cross me."

I helped Elena to the bedroom. She surveyed it with wide eyes. *"Bueno aquí."*

"Clarence and Joe will take good care of you, but I need to get back to my cabin to make sure my dog is all right."

She frowned. "No stay here?"

"I'll come back as soon as I can. You are safe here."

"The Conways no come for me?"

"No." I patted her on the shoulder. "You rest now."

Elena curled up under the covers and closed her eyes. With her face so relaxed, she looked younger. I wondered if this was the first time she'd felt safe in a while. I hoped that was true.

Downstairs Clarence beckoned me to the kitchen where we had coffee and sandwiches Lorraine had left for them that morning. Joe sat listening while Clarence relayed to us what he'd learned from Elena.

"Admittedly my Spanish is pretty rusty, but I think I got the gist of what she was saying."

"Is she undocumented?"

Clarence pressed his lips together in a grim expression. "That's only a piece of it."

I took a bite of the ham and cheese sandwich savoring the thick rye bread. Clarence watched me with a slight shake to his head. "What?" I set the sandwich down.

"Lorraine is as bad as my wife. Whole grain this, whole grain that. What's wrong with nice soft Wonder Bread?"

Joe chortled and said nothing.

Leaning toward Clarence I asked, "What do you mean 'only a piece of it'?"

Clarence opened his sandwich, took the ham and cheese out, cut them into little bites, and ate them before he answered. I wanted to poke him. Joe sensed my impatience and finally spoke. "Clarence, Jamie needs an answer before she throws a butter knife at you."

I looked at him sitting with a slight smile on his face. "Is it that obvious?"

Setting his knife and fork down by his plate, Clarence finally spoke. "She said she was seeking asylum. She paid a lot of money to be taken across the border in Texas. The man she paid told her to surrender to the authorities and ask for asylum. They would take her somewhere to apply for it."

I nodded. "Okay."

"They locked her up in what she thought was a jail with many other people including children. It was loud and uncomfortable—hardly any food or water and people were using the corners of the room for—uh—the facilities. When nothing happened for several days, she used her English to get the attention of one of the guards. She told him she was pregnant and might be in labor."

I thought about how I'd once been jailed in a crowded cell and how panicked I'd felt. My hands suddenly turned cold as I remembered the smell of unwashed bodies and fear. In my case, I was in Queens, not a foreign country.

"That's when the guard took her to another room and someone from Viaje Seguro talked with her."

"I wonder if it was Rex? He's a lawyer from Viaje Seguro."

"Whoever it was told her they would take care of her but she needed to sign some papers."

"And that's how she got to Mary's Place?" Maybe some of the pieces were falling in place.

Clarence shrugged. "That's as far as we got. Poor girl was exhausted talking to me. And I was exhausted trying to understand her."

"Why did you say it's complicated?"

Joe stood up to clear the table. He spoke in a quiet voice. "It's the papers, isn't it?"

Clarence pushed himself up from the table. "They said if she signed the papers, they would take care of her." When he stood he sighed. "She doesn't know what those papers were."

I ran all the possibilities through my head and stopped. How many times had I heard Carmela plead to keep her baby? "Oh my god, do you think it had something to do with surrendering the baby?"

Instead of answering, Clarence walked slowly out of the kitchen. "Naptime for the old geezer. Joe and I will do some research. You go home and tend to that dog of yours. Our little mother-to-be should be safe for the time being."

Before leaving, I called the hospital to check on Yoli. Fortunately, Norma answered.

"It's Jamie. I'm checking to see if you have one of the girls from Mary's

Place. Her name is Yoli. I don't know her last name."

"You know I can't give out patient information."

I heard the tap on the computer. "How about general information? You know, like whether you have someone in labor?"

Norma laughed. "Only for you. We have a young woman—probably not more than fifteen. Doesn't speak English. Nita, our LPN speaks Spanish. She said the girl doesn't speak Spanish either. She thinks it might be a local dialect."

"Oh man, poor Yoli. Are the Conways with her?"

"She's here alone. I'm told a couple brought her in and left."

"She must really be scared. How is she doing?"

Norma hesitated. "Again, I can't give out medical information. However, I'd say this one is high risk. We're going to transfer her to Duluth as soon as the ambulance gets here."

I pictured Yoli so small and frightened. "Would it help if I came? She would recognize me, at least."

In the background, I heard the sound of a bell. "Oops, gotta go. Maybe if you could stop by and hold her hand for a minute that would help. She's pretty agitated."

Out the window, the slow fluffy flake had turned hard and icy. I needed to get home before my road closed, but I couldn't abandon Yoli.

At the door, I told Joe, "I'm going to stop at the hospital to check on one of the Mary's Place girls. Once I get home, I'll see if I can find out more about Viaje Seguro. Maybe when Clarence gets up he can try to get hold of Rex—you know lawyer to lawyer—and figure out what papers have been signed. I'll text you the number."

He frowned with a troubled expression. "I'll do what I can here." Joe knew what it was like to be alone and in trouble. I trusted him to watch over Elena. I knew Norma would watch over Yoli. But what about Carmela and Bonita Amy?

I arrived at the hospital as they were putting Yoli on a gurney to transfer her to the ambulance. I looked around for Brewster or Kiley but saw only the ambulance staff, the doctor and Norma. Yoli's eyes were wide with fear and pain. As they strapped her down, she writhed calling in a language I didn't recognize.

Taking her hand, I leaned close. "Yoli, I know you can't understand me, but these are good people and they will take care of you and your baby."

She looked through me as if I wasn't there. Perhaps her fear blocked her from seeing me.

"It's okay." I kept my voice soft. "You'll be okay."

As they started to roll the gurney out, she blinked and squeezed my hand. "Sankew," she whispered. I smiled, touched her cheek, and said under my breath, "Godspeed, Yoli. Godspeed."

Dead Presidents

The snow swirled across the highway in a dizzying and macabre dance. I prayed the ambulance taking Yoli to Duluth was able to keep ahead of the storm.

By the time I turned off at the lodge for my road, I was having difficulty telling where the road ended, and the ditch began. My head and shoulders ached from the effort. As I drove past the lodge, the tracks through the snow in the driveway indicated another vehicle had driven this way and turned around. A white van? The imaginary spider crawled up my back. What if someone was waiting for me?

I almost stopped. If I had, I wasn't sure I'd get traction to go again. Driving was still new to this New York City girl and driving in the snow was even newer. I'd actually watched some YouTube videos to prepare myself. They didn't capture the sensation of sliding and barely controlling the car as the wheels spun through the snow. My fingers clamped onto the steering wheel as I peered through the veil of snow hoping I was keeping to the track.

I'd left my back porch light on and I took a deep breath of relief when I saw the glow through the gray-white curtain. The parking area was empty, but tracks indicated someone had been here and turned around. I could hope it was the UPS driver with another manuscript, but something told me it wasn't.

As soon as I turned off the car, I heard Bronte barking her greeting. Carrying my bags of groceries, I slogged to the front door. I estimated about six inches of snow had fallen and more was coming down.

Inside Bronte greeted me, tap dancing her enthusiasm. "It's okay. I'm here now. Did we have visitors?" UPS usually put the package between the screen and the door, but I saw nothing.

Before settling in for the evening, I made my way through the snow to the woodpile. I hefted several loads of logs to the fireplace and stacked them. Rob had delivered a cord of mixed oak and birch this fall. As I hauled the wood in, I felt a pang of guilt because I hadn't paid him for it yet.

"You've got to get yourself a steady income or you won't survive out here." A gust of wind tore my voice away.

The exercise in the blowing snow did me good. For a little while, all I concentrated on was carrying the wood into the cabin and stacking it. No worries about Yoli or Carmela or the baby with my name. No worries about who would pay for the dent in my car. No worries about paying next month's electric bill.

From the shed behind the cabin, I took out an old plastic sled. Who knows, maybe I could slide down the incline to the lake? After everything that had happened the idea of playing in the snow appealed to me. I also leaned my cross country skis up against the outside of the cabin and made sure the poles were with them.

With the wood stacked by the fireplace, I gathered everything I thought I'd need if the electricity went out. On the kitchen counter, I lined up a flashlight, several candles, and a box of matches. I was ready for whatever the blizzard had in store for me. Or so I thought.

The snow kept pouring down. In the hour since I'd arrived home another four inches had fallen. As best as I could tell, I could still get out if I needed to. I stood on the back steps watching the snow swirl makings its ghosts and curlicues. Bronte charged off into the woods with a delighted yip. The energy of the storm created an excitement similar to the one I had felt in New York when we'd had a big snowfall. It wasn't life as usual.

Grabbing the sled, I sat on it, urging it with my body until gravity took hold. With a sense of freedom and delight, I whizzed down the slope of the yard onto the lake, skidding and twirling with Bronte dashing after me. For those moments, I felt so exhilarated I didn't worry that I'd slid out on the lake.

Three runs later, both of us were exhausted. "Enough, girl. Time to be an adult again and sit down to figure out all the weirdness with Mary's Place and the pregnant women."

Although the lights flickered, they stayed on even as the wind increased. Dustlike snow seeped into the kitchen under the back door. I rolled up a rug and stuffed it against the door.

On a piece of paper, I jotted down the questions I wanted to ask Elena. What did she know about the other women? Did she know anything about Rita and why she was found in Black Crow Pond? What did Viaje Seguro promise to her and what were the papers she talked about? Why was Carmela out on the road the day she gave birth? The more I thought about what to ask her, the more questions I had.

I put them into an email to Joe Clarence's assistant because Clarence still hadn't entered the twenty-first century. I laughed thinking about my octogenarian lawyer friend who was still stuck in the days of telephone calls and snail mail.

Time for a glass of wine. As I poured it, my phone pinged with a text from Jim.

Are you okay?

I answered, **So far.**

Stay put.

I looked out the window and saw nothing but a gray-white curtain. **Can't go anywhere right now.**

He replied, **Take care.**

I sighed. I had to give Jim credit; he wasn't one for affectionate texting. No heart emojis, no "I luv you." Andrew, my ex was great for all that stuff including sending me flowers, which I ended up paying for.

Before logging onto the internet to find out more about Viaje Seguro, I called Rex. Once again the call failed message came back. "Where are you?" I muttered to my phone.

Bronte thumped her tail on the floor. I patted her on the head. "Not you. Rex the lawyer seems to have disappeared."

With some trepidation, I found Brewster's number. Before I called, I took a deep breath and thought through what I would say. If he was the one who locked Elena in the closet, I didn't want to reveal that I'd gotten her out. On the other hand, if he was the one, he probably already knew. If not, who had done it, and who was the "he" the big guy and the skinny guy were talking about?

Life was so much easier when I was studying poets and how to write a sestina. Whatever happened to those days? It reminded me that I was still in the midst of Queen Alusra and Levy's quest to save the planet from dehydration.

Brewster's phone went immediately to voicemail. I hesitated, unsure whether to leave a message. Since he probably knew it was me by caller ID I simply said, "Hi, it's Jamie. I'm checking to make sure everything is all right at Mary's Place." I ended the call knowing nothing was all right there. I doubted he would call me back.

Setting the phone down, I went back to my laptop which thankfully was still connected to the internet. When the Viaje Seguro site came up, I scrutinized it. Maybe I'd missed something about their mission or how they worked. The "about us" page featured a photo of a smiling woman holding a toddler with thick dark hair and deep brown eyes. Beneath the photo was the quote, "We are so happy to have a forever home for our Cassie." The quote was attributed to someone with the initials L.B.J. I studied it and wondered if Viaje Seguro provided international adoption services.

Only three other pages opened—our staff, donate and contact us. When I clicked on "Donate" I found little more than instructions on how to make an online donation. "Contact us" had a form to fill out but no telephone numbers or addresses either physical or email. I clicked on the page listing staff and board members.

The only staff members listed were John Adams as executive director and Jane Madison as office manager. The small size of the staff didn't surprise me. Many NGOs operated on a shoestring with mainly volunteer help.

I moved to the list of the eight board members. Starting with the chair, Andrea Jackson, I googled her but came up with nothing useful. Going down the list, next I tried J.K. Polk. Unless he was the dead president, nothing came up that I could use. The third one was Jay Tyler.

A blast of wind knocked against the front window, startling me. What was wrong with this list? Polk, Madison, Adams, Jackson, Tyler and Taylor?

"Bronte," I exclaimed, "this has to be bogus. How many organizations have dead presidents as board members? Is this a joke?"

I looked up a couple of sites that listed legitimate charities and charities that had 501c3 tax-exempt status. Viaje Seguro was not listed. "Why didn't I look this up in the first place?" Maybe because I was charmed by Rex Jordan's good looks and expensive watch.

Bronte ignored my mutterings, sat up, yawned and sauntered into the living room. She wasn't interested in my detective work.

The cabin rattled with a strong gust of wind and I heard a cracking noise outside. Bronte trotted to the back door with a little bark.

"What do you suppose that was?"

When I opened the door, snow slammed into my face, blurring my vision. "Tain't a fit night out fer man nor beast." Bronte gazed up at me as if to say, "Knock off the clichés." A large branch had fallen from an ailing birch tree at the edge of my lawn. Rob had recommended I take the tree down last September. Because of where it was located, he'd suggested hiring someone who knew what they were doing and wouldn't land the tree on the cabin. With the thought of more dollar bills floating away, I'd told him maybe next spring.

Over the roar of the wind and the slap of the icy snow, I thought I heard the buzz of a snowmobile. "Who would be out in this?"

I closed the door and made sure it was locked.

Sipping a warmed-up bowl of turkey soup, I logged into my email. Joe had replied in his usual parsimonious style. "Clarence will call."

Back to Viaje Seguro, I looked at the Federal Website providing information on international adoptions. It listed approved agencies. Viaje Seguro was not on that list either.

Clarence didn't call nor did Brewster return my call as the storm raged and the evening wore on. At one point I turned on the outside light and looked out at nothing but the gray swirl of snow. I figured at least a foot of snow had piled up on my car. By now, I expected the driveway to be impassable.

"Oh please, Lars, let me be your first customer tomorrow when you get the plow out."

Bronte woofed in agreement and stepped gingerly into the snow to do her bedtime business.

"Thank god I have indoor plumbing." The thought of running out in this to an outhouse brought back a longing for my Queens apartment with its leaky toilet and hissing radiators. I had Native American blood in my veins, but you'd never know it. "Whose idea was it to move here?" Bronte ignored me as she shook snow off her coat.

The lights flickered again. When I checked the laptop, the internet was gone. My hookup was sketchy in the first place. I relied on the internet at Larissa Lodge and a hot spot on my phone. Research time was over.

As I stood in the bathroom in front of the mirror brushing my teeth, the lights flickered once more. To be on the safe side, I filled several empty plastic jugs with water in case I had no electricity for the well pump. I must have been prescient because as soon as I turned the tap off, the lights flickered and the cabin was thrown into darkness.

Fully dressed, I settled under the comforter with Bronte next to me. I was just dropping off to sleep when Bronte growled. As the storm raged, holding the cabin in its icy grasp, I thought I heard a noise like a tapping at my door. "It's okay, girl, just the wind." The tapping grew as Bronte's growl turned into a bark. Someone was pounding at my door.

She scrambled out of the bedroom barking as she ran to the backdoor. I made my way through the darkness hoping the sound I heard was only the brush of the wind against the side of the cabin.

The pounding grew louder and Bronte's bark grew more frantic. My eyes adjusted to the darkness in the kitchen as the knocking continued. A female voice called out, "Help! I need help!"

Grabbing a flashlight from the counter, I pulled Bronte away from the door and opened it. Kiley stood shivering on the step wearing only a thin windbreaker and carrying a green backpack. Her hands were bare and she'd pulled the hood up over her ears. "Please." She stumbled inside. "I'm so cold."

A Snowy Rescue

I led her into the living room to sit near the dying fire. Melted snow dripped off her face and her teeth rattled from shivering.

"You...you have to get them..."

I threw a couple of logs on the fire and blew on the embers to build it up. "Get who?"

"They're...in the car. Stuck...couldn't get all the way here."

"Who are you talking about?"

Kiley drew the blanket I'd draped over her shoulders closer. "C...Carmela and baby. Couldn't have him take the baby away." She blinked tears out of her eyes. "Couldn't do it."

I was so focused on warming her up that I wasn't tracking what she'd said. "Carmela and the baby are where?"

"Car. Stuck in the driveway."

It finally dawned on me. "Oh my god. They're outside?"

"Y...yes." Her eyes were feverish in the dim light of the fireplace. "But I left the car running so they'd have heat."

"How far away?"

"I...I don't know. I just kept walking."

Immediately I thought about the snow piling up and the car running. Even as a novice driver I knew that if the tailpipe got plugged they could die of carbon monoxide. I was up and heading for my down jacket and boots before Kiley could tell me more. "I've got to get them out."

I grabbed my phone to call 911. It had no bars. The storm must have knocked out the cell tower. At least I'd had the sense to charge it.

When I opened the door, the wind blasted me. Bronte whined at my feet. I turned to her. "Stay and keep Kiley warm."

In my haste, I forgot a scarf and managed to drop one of my gloves. I slogged through the snow for about six feet. It was like trying to run in water. How had Kiley made it here? I stopped to catch my breath. "Okay, Jamie. Get hold of yourself. What do you need?"

If I were to bring Carmela and the baby back to the cabin, I was sure she wouldn't be able to walk through the snow carrying a baby. The red sled leaned against the wall of the cabin. I would have to pull them in the sled.

"Snowshoes. I need snowshoes." Rob had brought me a pair of used ones in early November. He'd showed me how to strap them on and said, "These could be handy."

I pushed my way through the snow that had drifted against the door of the shed. I couldn't pull the door open and a flush of panic crept up my body as I tugged at the door. "Calm down," I said out loud. "Think."

The snow against the door was light enough that I could scoop it away with my hands. I worked until I had cleared enough to open the door a crack. Clicking on the flashlight, I eased into the shed. Already my hands were numb. The snowshoes were hanging by the door. I slipped them off the hook praying I could remember how to put them on.

Snowshoes in hand, I slogged back to the cabin and opened the door.

"Kiley, how far do you think the car is?"

Kiley huddled by the fireplace, her back to me. "I was driving fine even though the snow was deep on the road and then the road curved a little and I went off onto the side. I couldn't get it going again." She sniffled. "I'm so sorry. I screwed everything up."

"It's okay. We'll get them out."

On the back step, I struggled to strap on the snowshoes. My hands felt like paws as I pulled the strap over the front of my boot and ratcheted the strap around the back. Looping the rope to the sled around my wrist to drag it behind me, I set off using the cross-country ski poles to keep me steady. In the darkness and the swirling snow, I tried to keep to Kiley's footprints. In some places, they were already drifted in. In others, the snow was compact enough that I could move forward easily. I cursed my awkwardness and the wind that whipped at the plastic sled. A gust lifted it up and pulled me so hard I fell over. "Damn it!" Struggling to get up, I nearly lost my glove.

The wind tore through my jacket, but I wasn't cold. In fact, as I trudged ahead, heat rose through me from all the effort. For the first time, I understood the slim, body-hugging suits skiers wore in the Olympics. The jacket was cumbersome and caught the wind.

The part of the road Kiley described was about halfway between the cabin and Larissa Lodge. As I struggled with the snow and the wind and the sled, I wondered if I would ever reach the car. At one point, I stopped to catch my breath straining to hear the sound of a car engine above the roar of the storm. It was so dark and the snow so thick, I wasn't sure where I was. If it hadn't been for the faint tracks Kiley had left behind, I wouldn't have known I was on the road.

I trudged on, straining for the sound of a car engine. I'd lost all track of time and distance. How much farther could it be?

I stopped for a moment to catch my breath, feeling an overwhelming sense of tiredness. My arms and legs grew heavier and for an insane moment, I considered sitting down. Maybe I could take off my heavy jacket and burrow into the snow, muffle the grating whine of the wind and take a little rest. Just before the wind died down to a lull a branch snapped in the woods. The voice in my head whispered, *Not now. Keep moving.*

In the brief quiet, I heard the low rumble of a car engine.

"I'm coming," I mouthed, tugging the sled behind me.

Up ahead, I saw a blurred light. Kiley had left the lights of the car on. With renewed strength, I pushed myself forward. The car was sitting at an angle, partially on the driveway but mired in the snow beside it. The snow around the car was disturbed. Kiley must have tried to dig it out before she gave up and stumbled to the cabin.

"Carmela! Are you in there?" What if she'd gotten frightened and tried to walk out? I heard nothing but the blast of the snow and the wind whistling through the treetops.

I called again. "Carmela!"

The backdoor flew open and Carmela, hugging Bonita Amy close to her body stared at me in the sickly yellow dome light of the car. "Amy! Amy you come!"

I knelt down by her. "We have to get you back to the cabin. Not safe here."

Carmela stared out at the wall of snow and shook her head. "No!" She pointed, *"Frio. No bueno.* Cold for baby."

Convincing a frightened mother to abandon the warmth of the car for a raging blizzard was not part of my skillset. I was hot and cold and frightened myself. Instead of patiently working with her, I ripped open the driver's side door, reached in, and turned the car off. "We have to go!"

I'll never forget the look of fear and betrayal on Carmela's face as I tugged her out of the car. I pulled the sled to her and motioned her to sit with the baby still wrapped inside her shabby coat. Without questioning whether this was a good idea or not, I slipped off my down jacket and put it on her. "You keep Bonita warm, okay?"

The wind ripped through me as I struggled to pull the sled. It chilled me to my bones. Underneath the sweater I wore, my cotton turtleneck was soaked with sweat. I was ripe for hypothermia, but I had to keep going.

I knew the body did strange things as it slowly froze. People had been found naked as hypothermia set in and the brain said it was too hot.

Great, I thought. This is what I need to have running through my head. Behind me, the baby started to cry. It was like a prod in my back to speed up. My face was frozen, and I couldn't feel the tips of my fingers as I gripped the poles. The sled bumped up against the snowshoes whenever I lost the forward rhythm. If I didn't get to the cabin soon, I'd be shedding all my clothes.

"¡Dios mio!" Carmela cried over and over.

When I reached a point where I couldn't catch my breath and my lungs ached and I had a severe stitch in my side I thought we were all lost. Just then, I heard Bronte's muffled barking. Up ahead through the dizzying snow, I saw the faint yellow of a candle Kiley had put in the window. We'd made it.

With one big surge of energy, I pulled them to the cabin. At the door, I motioned Carmela inside while I worked my numbed fingers to unstrap the snowshoes. Tears from the wind and the snow froze on my cheeks. I wondered if I'd ever be warm again.

Kiley's Story

Kiley had stoked up the fire and lit several candles. The cabin smelled of woodsmoke and pine-scented candles. I'm not sure I'd ever felt such relief as I did holding my numbed tingling fingers near the fire. Bronte sat next to me, a worried expression on her face.

"It's okay, girl," I mouthed to her.

Carmela, still wearing my down jacket, huddled close to me cradling the sleeping Bonita Amy in her arms. No one spoke for a long time. Outside the wind continued its siren call. Inside, at least for the moment, we felt sheltered and safe.

My chest and hands ached as I warmed up. Despite a slight nausea, I knew I had to rehydrate. I stood on shaky legs. "I'm going to make us tea."

I set the tea kettle on the burner, thankful to have a propane stove and not an electric one. While the water heated, I checked my phone. I still had no bars. For the time being, we were isolated. I doubted Lars would plow the road until the storm abated. And who knows when the electricity would come back on.

We sat with our tea, three adults, one baby, and one dog on the floor in front of the fireplace. As the wood crackled and spit, Kiley slowly told her story. Bonita Amy slept in her mother's arms.

"I met Brewster in a twelve-step program after my dad threw me out." Kiley spoke in a flat voice, pointing to the scar on her face. "My dad…well, he was pretty mean and I was drunk and high most of the time. We got into a fight and I ended up in rehab. I was living in a shelter when Brewster kind of took me under his wing. He got me a temp job where he worked in a detention center. After a couple of months, he said he was going to work for this new place that helped some of the girls who were pregnant and asked if I wanted to come along."

Outside, above the wail of the wind, I heard a cracking sound. Jim had warned me that as the lake froze over, it spoke. If it was the lake, I decided it was in agony as the ice deepened and the temperature dropped.

I prompted Kiley. "You fell for him?"

She nodded. "He's older than me but I didn't care at the time. He was the nicest man I'd ever met."

Carmela, who had been straining to understand, shook her head. "No is nice now."

Kiley took a deep breath. "We're not married. We just say we are. The people—the Viaje Seguro people thought it best to say we were married."

I pictured the website with dead presidents as board members. "Who are they?"

Kiley shrugged, shaking her head. "I thought they were good people. They wanted to help pregnant girls who were trying to get away from bad places—you know, like Carmela." She fell silent.

"But?"

"They don't care about the girls. All they care about are the babies."

It took time, more tea, and a helping of leftover turkey soup before Kiley was able to tell the whole story. She didn't know who was behind Viaje Seguro, she thought Rex might have been duped into providing legal services and she thought Brewster knew more than he was telling her.

"We came in a van from Texas to here. I don't know why they decided this was a good place except someone had offered a house for us."

"Bevins?"

"I don't know."

Carmela dozed on the couch as we talked. Bonita Amy continued to sleep peacefully. I worried that when she woke up she'd need a diaper change. I hadn't prepared for infant guests or any guests for that matter.

"What happens to the babies?"

Kiley wiped her face with the sleeve of her sweater. "I don't know, but I think they're put up for adoption."

I pictured the Viaje Seguro site with its lack of concrete information.

"Our job, Brewster and mine, was to keep the girls healthy and make sure they had a safe delivery. After they came back to the house, usually a day or two later, someone would come and take the girls and their babies." Her eyes grew moist. "They...they said they were taking them to get asylum. I never saw them again."

A stab of cold shot through my body. "What do you think happened to them?"

Kiley picked up the mug with her tea. Her hand shook. "I overheard Brewster on the phone just before Thanksgiving. He said something about someone taking Rita back to the border."

"You think Rita ran away because they were going to deport her?"

Bonita Amy squawked in her sleep. Carmela shifted a little and Bonita began fussing. Carmela sat up. "*Bebé* need change."

I wondered how to handle this diaper change. I knew we couldn't put paper towels on Bonita Amy. Fortunately, I'd once copyedited a memoir by a woman who had grown up a middle child in a large Catholic household. She wrote about how her mother kept running out of diapers and had to use dish towels as a backup.

"Come. We'll find something to use."

The temperature in the bathroom had dropped to the low fifties. I grabbed some towels and washcloths and brought them out. We heated water in the tea kettle to use to wash Bonita's bottom. I wondered what it must have been like for the pioneer women or the Native Americans to live here in the winter. I decided the babies had to be strong to survive.

After she was changed, Carmela nursed her while I talked more with Kiley. Bronte must have sensed Kiley's distress because she settled in closer to her. I prompted, "Why did Rita leave?"

"I don't know. But I do know someone came to the door after Rita got back from the hospital. Brewster asked me to take Rita into the kitchen. I heard her baby cry and then the door closed and the baby was gone. Rita nearly went crazy."

"What did you do?"

"Brewster gave her some pills and told her they were just taking the baby for a check-up. The next day Rita was gone and…well you know how they found her." Kiley stared into the fireplace. "I think she killed herself."

No, I thought. Someone killed her. Brewster? Or was Kiley lying to save herself? She seemed harmless enough but what did I really know about her? Maybe she was after Bonita Amy.

My shoulders tensed and Kiley must have noticed. "I'm so sorry about all of this."

I put the last log on the fire. Instead of catching fire right away, it smoked and appeared to be smothering the embers. "I need to get more wood. Can you poke the logs? I think this last one might be too wet or too green."

I hated the thought of going back outside but we needed to keep the fire going. My boots were wet. Bronte came trotting over to me as I tied the soggy laces. "Want an adventure?" She wagged her tail.

She kept wagging her tail until I opened the door. As the wind and snow blasted into the kitchen, she backed up. "Oh no, girl. You're coming out with me. No peeing on the floor."

Outside, the snow had subsided enough that when I used the flashlight to check the thermometer mounted on the ailing tree, I saw it registered zero. If what everyone had told me about winter storms was correct, as the weather cleared the temperature would go down. I hoped I could keep the cabin warm enough until I could get a cell signal and call for help.

I hauled in three more loads of logs before I thought my fingers would freeze off. It gave me some "think" time as I lifted the logs from the pile, carried them inside, and stacked them by the fireplace. Something about Kiley's story was off, but I wasn't sure what it was.

Before I settled in front of the fire again, I poured myself a glass of red wine. I offered one to Kiley but she shook her head. "I'm six months sober."

It was clear to me that Kiley had lived a lot in her short years. Settling down next to her, I took a sip of the wine. It tasted a little vinegary, but I didn't care. "Okay, Kiley. I'm tired, this hasn't been my idea of a fun campout and I need you to tell me how you ended up here in the middle of a blizzard.

The truth please."

She looked at me with a startled expression. "You don't believe me?"

"I think you're holding something back. I don't think you are a bad person, but I also don't think you would risk what you've risked simply to save Carmela and her baby. Something else is going on."

She pressed her lips together and I could see the sullen teenager that still resided in her.

"Well?"

She weighed her words and took a deep breath. "Okay. Brewster and I had a fight. We'd taken Carmela to the motel on the edge of town, you know, the Pine Tree Inn. Brewster said that's where we'd get our ride to the new safe place. But something wasn't right. Why not pick us up at the house?"

"And you didn't believe him."

"I think he was going to take the baby and leave us. He was making a bunch of phone calls outside the room."

She was still holding back. She must have known about locking Elena in the closet. Yet, she said nothing about it.

"What about Elena?" I gripped the fireplace poker hard as I stirred the logs.

"Elena? They'd taken her already."

"Who had taken her?"

Kiley shrugged. "You know, a couple of guys from Viaje Seguro. They had a van like the one we rode in from Texas. They were taking her to another place, I guess."

I'll give Kiley credit, she lied with a straight face. "What happened at the motel?" I found I was poking harder at the logs, trying to stay calm.

"I think Brewster was making arrangements for someone to come and take Bonita Amy. I knew Carmela didn't want to give her up and I panicked. While he was out using the phone, I grabbed the keys from the car Viaje Seguro had lent to us. Then I led Carmela out the back way to the parking lot and headed here. I didn't know how bad the snow would get."

"Kiley." I set the poker down beside me. "How did you know to come here?"

She motioned with her head to Carmela who dozed on the couch. "She wanted you. I didn't know where else to go. I stopped at the grocery store and asked how to get here."

I believed that part of her story. In a small community like this, people knew where I lived. A chill swept through me. If Kiley could easily find me, so could Brewster. I was sure the guys in the van had already been here. Was Elena safe at Clarence's? What had I gotten the old lawyer into?

I took a drink of the wine and decided it tasted more like salad dressing than wine. "What next?" My words were more to myself than to Kiley. A heaviness descended on me. My body and mind were both exhausted. I didn't have the energy to ask more questions and Kiley appeared to be dropping off to sleep.

As the wind continued to howl through the trees, I decided we all needed to sleep near the fireplace. I brought out a sleeping bag for Kiley and extra blankets for Carmela. We settled in front of the fireplace with Carmela and Bonita Amy on the couch, Kiley, Bronte, and me on the rug between the couch and the fireplace. I stoked the fire hoping I'd wake up before it needed more wood.

With a deep sigh, I closed my eyes and fell into a dark sleep, haunted by images of snow ghosts. In my dreams, I was huddled on the sidewalk next to Queens Boulevard with the constant roar of traffic streaming by.

Carmela

Sometime close to dawn I awoke with a start to a chilly cabin. The temperature had dropped and the fire was out. Bronte stood by me, her ears alert as she watched the door. With the wind quieted, the cabin had an eerie stillness to it. On the couch, Carmela breathed in an easy rhythm while Bonita lay beside her, making little grunting noises.

"What is it?" I whispered to Bronte. She continued to watch the door as if she expected someone to come in. I glanced at Kiley to see if she was awake.

"Oh no."

The sleeping bag was empty. Throwing off the heavy comforter, I hurried to the door to see if she'd stepped outside for some reason. My down jacket that I'd draped over the kitchen chair was gone along with my winter boots. Opening the door, I saw snowshoe prints in the snow heading down the driveway. Kiley had made her escape.

The thermometer registered fifteen below zero as weak sunlight rose from the east. If Kiley hadn't run off, if Carmela and her baby weren't on my couch, if I had electricity and water and a phone, I might have reveled in the sparkling beauty of the newly fallen snow. Instead, I stood in the doorway and selfishly despaired over the loss of my warm jacket and boots.

Bronte whined and walked gingerly into the snow. For a moment, I wished I was a dog with a thick furry coat instead of a human who'd just had her winter jacket stolen.

The contents of my purse spilled onto the kitchen table. I rushed over to find my wallet intact. At least she hadn't taken my ID and credit cards. However, all the cash, the precious dollars for Lars and for groceries, was gone.

Behind me, as if she could read my thoughts, Bonita Amy let out a squawk and a lusty cry. Carmela groaned as she picked up the baby. I walked over to her noting how washed out she looked. She had a paleness and sheen to her cheeks that her light brown coloring could not cover.

"Are you okay? ¿Está bien?" I hated that I could not communicate with her.

She shook her head. "No feel good."

I remembered from one of the romances I'd edited that the sister of the heroine died from "child bed fever." With all the activity of the last couple of days, I wondered if Carmela had an infection. The backseat of my car had hardly been germ-free when she'd given birth. I stepped over to her and touched her forehead. She was warm, too warm.

Right now, I wished I was by myself plowing through the hot sands of C.P. Dowling's book, not sitting in a cold cabin with a newborn and a sick mother and no electricity or phone.

I brought her a couple of Tylenol tablets and a glass of water. "This should help."

If she had an infection, the Tylenol wouldn't fix it. I needed to keep her warm and get her to the hospital as soon as I could. My cellphone was still dark. No service.

While she nursed Bonita Amy, I slipped on a pair of hiking boots, found my dress coat in the closet, and stepped out into the frigid air to bring in more wood.

"Damn you, Kiley," I huffed as I waded through the snow in a coat meant for going to the opera not hauling wood. My arms, shoulders, and thighs ached from pulling Carmela in the sled. The air was so cold that when my eyes watered, the tears froze on the lashes. At least it was light out now and the wind wasn't driving snow into my face.

While I built up the fire, Carmela sat rocking the baby. Her eyes were glazed with fever. If we didn't get out soon, I would have to ski to the lodge and hope they had a working telephone.

In the backroom with the furnace and the water heater, something mechanical squeaked. The light over the kitchen sink glowed a sickly orange, went out, and then snapped on. The electricity was back. Now if we could only get out.

Outside in the distance, I heard the rumble of a vehicle. "Please be Lars with the snowplow."

The progress was slow, but the drone of the plow grew louder. I heard thumping noises as he pushed the snow to the side of the road. I buttoned up the dressy coat, wrapped an old scarf I'd found in the closet around my neck and pulled on a knit cap. With Bronte by my side, I used a broom to wipe the snow off the car. Bronte happily woofed as the snow came spraying down and the plow made its slow progress to the cabin.

My toes were numbed by the time Lars arrived, pushing the snow in front of him. I waved, feeling a sense of relief. Bronte barked her happy bark.

He pulled up carefully clearing a path to the car. I walked over to the cab of the truck. "Thank god you are here."

"Had some trouble getting by that car down the road. Had to plow around it."

I pointed to the cabin. "I need to get out as soon as possible. I have a sick new mom in the cabin and I have to get her to the hospital."

Lars appeared unfazed as if this happened all the time. "I'll help you clear out behind the car and then I have to get to my other customers."

He had a snowblower in the bed of his truck. I was amazed at how quickly he was able to get it out and blow out the snow behind the car. He pointed to the frozen Subaru, "Better get her started and warmed up."

The car groaned, creaked, and grunted but finally caught. I almost cried, I was so relieved. Lars turned around and headed back to the Larissa Lodge. "I'll call a tow truck to get that other car out."

With the car warming, I bundled Carmela up with blankets. As I helped her to the car, I could tell how sick she was. She walked slowly, groaning softly, her teeth gritted. The fear that had faded in the cabin, registered on her fevered face again.

"No one will hurt you and no one will take Bonita Amy, okay?"

She hardly acknowledged me as she cradled the baby against her chest.

Locking up the cabin I instructed Bronte to guard it well. Who knew what Kiley was up to? If she found Brewster, would she tell him that Carmela and the baby were with me?

When we reached the snowed-in car, I stopped long enough to wipe the snow from the license plate and take a photo. I planned to report it as soon as I got Carmela to the hospital.

Back in the car, I eased around it, praying I wouldn't get stuck. Thank God the Subaru cooperated and stayed on the track. Even with Lars's careful plowing, the drive to the highway was slow. The car slid on the compacted snow. None of the YouTube videos had prepared me for the slipperiness. I ran into the same thing on the highway. Despite the heroic work of the Department of Transportation to keep the highway open, it was slippery. In places where the pavement appeared to be clear and dry, unexpected patches of ice caused the car to slue.

Next to me in the passenger seat, Carmela clutched the baby. If I was pulled over, I could be cited for not having an infant car seat. As slow as we were driving, I feared Carmela might fall asleep and drop the baby. Between trying to stay on the highway and worrying about Carmela and the baby, my head felt like something black inside it was pressing on my eyeballs.

Town was eerily quiet of traffic but filled with the noise of snowblowers. The hospital lot had been plowed and the emergency room entry liberally sprinkled with salt and sand. When I tried to help Carmela out of the car, she struggled to stand and then collapsed back on the seat. *"No puedo."* She handed the baby to me. *"Por favor."*

"I'll get help."

Carmela merely nodded.

Bonita Amy started to cry as soon as I held her. I ignored her wail and ran for the emergency room door. Once inside, I called. "I need some help here."

Norma came hurrying down the hall, her shoes squeaking on the polished floor. She looked at me and at the baby. "Is the little one sick?"

"No. It's Carmela. She can't get out of the car."

I stood aside holding Bonita Amy as Norma and her staff pulled out a wheelchair and brought Carmela in. They whisked her away while I rocked Bonita Amy. She was soaked through the makeshift diaper and the little sleeper. As I tried to calm her I felt clumsy and completely out of my element. I wanted to cry out, "I need help, too," but I knew the hospital was running on a skeleton staff and no one was available.

I stood in the waiting area feeling helpless and dumb until an aide scurried out "She won't let us do anything until she has her baby."

Still trying to calm Bonita Amy, I followed the aide to a curtained cubicle. Carmela lay in the bed looking even more ashen. Norma rolled a bassinette in. "We'll take care of the baby."

I squeezed Carmela's hand and left them to tend to her and the baby. Right now, all I wanted was a strong cup of coffee and Jim at my side. A coffee urn in the waiting room dispensed day-old sludge. It wasn't even warm anymore. I took one sip and threw the cup away.

The janitor came out pushing a mop and a pail to wipe the area around the front door. He muttered as he worked. "Damn winter. Shoulda retired to Florida like my brother."

He had the name Ed embroidered on his shirt.

"Ed?" I pointed to the urn. "Do you think someone will bring fresh coffee?"

He scowled at me. "Volunteers take care of that. Probably won't come today. Damn winter. Shoulda retired to Florida." He finished mopping and disappeared behind the double doors.

I shook my head. And I should have stayed in New York.

As I sat on the hard plastic chair, I knew I should check my phone. I didn't want to. I was suddenly exhausted. I didn't want to respond to messages. I didn't want to figure out how to deal with Carmela, Elena, Kiley or anything else associated with Viaje Seguro. I wanted to go home and sit at my kitchen table with a decent cup of coffee, my blue pencil and *Survivor of the Darkening Sand*.

Before I could continue feeling sorry for myself, the phone binged with a text from Jim.

Are you OK?

I hoped he was frantic with worry. Had he been around maybe I wouldn't have had to rescue Kiley and Carmela. If he'd been around…

I texted back. **OK. Long story. At hospital emergency room.**

The phone rang almost immediately. "Jamie, what's going on?"

For the next ten minutes, I filled him in. I was interrupted when a man holding a bloody towel over his hand walked in. Norma led him back to one of the treatment rooms.

I continued with Jim. "I'm waiting to find out how Carmela is. After that, I'll check on Elena and then I'm going home, shutting myself in the cabin and never coming out."

Jim didn't laugh. His voice carried a serious tone. "Listen, Jamie. You need to involve the sheriff."

I let out a deep sigh. "I know."

We ended the call when Norma beckoned me through the door to the treatment rooms. She stopped by Carmela's room and whispered. "She's got a bad infection. We're giving her IV antibiotics."

"Will she be okay?"

Norma stretched tension out of her back. "I hope so. This can happen when they discharge new moms too soon."

"Can I see her?"

"She's sleeping. Maybe later. But, I did get some information. My LPN speaks Spanish. Carmela says she has a brother who will come for her if we can locate him."

"Did she say he lived in Vancouver?"

"You know who he is?"

I shook my head. "Only a name. If she can tell you an address or phone number or something, I think we can find him."

Norma touched my arm. "I know you are worried about her but let us take care of this now."

I nearly cried in her arms. I might have, except my phone rang. "Unknown number." Could it be the elusive Rex? If so, he had a lot of explaining to do.

Elena's Story

Norma slipped into Carmela's room while I answered the phone. "Jamie? It's Kiley. I'm sorry, really but I had to get out of there. I left your snowshoes at the Lodge."

"Kiley." I wanted to yell at her and ask her if she knew the jacket she was wearing was my only sub-zero weather gear. But the line went dead. I stared at the phone wondering what to do next. I needed to get out of the antiseptic smell of the hospital and find some decent coffee. Time to see Clarence and decide what to tell the sheriff.

The street in front of Clarence's house had been plowed, leaving a high bank of icy snow along the curb. I looked for a way to get around it to the sidewalk and finally scrambled over it. My foot sank to the knee and I almost lost my hiking boot as I struggled to get to the shoveled part of the walk. At this point, the subzero air and the snow helped me to understand why Ed the janitor was talking about Florida. I'd heard about the "snowbirds" who fled for the south every winter and now I knew why.

Joe answered the door as I stood on the porch brushing off the snow. Just the simple walk to the house chilled me to the bone. Once inside, Joe led me to the kitchen. Clarence sat across from Elena with coffee and a muffin. She appeared calm and rested.

"Amy, *muchas gracias* for bringing me here. *Señor* Clarence, he is a nice man. And so is Jose."

Clarence motioned me to sit. "Joe here has been trying to reach you."

"Sorry, phone out, electricity out. I've had a challenging time."

While savoring the coffee and the muffin, I told them about the snowstorm,

Kiley, and Carmela.

When I reached the part where Kiley left with my only decent winter jacket and boots, Elena interrupted. "That Kiley. She no good."

"Maybe but she's not all bad either. I think Brewster was going to do something with Bonita Amy and Kiley got her away."

Clarence scratched his head with a contemplative expression. "I wonder if we have an adoption scam going. It's probably time to get Rick Fowler involved."

"¿Quién? Who?"

"He's the sheriff here."

Elena tensed up. "They take me to the border."

Clarence raised his hand in a gentle gesture. "No one is going to deport you. We'll figure things out."

Because Elena was growing more agitated, I stopped the conversation. "Let's not worry about it right now. You are in safe hands."

"That what señor Rex say, too." Elena's brow was knit as she gazed down at her hands.

She'd been through so much. It was no wonder she didn't trust anyone.

After we finished eating, Elena excused herself to lie down. I watched her walk heavily down the hallway massaging her lower back. I wondered when she was due.

"Poor little lady," Clarence commented when she was out of earshot. "She was a school teacher in a small village. One night the militia came killing the men and raping the women. She fled before she knew she was pregnant. Her journey here has been a nightmare. If she's sent back, she's sure she will be killed."

I'd read recently that over 200 people who were deported after seeking asylum were murdered once they were returned to their own country. The cruelty was beyond me to understand—both on the parts of the gangs and the militia and the United States government.

I told him about my search of Viaje Seguro and the discovery of the dead presidents. "Whoever is behind the organization certainly has a weird sense of humor. I looked into legitimate NGOs and it was not listed. Nor was it approved for adoptions."

"It's an intriguing puzzle."

Joe, who had been quiet throughout the conversation spoke up. "My auntie couldn't have a baby but she wanted one really bad. She asked around. She said for a price, you could find a baby."

"Someone sells them?"

"They call it adoption fees. She couldn't pay so she gave up." He sat back with a little smile. "Good thing. She'd be a bad mother."

Despite the coffee and the muffin, I felt cold. "Is that what's going on here?"

None of us had the answer. Clarence groaned as he stood up. "I'll have a chat with the sheriff. Right now, I'm considering Elena to be my client. I'll keep her out of trouble."

"One more thing." I stopped Clarence before he could shuffle out of the kitchen. "Kiley said something to me about the dead girl, Rita. She said someone came and took her baby. Rita was so distraught they had to give her drugs. I think Kiley knows more about what happened. Of course, Kiley's in the wind right now."

"I'll pass that on to Rick. Do you want me to mention your stolen jacket and boots?"

"Considering I bought them at the thrift store, no. I'm sure the sheriff wouldn't be interested."

Before I left, Clarence insisted I look in the upstairs closet for a jacket. "My wife, she bought expensive things. Lorraine has been after me for years to clear her clothes out. See if something fits you." His voice softened as he gazed up the staircase with a faraway look.

For all his wit and complaints about her, it was clear that Clarence still mourned her loss.

To my delight, I found a new North Face down jacket complete with the ten-year-old price tag and a pair of winter boots only a half-size bigger than mine. My opera-going coat could be retired once again.

I made a quick stop at the hospital to find Carmela and Bonita Amy sleeping. I asked Norma to keep a special eye on them. "I'm worried someone will try to spirit them away."

"You mean like kidnap?" Norma's eyes grew big. "Does the sheriff know?"

"Clarence is talking to him. He suspects something is very crooked with Mary's Place."

Norma frowned, clearly unhappy with the conversation. "I'll do my best and hope it doesn't get too busy here."

By the time I reached the highway, much of the pavement was completely clear. Even so, I drove slowly, wary of the ice patches. It gave me time to admire the way the wind had sculptured the new snow as it swept across the open area.

I stopped at Larissa Lodge and found my snowshoes leaning up against the outside of the lodge entrance. Inside, Mavis stood at the reception desk studying a memo. She greeted me in her usual breathy voice. Mavis was middle-aged frumpy with dyed hair and reading glasses hanging around her neck.

"Hi, Jamie. Cold enough for you?"

"Oh, I don't know. Maybe it should drop another ten degrees."

She laughed. "You New Yorkers you have such a sense of humor."

Actually, I feared my sense of humor had fled when I'd gotten involved with Mary's Place and Viaje Seguro. My smile felt tight on my face. "Did you happen to see a girl in her mid-twenties this morning? She left my snowshoes here."

Mavis raised her eyebrows. "I heard about her from the night person. Said she asked to use the phone, called someone and a while later, she was picked up."

"Do you know who she phoned?"

"Nope. He only said the car that picked her up was a van with out-of-state plates and that the driver didn't know diddly-squat about driving in the snow. Got stuck in front because Lars hadn't plowed yet."

I wondered if it was Brewster, the Texan. I also wondered who owned the car stuck in my driveway. As if she read my thoughts, Mavis leaned toward me. "Lars had them tow that other car. I heard it was stolen."

"Interesting." I was learning "Minnesota talk" indicating I had nothing more to say.

Her eyes were bright with curiosity. "Funny having a stolen car in your driveway."

I didn't want to explain Kiley or Carmela to her. Instead, I shrugged. "Must have gotten lost or something."

Exhaustion seeped through my body as I climbed back into the car. I needed to get home to my dog, clean up the mess of dishes and sleeping bags from last night and take a long winter's nap.

All of that would have happened if my phone hadn't started to ring as soon as I walked in the door of the cabin. I fumbled with it while Bronte danced around me.

Unknown name. "Hello?" I held the door to let her out.

"Jamie? It's Rex. Sorry I didn't get back to you. Phone died." He told me he was calling from El Paso and wondered how the transfer to another Viaje Seguro residence had gone.

"You don't know?" I stood at the window waiting for Bronte to come back in.

"I heard from Brewster that everything had been set up. I would have been there but I have a court case here."

Bronte barked at the door. Even as an outdoor dog, she didn't appreciate the below zero weather. Suddenly I felt too tired and too exhausted to have this conversation. I simply answered, "Carmela is in the hospital with an infection and Yoli had complications and was transferred to a hospital in Duluth. I'm sure Brewster can fill you in." I didn't tell him about Elena or about Kiley. If he was part of whatever was crooked about this organization, he would find out soon enough.

"My god," his voice rose in concern. "I had no idea." He paused, "Uh, what about the baby? Is the baby okay?"

Enough. I wanted to take a hot shower and crawl into bed. I waffled about revealing my suspicions or staying quiet. If Rex was in El Paso though, he clearly wasn't part of whatever was going on with Brewster. "Something isn't right about Viaje Seguro and all of this."

I heard an overhead announcement in the background but couldn't place it. Would they have such a thing in a courthouse?

"What do you mean?"

"I mean, I looked more carefully at the Viaje Seguro website. It's a scam. The staff and board of directors are all dead presidents. What are you into?"

I sat at the kitchen table rubbing the back of my neck while Bronte looked at me with anxious eyes.

I expected a rushed explanation, a lie, or a claim of ignorance. Instead, to my surprise, Rex simply groaned. "Oh god, did that site go public?"

"What do you mean?"

"Jamie, it's a beta site and wasn't supposed to go public yet. We're working with the designer. He must have dummied up the board members."

All the anger I'd built up fizzled out. Now I was more confused than ever.

Rex continued. "I'm flying back to Minnesota tomorrow. I'll get in touch once I've figured out where people are and what's happened. Believe me, Viaje Seguro is a good organization."

Whether I believed him or not, I planned to talk with him in person. "Call me when you get in."

He had some explaining to do. I ended the call and shut off the phone. I needed a break.

Adoption

After I tidied up the cabin and ate a late lunch, I was so tired I collapsed on the couch into a deep sleep. While I slept, the temperature outside warmed up to five below zero. I woke up two hours later to the sound of snowmobiles on the lake. When I peered out the window, I saw something I'd never experienced before. It looked like two glowing lights with faint rainbow colors on either side of the sun.

"Hey, Bronte. You have rivals. Two sundogs outside."

Bronte lifted her head with little interest. She didn't understand that winter, even at its worst up here in the Northwoods had an ethereal beauty I didn't have the words to explain.

"And you call yourself a poet," I uttered under my breath trying to conjure couplets to describe the view outside my window.

I watched the snowmobiles on the lake circling each other like a couple of kids playing keep away. It actually looked fun until I thought about how cold it must be. I'd learned that Minnesotans loved to talk about the windchill. What had Mavis said? "Windchill at thirty below." After my night in the snowstorm, I could believe it.

"Time to go to work." I took out C.P. Dowling's manuscript. After two pages describing Levy's trek through the burning sand, my mind wandered back to the last week and everything that had transpired. Baby born, a mother died, refugee women, kidnapping, weird website. Oh yes, I added, smashed car.

Instead of editing, I set the manuscript aside, poured myself a glass of wine and opened the laptop. Nothing had changed on the Viaje Seguro webpage.

It was still filled with dead presidents.

Thinking about adoptions reminded me of my college roommate Madison who had been so focused on having a baby. I still had an email address for her. I sent a message asking if she'd been able to adopt and if she had time to talk with me. I included my phone number.

Fifteen minutes later she called me. "Jamie, long time."

"Wow, that was a quick response."

She laughed and I pictured how her eyes came alive when she was amused.

"You caught me during my 'mope' time. I'm feeling sorry for myself because it's cold outside and the snow is nothing but crusty dirt. Welcome to Boston."

We spent time catching up. I told her about my divorce and move to northern Minnesota. I omitted details of my adventures since coming here and told her I was living happily with my dog and occasional visits from a state trooper named Jim.

She told me about her divorce. "I think it was the tension over having a baby. We gave thousands of dollars to fertility clinics but it never worked. We even looked at surrogacy. Then we spent more time applying to adopt but in the end, it turned out Mannie, my ex, really wanted a child of his own seed." She sighed. "He's now got three of them."

"I'm sorry." I told her about Mary's Place and Viaje Seguro and wondered if she knew about the organization.

"Jamie, I can tell you I was so desperate that I looked into everything I could, including private adoptions. You know, where it's between the birth mother and the adoptive parents." She paused. "It was a disheartening time in my life."

Bronte stood up, yawned, and trotted to the door. Outside the snowmobiles had disappeared along with the sundogs. As I let her out the door, I saw the temperature had dropped to a minus fifteen. Even opening the door sent a chill down to my toes.

"What do you mean by disheartening?"

Almost as soon as I had let her out, Bronte barked to come in. I was sure her poor paws were nearly numb.

"I found online support groups that led me to some questionable people. It seemed like the more I explored, the sleazier it got. At one point I found a lawyer who only saw clients referred to him by other clients. When I finally met him, he guaranteed a healthy Caucasian baby for a half a million dollars."

"My god. You mean it was a business deal?" I sat on the couch looking at the empty fireplace and thinking about Bonita Amy.

"To put it simply—I'd call it human trafficking. I don't know exactly how it works, but once I talked with him, I was done." She paused. "And Mannie and I were done."

"I'm so sorry it turned out that way." I remembered their wedding and how gentlemanly Mannie had been to her.

She said she still had some contacts and she would get back to me with any information she could find on Viaje Seguro. We closed out the conversation with mutual invitations. She'd love to see me in Boston. I thought she should experience Minnesota. It would be nice to have an old friend from back east visit. "But don't come in the winter unless you like to suffer."

She laughed. "Winters in Boston are bad enough. I'll get back to you."

After the call ended, I sat for a long time thinking about the Mary's Place girls. Was someone using them in order to sell their babies? Or maybe I was headed down a rabbit hole. The key seemed to be Viaje Seguro.

Jim called later in the evening. I asked him what he knew about human trafficking.

"Oh, Jamie. You need to get out your blue pencil and go back to editing."

I felt like a little kid who had just gotten a pat on the head. I bit back a sarcastic comment and asked instead, "Have you made your decision yet about the training?"

He paused long enough that my grip on the phone tightened. "Not yet. We'll know if Jake is in remission next week and I'll decide after that."

Sure, I thought. You've decided and I won't be sharing a bed with you much longer. Before we ended the call, he told me he was on for double shifts because of the weather. "Maybe I can get up there next week for a day or two."

I was about to tell him to skip it and save the gas, but Bronte looked at me with her soft brown eyes and I relented. "Can't wait." As soon as I set the phone down, I pictured Rex with his diamond earring and expensive coat. What a contrast to Jim's crooked smile and faded jeans.

In bed that night under the warmth of the comforter, I thought more about adoption. I once fancied the idea that I was adopted. If that was the case, I couldn't inherit whatever it was that ate away at my mother's brain. After a disturbing visit to see Mother in the nursing home, where she cried when she saw me and called me Patty, I asked Dad, "Was I adopted?" I remembered the pain in his eyes when he replied. "Jamie, you have the good of your mother in you. Never ask me again." Years later, I fact-checked an article about early on-set Alzheimer's and how it could run in families. I had to fight off an icy knot in my stomach to finish editing the article.

I pulled the comforter up to my chin and vowed not to think about Mother and heritage. Still, I had a hard time falling asleep.

The next morning dawned clear and cold once again. I was thankful for my new furnace although I worried about how much LP gas it was using. In my current financial condition, I wasn't sure I could afford to fill the big silver tank behind the cabin. I kept the thermostat at 62 and dressed in layers as I worked on the manuscript.

Levy of *The Darkening Sand* used the glowing talisman her grandfather had given her to travel at night in the coolness of the desert. I found this section of the novel to be surprisingly well-written. Other than her confusing fantasy world names, C.P. Dowling had created a compelling plot. As Levy moved through the darkness, the maleficent force of Aga Pumpert and his scorpion-like Ticks followed close behind. In some ways, I felt the same. Something dark was following the girls of Mary's Place.

The novel stalled, however, in the next chapter when it devolved into a long description of the tales of the two moons of Watersmeade and how they were formed. The writing left poor Levy stuck halfway between her lush homeland and the Kingdom of Watersmeade where Queen Alusra awaited her.

"I'm stuck, too," I reached down and scratched Bronte behind her ear. "I feel like I need to know more about Viaje Seguro, and I don't know where to start."

Before I could get back to the tale of the two moons, Bronte growled, and I heard the crunch of tires against the packed snow of my driveway. I hoped it was the UPS driver with another manuscript. Instead, when I looked out the window, Greg, the sheriff's deputy stepped out of his cruiser.

"This was not my idea of getting unstuck," I said, grabbing Bronte's collar and hauling her into the bedroom before she could assault the deputy.

When I opened the door he stood, looking uncomfortable. I hadn't noticed before, but with a wisp of a mustache and a few acne scars, he reminded me of a kid just out of high school. "Uh, do you have a few minutes to talk?"

My unfortunate experience with law enforcement told me this was serious. Otherwise, he would have simply called, or he would have called to set up an appointment to see me.

I motioned him to sit at the kitchen table where several chapters of *The Darkening Sand* were spread out. While I cleared a spot, I pointed to the coffee. "I'll brew a fresh pot."

Greg slipped off his heavy jacket. "You don't need to bother. I just need to ask you some questions."

I filled the coffee maker anyway and pressed the button. I wondered if Clarence had talked with the sheriff and the sheriff had sent Greg. What could I tell him about Kiley and Carmela?

Bronte whined in the bedroom. At least she wasn't barking like crazy. She must not have sensed that Greg was a threat.

Greg pointed to the hallway. "I hear your dog doesn't bite. You can let her out. I like dogs."

Amazing what people know about you in a small community. I let Bronte out. She trotted over to Greg, sniffed his hand, and settled by his feet.

I smiled. "I guess she thinks you're okay."

The coffeemaker sputtered and hissed as it brewed. Greg took a small notebook out of his pocket. "I'm wondering what you know about the car found on your road."

With all that was going on, he wanted to know about the car? What should I tell him? I knew Kiley had taken it without permission. I also knew it had been reported stolen. I decided to answer Greg's questions as simply as possible.

He sat with his pen poised. I sat up a bit straighter. The voice in the back of my head said, *take it slow*. "Uh, I heard it was used by Mary's Place."

"Who told you that?"

"Kiley Conway. She works for Mary's Place. She said it was their car."

Greg said nothing and the silence filled the cabin until the thermostat clicked and the furnace fan whirred. I was too much of a New Yorker to let the silence grow. I didn't have any obligation to protect Kiley. "Kiley Conway was driving. She brought Carmela and her baby to my cabin the night of the storm."

Greg appeared unimpressed with my response. "Is that all you can tell me?"

"She left early yesterday—took my snowshoes and walked to the lodge. They said someone picked her up from there." I shrugged. "Really, that's all I know."

"Did she tell you she'd stolen the car?"

I shrugged. "She told me she'd taken the car. I didn't ask her whether she'd stolen it. I asked her why she came to my cabin."

"What did she say?"

"She was worried about Carmela's safety." I didn't want to spew out all my half-baked concerns about human trafficking. "Listen, Greg, I really don't know anything about the car. What are you trying to find out?"

Greg set the pencil down. "The car belongs to Bevins Transport. M.C. is quite upset that it was taken."

Now it made a little more sense. I poured him a cup of coffee. "He has the car back and you wouldn't have come all the way out here for a recovered stolen car. Why is this so important?"

"Sheriff thought it might be connected to another crime."

Now I was intrigued. "Does it have anything to do with the murder?"

Greg blinked like he'd been flicked in the cheek. "What do you know about that?"

I backtracked because I wasn't supposed to know anything about what the coroner found. "Sorry, I mean the drowning. Don't you have to figure out what she was doing at the pond?"

Jamie, you're an idiot. *Keep your mouth shut.*

Greg squinted at the steam coming off the coffee mug as if he was trying to decide what to tell me. Chewing on the inside of his cheek, he finally spoke. "Okay. Well, I think I have all that I need." As he pulled on his jacket, he glanced at his notebook once again. "Oh, I was supposed to ask if you found anything in the car."

"Like what?"

He shrugged. "Someone asked the sheriff to ask."

"Sorry. I really didn't look inside the car. It was dark and snowing and I needed to get Carmela and the baby back to the cabin."

I watched him walk out the door, feeling a little confused. Why was he more interested in the driver and "something" in the car than why Carmela and the baby were in my cabin?

"Not my problem, I guess."

Bronte wagged her tail before settling on the rug in front of the fireplace.

Fish House on the Lake

I called Clarence to let him know about the visit.

"Engstrom," he barked into the phone.

"Ah, it's Jamie?" I was taken aback by his harsh tone.

"Oh, Jamie. Sorry." His voice softened. "I've been on the phone with the sheriff's office. What a bunch of incompetents. It's time for the Rick Fowler era to be over."

I'd rarely heard Clarence so worked up. Rick Fowler, the sheriff, and I had an uneasy relationship due to several incidences since my move to Lake Larissa. His father and grandfather had both been Jackpine County sheriffs in their time.

"What is it?" I settled on the couch with Bronte at my feet.

"Tried to tell him something was cattywampus with Mary's Place."

Cattywampus? I almost asked Clarence if that was a legal term, but it was clear he was in no mood for humor.

"He told me to come in and fill out a complaint if I wanted something investigated. Can you imagine? Fill out a complaint—like I was reporting someone stealing my hubcaps?"

I wasn't sure what he meant by "stealing hubcaps" so I simply murmured in agreement. "Did you tell him about Elena being locked in the closet?"

"Didn't get that far into the conversation," he growled. "There's a conspiracy somewhere."

From my experience with Clarence, he wasn't one to look for conspiracies. Clearly, he was angry. I told him about my visit from Greg. "He seemed far more interested in finding who stole Bevins's car than finding the truth about Rita's death."

"Bevins holds a lot of power in this county. But a stolen car that has been recovered? I'm surprised the sheriff would care one whit about it. I don't like this at all. I think I'll make some more calls." He covered the phone and I heard a muffled, "Be right there." To me, he said, "But first, lunch. Lorraine has been fussing over Elena like she's her daughter. I'm not sure my old body can stand all the excitement."

"Wait," I had a sudden sense of foreboding. "Has she told anyone Elena is with you?"

"Sworn to secrecy."

"What's going to happen to her? Or Carmela or even Yoli?"

Clarence cleared his throat. "I've got the team working on it."

"Meaning?"

"Friends in high—or maybe not so high—places."

"I'll come by tomorrow. I might have more information on Viaje Seguro by then." I didn't tell him that Rex had promised to talk with me. Nor did I tell him about the beta website.

When I called the hospital, the person who answered wouldn't give me any information about Carmela except to let me know she was still a patient. I debated asking to be put through to her room and decided it was hard enough to communicate in person let alone over the phone. I asked the receptionist to give her a message that I would see her and the baby tomorrow. To my shame, I had no desire to drive into town.

After the call ended, I peered out the window. The thermometer was still below zero but had inched up a bit. The light sparkling off the snow was eye-achingly bright. By early afternoon, despite the thermometer, I realized I had to get outside. In my Manhattan and Queens days, I enjoyed being outside but didn't crave it. After living here for nine months, I couldn't stand being cooped up inside for too long.

"Wanna go out and freeze your paws with me?"

Bronte responded like a little kid who had just been offered a trip to Disneyland. I put on two pairs of thick socks and the boots Clarence had given me. I snipped off the price tag on the jacket pulled a woolen cap over my ears and finished by wrapping my neck with a scarf. With all these layers, I could hardly walk.

"At least if I fall over, I have a good cushion."

Before going out, I noticed the green backpack Kiley had brought with her. She must have forgotten it. As I glanced at it, I realized it looked a lot like my day pack that I kept in the coat corner with emergency supplies like granola and energy bars. I did a quick search for my pack but couldn't find it. "Great, she took my coat, boots, and emergency supplies. I hope she left something useable behind for me."

Bronte woofed with impatience while I muttered. Outside, though, she sniffed, figured out how cold it was, and immediately turned back to the door.

"Oh no. You're coming with me." I surveyed the yard and the woods and decided the snow was too deep to plunge through it. Instead, I headed down the plowed driveway. As I walked, I felt a weight slowly melting. Something about the woods and the calm and the quiet helped me relax. The scarf covering my mouth iced up with the vapor from my breath. I let my thoughts wander.

Surprisingly, what kept creeping back into my head was not Viaje Seguro or Elena or Carmela. It was my visit to see Sheryl Bevins about the damage to my car. Clearly, M.C. had been drinking and something was off with Sheryl. Looking back on it, I wondered if she was afraid of him. That tickle on the back of my neck told me something was going on.

"Bevins, girl, that's what has me puzzled." Bronte charged ahead of me, oblivious to my thoughts on the Bevins. "You, see," I insisted. "The two men at Mary's Place, the car, and the fact that the house was owned by him tells me they are connected with Viaje Seguro, but I don't know how."

Bronte didn't care. I picked up a handful of snow, fashioned into a ball and threw it for her. She turned around and stared at me like I was crazy.

"You're supposed to fetch it. Just like on some of those cute-dog YouTube videos."

I guess my dog was smarter than that.

Once back inside the cabin, I built up a fire in the fireplace, brewed some tea and pulled out the manuscript. I was over half done with the first read-through. If I correctly guessed the plot, it would turn out that Queen Alusra was Levy's mother (or maybe grandmother) and the evil Aga Pumpert her father (or grandfather.) There would be a battle and Levy would show the physical strength her small body had gained from all the years of living on the lush island with her grandfather. After that would be some kind of a reveal and reconciliation.

"What do you think?"

Bronte offered no opinion as she licked ice balls from her paws.

The sun was beginning to set when I heard a noise coming from the lake. It sounded like a plow. When I looked out the window, it appeared that Lars was plowing a road on the lake and banking snow to make a clearing. Rob had told me that the ice wasn't safe until it was eight to twelve inches thick and cars and trucks needed to stay off until it was at the twelve-inch mark. I hoped Lars knew what he was doing, and I hoped as I watched him, I wouldn't suddenly see his truck sink into Lake Larissa.

Bronte, who usually perked up when there was activity on the lake didn't move from her spot in front of the fire. I guess she wasn't a below-zero dog.

My phone rang just as the predicted big reveal in the manuscript was about to start. Madison was calling me back.

"Hey," she greeted me. "You sent me on an interesting assignment communicating with some of my old acquaintances from the online adoption groups."

"Did you find out anything about Viaje Seguro?"

"Alas, no. But I did get the name of an adoption lawyer you might try talking to. He's out of Arizona and one of my sources says he's one of the best for private adoptions. She adopted her daughter through him—but the process was very pricey."

"Like the lawyer who promised you a nice Caucasian baby for a half-million dollars?"

She laughed. Her laugh had a windchime quality to it. "My friend says he's legit."

I wrote down his name. "I have a lawyer friend and I'll sic him on it."

"Jamie," she had a note of warning in her voice, "Some of these people can be dangerous, I'm told. Tread carefully."

We talked a little longer about the adoption world. I assured her I would be careful. I hardly saw myself as a hard-hitting investigative journalist. Plus, I wasn't convinced that was the issue with Mary's Place.

After the call ended, I reflected on how nice it was to talk with to a familiar voice from my New York life. "I guess I didn't have much of a social life those last couple of years."

Bronte sighed and shifted, settling on her side.

Thinking about it, I realized how controlling Andrew had been. When we'd first gotten together, I had a group of friends that I went out with on a regular basis. Mainly we were struggling college graduates trying to make it in the New York publishing world. Andrew didn't like many of them and over the course of the first year or two of our marriage, they fell away. In retrospect, wasn't that one of the signs of an abusive relationship? Isolation?

Despite my financial struggles, I was happy here even though I did miss people like Madison.

As the sunlight waned, I watched the activity on the lake. A truck unloaded a fish house and placed it in the cleared area. Rob had warned me that soon there would be a town out there. "It will be filled with those who really like to fish, and those who really like to sit in front of a hole in the ice and drink."

"How long will they be there?" I'd asked.

"Probably until March."

"Well, I hope no one falls in."

Outside, the temperature was rising. "We are above zero now, girl. Life is good." Still, when I opened the door to let her out, I was smacked with frigid air. Did it really matter if it was ten above zero or ten below?

I finally returned to the *Darkening Sand* in time for the big reveal. Except C.P. Dowling apparently wasn't ready for it to happen. Instead, she took the story down a side path with two chapters of a love story between Golix and Ms. Agatha of the Midgers. She went into far too much detail about how Midgers performed the sex act. Apparently, the Midgers weren't quite human. If this stayed in, the book would not be bound for the high school libraries.

Despite the supposedly steamy scenes, my eyes drooped and the words blurred. It was time to call it a night.

"What do you say, girl? One last step out into the winter night and then we head for bed?"

Bronte was hardly enthusiastic when I called her to the door. While I waited for her, I glanced out the front window at the lake. Bear Island was a distant shadow in the moonlight. In the area where Lars had plowed this afternoon, I saw the pinpoint glow from the lone fish house. I shivered, wondering why anyone would want to be out on the lake in the cold and dark.

When Bronte came in, she headed immediately for the bedroom and the bed. I made sure my doors were locked before crawling under the covers. I wanted a good night's sleep and no interruptions—especially not some drunken ice fishermen.

Night Visitor

Bronte's bark woke me up from a deep sleep. At first, I wasn't sure if I was awake or in a dream. She jumped off the bed and ran to the front door, her barks growing more frantic. I looked at my phone. It was a little after two in the morning. Light from the half-moon filtered through the bedroom window.

Someone was knocking on the door.

Don't answer it! You're in an isolated cabin and it's the middle of the night!

"Help! I need help!"

I couldn't ignore the voice. It had a sound of desperation. I threw on my robe and slippers and took stumbling steps to the living room. My body was not completely awake. "Who's there?" I shouted grabbing Bronte with one hand and my phone with another.

Flipping on the outside light I saw a man in a snowmobile suit and ski mask. This would have been the right time to call 911, but I wasn't thinking clearly. I could only see his eyes, and they were wide with panic.

Holding Bronte back, I unlocked the door and motioned him in. If he was an axe murderer at least I didn't see the axe. If he went for me, Bronte would put up a good fight.

He lurched inside, pulling the ski mask off to reveal a man about my age with pitted cheeks from a bad case of acne.

"Matt?" I knew him from the hardware store. Last summer he'd walked me through fixing a leak in the bathroom faucet.

"Thank god. I thought I'd freeze to death." His teeth chattered.

Bronte sniffed at him, gave one little woof, and sat down by my side.

"You're an odd midnight visitor."

Even in his heavy snowmobile suit, I saw how he shivered. "Yup. You can call me Matt the dumbass."

I motioned him into the kitchen and pointed to the chair nearest the stove. "I'll turn the oven on to warm you up."

He collapsed onto the kitchen chair. "God, I've never been so cold."

After I fixed him a cup of hot tea, I sat down across from him. "So, what's your story? Car trouble?"

He rubbed his face. "Stupid. Just stupid. The wife and I, we had a little spat. I thought since I'd set up the fish house I'd spend a little time letting her cool down."

"Sounds like you 'cooled down' instead."

"Drank a little too much Schnapps, I guess. Must have fallen asleep and when I woke up, I tripped and knocked the truck keys and my phone into the ice hole. Oh man, she's going to be pissed."

I held back a laugh. It wasn't funny to him.

"Saw the smoke coming out your chimney and walked over." He tried to smile but it looked more like a grimace. "Man, that was an awful walk. Kept falling in the snow. At one point I thought I'd just stay there until spring."

"Not a good idea. You'd better call your wife. I'm guessing she's pretty panicked right now."

With a sheepish expression, he accepted my phone. I took the opportunity to head to the bedroom to change into warmer clothes. I guessed Matt would be here for a while.

When I emerged, he sat staring at his empty teacup. "She'll be coming to pick me up. Might take an hour 'cause she's got to get someone to sit with the kids." He rubbed his face. "I'm a dumbass. Just a plain old dumbass."

While we waited, we talked about the weather. Any discussion around here with someone you didn't know seemed to start with, "Cold enough for you?" or in the summer, "Hot enough for you?"

I asked him how sure he was that the ice was thick enough now.

"Lars and me, we augered the hole. It's at least twelve inches. Cold fall, you know. Should hold a whole colony out there."

I shuddered thinking about the freezing water beneath the ice. "I wouldn't want to fall in."

"Like that woman last week at Black Crow Pond. The one who drowned."

"She didn't…" I was about to finish the sentence when I stopped myself.

"They say she was one of them Mexicans staying at the old Torgerson place."

"Do you know anything about the women staying there?" I was curious about the town talk. Since Matt worked in the hardware store, I guessed he heard all the gossip.

He pushed his chair back and regarded me with a hint of amusement. "I heard you delivered a baby for one of them."

I shrugged. "Happened upon her on my way home—that's all."

"I also heard Lacey got one of those babies."

"Lacey? You mean Sheryl Bevins's daughter?" I tensed. "What do you mean 'got' one?"

Matt blinked, surprised by my questions. "Like she adopted it?"

"Really. I didn't know her baby was adopted."

He looked down at the table. "I guess that's just what I heard—you know, talk. People get things wrong sometimes."

No kidding.

I nodded, hoping he would tell me more. After a little silence punctuated by a yawn from Bronte, I prodded. "Do you know Lacey?"

"We went to high school together." He massaged the back of his neck. "She was a wild one. I dated her once and all she wanted to do was drink and make out." He blushed. "Don't tell the wife that."

Reheating the water, I offered him more tea. "I've only seen M.C. Bevins a couple of times. What's he like?"

Matt guffawed. "Well, I know you don't want to cross him. Back in high school with Lacey, he scared the shit out of me. Took her out on a date and he was standing at the door when I brought her back. We were late for her curfew, and I thought he was going to take after me with a baseball bat. I hightailed it out of there before he could figure out that we'd been drinking beer. Whew!"

"Sounds like a scary kind of a guy."

"All I know is that he runs a tight business—works his crew pretty hard but he pays decent." He gazed up at the ceiling. "Poor Lacey didn't like being under his thumb. Wild as she was, she hooked up with a guy from another high school. Drove drunk and rolled the car. He died and she was pretty banged up."

"I heard she had a bad head injury."

Matt dipped his teabag in the hot water, wringing it out with a delicate touch. "Guess so. When she came back to school, she was different—not so wild, kinda quiet. After high school, she went to college in Texas. She's lived there ever since. Don't know much about the guy she married. I think he works for the Feds doing something."

Bronte pricked up her ears to the distant noise of an automobile. "Sounds like your wife is here."

Matt's wife pulled up beside the Subaru and honked the horn. She wasn't coming in for a chat. He zipped up his snowmobile suit, grabbed his ski mask, and turned to the door. "Well, thanks. Sorry for all the bother."

I smiled to myself imagining their conversation on the way home. I guessed Matt would be grounded for a while.

As soon as he left, I cleared off the cups, turned off the lights, and crawled back into bed. Curled under the covers I wondered about Lacey. She seemed off, like she wasn't quite tracking. Residual from a head injury or simply post-partum weirdness. What about the rumors the baby was adopted? If I had been text messaging all of this, I would have stopped right there with a big TMI. Too much information. Time to turn in. My brain skipped to Rita and her baby. Where was it? Hopefully in loving hands. I fell asleep with the image of Rita in my head, her wet hair clinging to the ghostly skin of her face.

Rex Returns

The next day, clouds moved in graying the sky. The thermometer rose to ten above zero as the clouds held in the fragile earthen heat. I woke up tired from my middle of the night adventure. My head ached with the change in barometric pressure. Sometimes I wondered if my head did a better job of predicting the weather than the meteorologists with their radar and satellites.

I hoped Rex would contact me today. I needed to ask him a bunch of questions including whether he knew what happened to Rita's baby. It might make the story of my roadside delivery more marketable.

An email from the editor I'd queried popped up as I was scanning the news for something local. The editor was indeed interested in another article from me. The paycheck from the last article on the school shooting in Cascade would be direct deposited into my account this week.

"Yay. Electricity for a little longer."

Other than the experience of delivering Bonita Amy, I wasn't sure what else to write until I had something more concrete about Viaje Seguro.

Clarence called while I was finishing a breakfast bagel. "Doddering old barrister here. Our guest is doing well but Lorraine says her time is near."

"Is she having contractions?"

He laughed, "I'm hardly the one to ask. Are you coming by to see her today?"

"Sure, I need to check on Carmela and the baby at the hospital."

"Good. Elena wants to talk to you."

Out in the plowed area of my driveway, Bronte frolicked with a twig, tossing it and chasing it. Would that life could be so uncomplicated.

At the hospital, Carmela sat up in bed nursing Bonita Amy. Her smile radiated peacefulness as she cradled the baby.

"Amy!"

It wasn't often someone besides my dog was so glad to see me. "Are you feeling better?"

She continued to smile. *"Mi hermano come."*

"Your brother is coming?"

"Sí. Alfonso come."

Norma walked into the room with a fresh IV bag and joined in the conversation while she took the empty one down and hung the new one. "We found the brother. He's flying to Minneapolis and driving up tomorrow. We're hoping Carmela can leave with him."

I wondered about all the paperwork to get her into Canada but decided to leave it to the brother to figure out.

Before I left, I kissed Bonita Amy on the head and Carmela on the cheek. "Take care of my namesake."

Her eyes sparkled. "I come visit? Okay?"

I sure hoped she would be able to do that.

Out at the nurse's station, I talked with Norma. "How did you pull off this miracle of finding her brother? I tried but got nowhere."

"Clarence, our town's elder statesmen got in touch with a group that works to link refugees with their families."

"He didn't tell me." But I remembered his statement that he had friends in high or low places. "He certainly is full of surprises."

Norma glanced down the hall as a light went on outside one of the rooms. "Sorry, gotta go. I only hope something doesn't get fouled up. That poor girl has been through enough."

My phone pinged with a text from Rex. **Meet at Loonfeather in an hour?**

See you there, I texted back.

Joe had shoveled a path from the street all the way up to Clarence's porch.

The snow was still a pristine white. By this time after a snowfall in New York, the snow would have been covered with dirt and soot. Killdeer, layered in a white sheet, looked like a calendar photo.

When I rang the bell, Lorraine answered. I'd never met her, only heard Clarence complain about how she tried to get him to eat healthy foods. I pictured her to be middle-aged and stout with a sternness to her that could keep Clarence under control. To my surprise, she was in her early forties, had short-cropped blonde hair and a heart-shaped face. She wasn't quite good-looking because her nose was a little too big for her face.

"Come in. You must be Jamie. Good of you to keep the old guy on his toes."

"I heard that," Clarence called from the kitchen. "I might be old, but I'm not deaf."

Lorraine laughed.

Clarence sat in the kitchen with a cup of coffee and a bran muffin. He motioned me to sit while Lorraine poured coffee for me. Once she served the coffee, she left. "I have to check on our mom-to-be."

"Oh, that woman fusses."

I drank my coffee and filled him in on my visitor from last night. "He knew Lacey Graham and said he thought she had adopted a baby. Jilly at the paper said she'd heard Lacey had some problems getting pregnant. I couldn't get the thought out of my head that it might be Rita's baby."

"Seems unlikely. People here sometimes put two and two together and get one." He chuckled. "On the other hand, what do I know? You've certainly gotten us into a circus with these girls."

I stirred cream into my coffee. Normally I like it black, but this coffee was so weak it looked like brown-colored water. Lorraine probably made it that way to keep Clarence from being over-caffeinated. "Norma told me how you found people to help Carmela."

"I used the miracle of the telephone. It's amazing, you call someone up instead of using that text and computer nonsense, and things get done. The grandson of a lawyer friend of mine runs a non-profit helping refugees. He jumped right in. Hopefully he can help Elena as well."

"Will Carmela be able to leave the country? I don't know what kind of papers she has."

He shrugged. "Let us hope."

I checked my watch. I still had a few minutes before meeting Rex at the Loonfeather. "You said Elena wanted to talk with me."

"She's sleeping right now, but between her pretty good English and my pretty bad Spanish, she told me Rita was afraid before she gave birth. She said the father was an American and didn't want the baby, but she did. She worried that she'd signed the baby away without realizing it."

"It sounds like the same thing Carmela was afraid of."

Clarence sat up straighter, taking a deep breath. "That's what I hope to get to the bottom of. Elena doesn't know where these 'papers' are. Maybe they're still at Mary's Place and maybe we can get Bevins to let us look."

"Aha, intrigue."

We talked a little longer about what the papers could be and who might have them. "Brewster Conway seems to have disappeared along with Kiley. They might be the key."

Clarence growled. "I'd like to get Sheriff Fowler off his fat butt to look for them. I can't imagine why he isn't doing his job."

I wondered if the problem might be that a crime—at least as far as the missing papers—hadn't been committed. On the other hand, I wasn't sure he was doing much to investigate Rita's death.

My phone pinged. **Waiting @ Loonfeather.**

"I have to go. I'm meeting Rex for lunch. Maybe I can lure some information out of him."

Clarence groaned as he stood up. "Well, the old guy here has to take little rest. Too much excitement around this place."

I walked with him to the door of his downstairs bedroom. I noted he walked with a little bounce to his step. Clarence thrived on all this intrigue. I hoped it didn't wear him out.

The Loonfeather was busy with the lunch crowd. Three days post snowstorm and people were happy to be out. Rex sat at a table in the dining room talking with the server. She giggled as I approached.

"Have a seat," he motioned to the chair across from him. "Kristy here is getting us something to drink."

Rex wore his pair of Ray-Bans even though the interior of the restaurant was dim. "What's with the shades?" I shrugged out of my new jacket and sat down.

Rex tipped them up revealing a swollen black eye.

"Wow. That must have been some court fight you were in."

He laughed, his lip slightly puffy. "More like a fight with an icy sidewalk. It wasn't pretty but I think I won."

"You're lucky you didn't break an arm or leg." I noted his diamond stud was missing and his hair appeared messy like the winter hat hair of the Minnesotans. Though he was still impeccably dressed in a cable knit sweater, he had a slight air of neglect. I leaned forward, "Rex, are you all right?"

"Fine. The fall threw me off, that's all. Too many years away from the snow and ice I guess."

The waitress brought our drinks. I had black coffee and Rex had a scotch and water. Once again, she giggled when she set them on the table. I wondered if under the sunglasses, Rex was winking at her.

He took a swallow of his scotch with a grimace as if the alcohol burned the inside of his mouth. "I hear you've had quite a last couple of days."

"Oh? Who told you that?" I wondered who he had been talking with.

"Kiley Conway left me a voicemail and said she and the new mother and baby spent the night at your cabin."

"You've been in contact with Kiley? Do you know where she is?"

He drummed his fingers on the table with a shrug. "I'm assuming she and Brewster are at the new place in southern Minnesota."

"But you haven't seen them?"

We were interrupted when the server brought our food. Rex ordered a steak and I had soup and a small salad. Somehow steak for lunch struck me as far too decadent, but I didn't mention this to Rex. For a few minutes, while he carefully cut his steak into bite-size pieces, we didn't talk. I watched, fascinated by the way he concentrated on making the steak bits equal in size. I sensed he did it to avoid my question.

152

When he had all his food in order, he looked over at me. "Sorry. It's a bad habit—goes back to childhood, I guess."

I tasted the soup. It was thick and filled with vegetables. "Rex, let's not beat around the bush here. Something is very wrong both with the people who are running Mary's Place and Viaje Seguro. I'm hoping you will set me straight because right now it looks like some kind of an illegal operation."

Rex set his fork down with a clatter. "That's pretty heavy."

Who says things are "heavy" these days?

I took another spoonful of soup, savoring the earthy spices in it. "Well, let's see. One of the girls is dead, another was trying to run away…"

I didn't finish because he put up his hand to stop me. "Listen, I know it doesn't look right, but Viaje Seguro is a good organization. Let me fill you in on a few things."

"Wait. Let me finish this amazing soup so I can take some notes."

"Notes?" He wrinkled his brow.

I smiled. "Don't you remember? I'm planning to write an article about my experience as an accidental midwife. A New York editor is interested. If Viaje Seguro is a good organization like you say it is, the article could be the kind of publicity they might want."

He picked up his fork and quietly tapped it against the side of the table. "I didn't know about the article."

I sipped my soup. He didn't know because I hadn't told him. I should have felt ashamed about leading him on. "Sorry, I'm sure I told you that was part of my interest in Mary's Place."

Rex's tone turned flat. "Listen. I'm a lawyer and a lot of what I do has to be kept confidential. I need to be careful about what I say."

Now I felt like a chump. A blush rose up my neck. "Really, I'm sorry. I won't write anything that would be considered privileged information."

The tension lines around his mouth stayed fixed. "Okay. What do you want to know?"

"I heard Rita was afraid someone was after her and her baby. Do you know anything about it that you can share?"

He leaned toward me. "Those girls ran from their countries for a reason.

I'm not saying this is what happened to Rita, but some of them were fleeing the drug cartels. The cartels have long, long arms and their revenge knows no bounds. It's possible that's what she was afraid of."

"You mean her death could have been a hit or revenge of some sort?"

He held up his hands in a gesture of surrender. "No, I don't think so. I think poor Rita got confused and wandered into the pond. It was an unfortunate, goddamn accident." He emphasized goddamn. "But things like that have happened. Please be very cautious about what you write—for the safety of the women and the babies."

I took a deep breath. "I didn't think of it that way."

We talked through the rest of the meal mostly about the unstable situation in some of the Central American countries and how this could affect the girls at Mary's Place. When I asked more about who was behind Viaje Seguro he was evasive, claiming again that public information about the organization might put more women in danger.

When the waitress came with the check he said, "Separate checks, please."

He watched her as she walked away and appeared to flinch when I spoke. "Rex, one last question. There's a rumor going around in town that Rita's baby was adopted by the Bevins's daughter Lacey. Do you know anything about it?"

Immediately he turned his attention to me. "Who? Bevins? I don't know them. Of course not!"

I was surprised he responded so quickly to the question and that he claimed not to know the Bevins. "Do you know what happened to Rita's baby?"

"He was taken to relatives who live in southern Minnesota." He glanced at his watch. "Oops, sorry, I have to run. I hope this was helpful." Before he stood up he leaned close to me, and whispered, "Please be careful. There are things about this situation that are dangerous."

I watched the way he walked to the door with a limping gait wondering again why he lied about knowing M.C. and Sheryl Bevins. "Rex, you certainly are a puzzle."

Jim's Warning

On the drive home I thought about the conversation with Rex. Yes, he clearly warned me about doing an article and yes, I believed Carmela, Yoli, and Elena could be in danger. What I wasn't sure about was his theory of the cartels or gangs or whatever pursuing the girls. It sounded too much like a television crime show plot. In essence, other than his denial that Rita's baby went to Lacey Graham, he had given me very little information. Ah, wily lawyers.

A familiar red pickup truck was parked in my driveway. When I spotted it, I felt a rush of relief followed by the rapid beating of my heart. Jim had figured out a way to get back to me. Despite my irritation with him, I desperately needed him right now. I needed the warmth and comfort of his embrace. I needed his practical wisdom and I needed to bounce all I'd learned about the girls off his law enforcement brain.

He stood at the door waiting for me as I stepped out of the car. For a second I had a picture in my head of running to him in slow motion with a graceful leap into his arms. Instead of a graceful leap, I hit a patch of icy snow and ended up on my butt skidding toward the door. Bronte, in her enthusiasm, rushed out barking with glee.

She licked my face as Jim stood laughing. "Jamie are you okay?"

"I should have taken the ballet lessons when my dad offered them years ago," I groused, letting him help me up.

Over coffee, I told him about my adventures, starting with Mary's Place and the locked closet. "They locked Elena in a closet for god sake. I can't believe they care about the girls when they treat them like that."

155

Jim shook his head. "I can't picture who would do that."

I'd deliberately not mentioned Elena to Rex. I didn't want him to know where she was, and I didn't want him to know I'd taken her from the house. I told Jim about spiriting her to Clarence's house. "Now I've put him in a precarious position." I pictured him with the sparkle in his eyes. "Although he seems to be enjoying it."

We talked about the snowstorm and Kiley. "I felt like she was trying to help. Then next thing I know, she's stolen my jacket and boots and disappeared."

Jim sat next to me with his hands on my thighs as I talked. Watching his face, I saw a collage of expressions varying from concern to amusement. Mostly, though, I saw the concern.

I finished by telling him about my night visitor. Laughing, I thought about the chagrined look on Matt's face. "I wonder what punishment the wife is giving him right now."

"Geeze, Jamie, for a naïve city girl, you certainly get yourself into messes."

I didn't like his tone. It sounded almost accusatory. "Honestly, Jim, I didn't ask for this."

He stood up pulling me to him. "Let's sleep on it." His eyes danced and he smiled in that crooked way that tended to erase all my doubts about him.

"Maybe we can try some Midger-moves."

"What?"

"Never mind. I'll explain later."

Bronte gazed at the two of us, sighed, and walked over to her rug in the living room. She knew she wasn't welcome in the bedroom.

Afterward in the tangle of sheets, I rested my head on his shoulder and apologized. "I was so caught up in my own drama that I haven't asked you about Jake. How is he doing?"

He absently rubbed my shoulder. "The lab tests all look good. He's on a vacation from the chemo and they don't plan to start it again if he keeps making progress."

"That's a relief." But when I looked at him, I saw something, a deep worry.

He sighed. "I've read the articles on his type of leukemia. I'm guessing you have, too. Long term it might not be good."

I kissed him lightly and he held onto me with a tight grip. After a few seconds of silence, he rolled toward me with a grin. "How about if we concentrate on the present, not the future for a little while."

"Okay?"

"What was that Midger-move you did a little while ago?"

"You want me to work on perfecting my skills?"

For the rest of the day, I forgot Viaje Seguro, *Darkening Sand,* and mothers with babies. Bronte spent a lot of time on her rug. We also skied the Lady Slipper Trail, drank wine in front of the fireplace, and watched as more fish houses went up on the lake.

Jim suggested we try ice fishing and I suggested we try more things under the warmth of the comforter.

The next morning dawned gray but again above zero. I was stiff and sore either from skiing or maybe the Midger-moves or both. Jim coaxed me into one final skiing expedition before he headed back to Minneapolis.

"You're getting the hang of it," he pointed out as I worked to keep up with him. The air was crisp and the track on the trail a near-perfect smoothness. I let Jim ski ahead, admiring the rhythm of his skis and poles and the tightness of his butt as he pushed forward. The quiet of the trail was broken only by the slight whisper of the wind through the evergreens.

I found a rhythm, a glide that was like being on ice skates. Periodically Jim turned around and came back to make sure I was still upright. At one point, I pulled off the trail and simply stood breathing in the freshness of the air. Dad used to talk about the rare moments of serenity, the time when all was right with the world. I experienced it in a way I would never have imagined as a city girl. Above me, an eagle soared as if to tell me I was in the right place at the right time.

After skiing and a lunch of grilled cheese sandwiches and tomato soup, Jim packed to leave. As I watched him, that sense of serenity faded. It was like we'd reached Sunday night and tomorrow would be work as usual. Twenty-four hours of activity and intimacy was too short. I treasured these hours and minutes. Somehow, though, it was hard to hold on to them.

When he was all packed, we sat on the couch and talked. I needed to have something more concrete about our relationship than these periodic visits. I wasn't sure what Jim wanted. I played with the zipper on my sweater as I talked. "We made a pact yesterday to only be in the present. I've loved it, but it's time to talk about the future."

He had his arm around my shoulder, squeezing it. "You're right."

Now finally we would have that serious conversation about where our relationship was heading.

"Jamie, I want you to think about some things. You're pretty isolated here."

I stiffened. "I'm not moving, if that's what you're talking about."

My reaction appeared to surprise him. He stopped caressing my shoulder and turned to me. "Not even close. I want you to think about this project with the refugee women."

"What?" What did this have to do with our relationship?

His jaw tensed. "I think you might be putting yourself in danger."

Was he warning me off the same way Rex did? "You don't believe gangs or whatever are involved, do you?"

He raised his eyebrows. "I don't know. But it all smells like rotting fish. Promise me you will hold off on writing the article until things are clearer."

I inched away from him so I could better see his face better. "What do you mean by clearer? Who's going to make things clearer?"

He dropped his arm and clasped his hands together, resting his elbows on his knees. Dad used to assume that pose when he had something serious to talk with me about. "I hear things. Rick Fowler is keeping a low profile with the murder investigation for some reason."

"Geeze. If the sheriff won't investigate, who's going to take this on?"

He leaned on his arms, staring at the empty fireplace. "Jamie, I don't know. But this isn't your crime to solve."

The heat rose up my neck and into my face. "What are you trying to tell me?"

"I'm trying to tell you that I don't want to get the call that says you're on the bottom of Lake Larissa."

"Wow." At this point, Bronte, sensing the tension, tried to crawl up on my lap. I pushed her down. "I don't want to end up there either. For one thing, it's freezing cold."

He didn't laugh. "I'm serious."

"Jim, that poor woman was probably murdered, and no one seems to care."

He hugged me so tight it was almost hard to breathe. "I suspect there are people behind the scenes working on this. Your expertise is in commas. Let the pros do their job and you can write about it later."

I let his warmth and the smell of his shampoo and aftershave lull me. "I'll think about it."

By the time he walked out the door with his gym bag, the tensions had eased a bit. I promised not to throw stones at the wasp's nest if he promised to check his sources about Rita.

"Honestly, Jim, I'd like to write the story. If for no other reason, it would pay me enough to stick around until spring."

"You know I could help with that. Pay you rent for the days I come. You could consider it an Airbnb."

I waved him away. "I'll be fine. Keep your rent for when I really need it." I didn't tell him it might come as soon as mid-January if I had to refill the propane tank.

Once again, I watched his taillights. And once again, we'd avoided talking about our relationship. "Jamie, you are such a fool. What would C.P. Dowling say about this relationship? She'd probably tell me to rub my talisman and see what color the light turned."

Summons

Clarence called later in the afternoon. I'd turned my phone off for much of the last twenty-four hours in order to live in the moment. Unfortunately, the moment was over.

"You're a hard woman to get hold of."

"I've been on a break."

He didn't skip a beat. "Jim showed up, I'll wager. Hope it was a good one."

I almost told him how worn out I was but decided that would be TMI for the old guy. "I would have called you if I'd gotten any information out of Rex. The best he could do was deny that Rita's baby went to Lacey and warn me about evildoers pursuing the women of Mary's Place."

"I've had a little more success. I found out they had tourist visas in case anyone checked."

"You're not serious. Tourist visas? How did they get them? I've read it's a long process that includes having to go through an interview at the embassy or consulate where they live."

"The team is looking into it. It's possible they were forged. Considering what Elena said about crossing illegally, I doubt she was holding a tourist visa when she arrived in Texas."

I thought about all the current complexities of being legally in this country if you happened to be Latina. "This strikes me as a pretty sophisticated set up."

We talked for a bit about next steps for Elena. Clarence thought he should keep her at his place until the baby was born. "I'm enjoying the company. Between Elena and Lorraine, I'm well-fed and busy enough to stay out of trouble." He chuckled. "Plus Joe's been around more. Seems Elena is teaching him Spanish."

"What will happen after the baby is born?"

"The organization is tracking down possible relatives and if they can't find any, they'll set her up with a sanctuary host family until we can work out the immigration issues."

I thought about the warnings from both Rex and Jim. "Is it possible the girls are being pursued by some unknown cartel?"

"I'm definitely not advertising Elena's location. At least for now." It sounded like any amusement drained from Clarence's voice.

A shiver swept through me. "What about Carmela? Will she be safe until her brother comes?"

Clarence was silent a little too long. "Let's hope he gets here quickly. Her location is public information right now."

"And Yoli in Duluth?"

"The team is working on it. She had her baby but it was pretty small. It's in a newborn ICU now. I don't know what will happen. No one except the folks from the refugee organization has contacted her."

"Really? Not even Rex for Viaje Seguro? I would assume he would want to know."

Rex was becoming more and more of a puzzle to me.

"I have someone checking on Rex, too. We're waiting for a call back from his law office."

After I finished talking with Clarence, I checked my texts. I had three from Rex, one from Travis, and one from Jilly at the paper. I read Jilly's first.

Weird rumors going round. Woman found @ blackcrow pond murdered???

I texted her back. **Where did you hear that?**

She didn't reply.

Travis's text was simple. **R u OK? Hear storm intense.**

My reply was equally short. **Fine. How r things in Cascade?**

Rex's texts were more complex starting with: **Sorry about short lunch. Can talk more about article.**

The next one read: **How far are you on story? Worried.**

The last one looked urgent.

PLEASE GET BACK TO ME. IMPORTANT!

It had been sent yesterday evening. I stared at the message. "Hmmm… I'm not sure what to do with this." I didn't feel liking talking with him right now. I replied. **Sorry, phone off. When would you like to talk?**

Bronte stood up, stretched, and walked to the door. "Need a break? Me too."

Instead of thinking about Viaje Seguro or the proposed article, I decided to spend time outside. Since I had my snowshoes back, I thought I'd take a walk onto the lake. Maybe being under the open skies would clear my head and help me focus.

Bronte's excitement about the walk waned when her paws sank in the soft snow and she had to leap to keep up with me. I turned to her and pointed back at the cabin. "Go play with your stick. I won't be long." I didn't intend to wander too far onto the lake. Despite what Matt said, I wasn't convinced the ice would hold me.

"Really, Jamie. If you look out there you see a couple of pickup trucks. It seems to be holding them. Why would your 110 pounds cause it to crack open?"

I stepped gingerly onto the snow-covered ice, bounced a little to see if it would hold me, and felt nothing but solidness beneath me. Out further, I stopped to take in the wide-open space. Closing my eyes, I imagined the summer with the water lapping against the shore and the warmth of the sun pouring down. About a quarter-mile to my left from where I stood, the ice fishing colony was growing. From the first house belonging to Matt, I now counted six more. Voices carried in the crystal-clear air.

"Did you catch anything?"

"Yah, sure, a cold and some frostbite."

Laughter followed.

To my right, nearer the shoreline, the landscape changed. The snow didn't appear to be as deep or even as white. That's where Rob had pointed out the underground springs. "Anyone dumb enough to snowmobile around there is likely to find himself very wet and possibly very dead."

I thought about Rita and suddenly I wanted to be back inside my cabin with a steaming cup of coffee and a fire in the fireplace. I turned back.

Bronte scratched at the door with an expression that said, "Enough of the outdoors. Let me in so I can warm up my paws."

After fixing a pot of coffee, I brought out *The Darkening Sand* once again. I'd left off with the love chapter between Midgers. Time to get back to the main story. I hoped C.P. Dowling wouldn't get distracted again. I needed to find out what happened to Levy, Watersmeade, and the evil Aga Pumpert.

C.P. belabored the plot with long paragraph descriptions of the interior of Watersmeade and the history of the castle with its labyrinth of tunnels and its moat of quicksand. It occurred to me that she was having a hard time bringing herself to make the big reveal. Either she was so caught up in the story that she didn't want to end it, or she didn't know how to end it.

Maybe that was my problem with Viaje Seguro and all the various pieces that didn't fit together. Maybe I was afraid to take a deep dive into the story and find out what was behind it. Or maybe I really didn't want to know.

I sat back stretching my arms over my head. "You're not an investigative reporter, Jamie." In fact, as an undergrad, I'd taken an intro to journalism class and found it wasn't all about rooting out evil businessmen and corrupt politicians. My heart was in poetry not reporting.

Bronte made slurping sounds as she licked herself. I watched her envious of how few worries she had.

I was in way over my head with Viaje Seguro and the stories of the women from Mary's Place. This was something I'd experienced before since moving to the cabin by the lake. The last time it happened I was also pursuing a story and found myself in a mess involved with very ugly people.

"Turn all these pieces over to someone who has the ability and resources to do a real investigation. Write a nice little puff piece about delivering a baby on your way home and leave it at that."

I'd almost convinced myself to let it go. Carmela's brother would take care of her. Clarence's contacts would take care of Elena and Yoli. I needed to butt out and put my energy into eking out a living editing passages describing erotic encounters between little humanoids. Jim would be so relieved.

I had my phone in hand ready to text Jim and tell him he was right. Time to drop the Viaje Seguro story. The text came in from Jilly: **minister found dead at Mary's Place. Sheriff investigating.**

I stared at the phone. Brewster dead? **Brewster Conway? How? Unknown. Will text if I hear more.**

Two deaths now associated with Mary's Place. My resolve to let it go evaporated. Immediately I texted Rex. **Heard about Brewster. What do you know?**

When he didn't reply, I phoned Clarence. Lorraine answered. "Oh Jamie, he's napping. I'll have him call when he gets up."

I called Travis to see if he could use his connections to find out what happened. The call went directly to voicemail. "Hi, it's Jamie. More excitement here. Can you call me?"

When my phone did ring, I expected to see either Clarence's or Travis's name pop up. Instead, it was the Jackpine County Sheriff's Office.

"Jamie Forest? This is Greg from the sheriff's office. I'd like to talk with you. Can you come in?"

Due to a bad experience in New York City with law enforcement, I wasn't keen on jumping up and visiting the sheriff's office. I kept my voice as polite and calm as I could. "Is this about the stolen car? I'm not sure what else I can tell you."

He cleared his throat. "Uh, no. It's on a different matter."

I held back from asking if it was about Brewster. "Can you tell me what you need to know? Maybe I can give you the information over the phone."

He hesitated a tick too long. "Ah, Sheriff Fowler wants to talk with you in person."

Outside the sun was setting and the temperature dropping. If I was going to see the sheriff, I wanted Clarence by my side. "I could come in tomorrow morning, if that would be convenient. I assume this isn't an emergency?"

He put me on hold. Probably checking with the boss. The line clicked back on. "Okay. Please come to the sheriff's office at ten. You know where it is?"

Unfortunately, I was well acquainted with the location of the sheriff's office. Also the location of the county jail. With a false perkiness to my voice, I ended the call. "Sure. That's peachy. I'll see you then."

Peachy? The last thing I wanted to do was talk with the sheriff—even though I had little to tell him. Bronte sauntered over to me and put her paw on my knee. "Yup, girl. Here we go again."

Death in a Van

Clarence called me back around supper time. I told him about Brewster and the sheriff's desire to see me. "I'm not going into that office without my lawyer."

"Well, I hope you find one who's competent."

Even though I managed a little chuckle, none of this felt funny. "You'll have to do."

I arranged to pick him up in the morning.

"You know," he said. "Lorraine and Elena will fuss about me going outside. They'll worry I'll fall and break a hip and they'll have to take care of me."

"Elena, too?"

"Worse than Lorraine. She's more like my wife than my wife except she speaks Spanish."

This time I did laugh, picturing the two women hovering over him. "I hope you can fight them off. I really need you. See you in the morning."

Travis returned my call as I was crawling into bed. "Got your message. What kind of trouble are you in now?"

I explained the text I'd gotten about Brewster. "Can you go to your sources and find out what happened? The sheriff wants to talk to me tomorrow. I'd like to be prepared."

He said he'd get back to me in the morning.

I thought about texting Jim, but once I was under the covers, I couldn't muster the energy. I slept badly, tossing and kicking at the covers. Bronte finally gave up and jumped off the bed with a big sigh. Jim's side of the bed still carried his scent. I grabbed his pillow, hugging it to my chest, and finally fell into a fitful sleep.

The morning arrived with a balmy south wind and temperatures in the mid-twenties. Outside, other than the distant buzz of a snowmobile, the lake, and the woods were quiet. When I let Bronte out, she spied a squirrel and chased it through the snow and up a tree. I watched her tail wagging as she stood at the base of the tree and wished I didn't feel cloaked in a gray cloud.

In Killdeer the banks of snow thrown up by the plow were beginning to crust over and take on a patina of dirt and soot. How quickly the pristine white faded, though not as quickly as it did in Queens.

Clarence waited for me at the front door wearing a woolen coat with a hat that he probably bought in the fifties. I took his arm and walked with him down the porch stairs which were covered in salt and sand. He pointed to it. "Lorraine went overboard, I'm afraid. We have enough salt on these steps to pollute Lake Superior."

I tsked. "Better that you should stay on your feet as my grandmother Forest used to say." I smiled thinking about her living in a stuffy Victorian near Boston. As far as I could remember, she only left her house to attend church on Easter.

Greg met us as I escorted Clarence through the doorway at the sheriff's office. For a law enforcement agency dealing with two deaths, it was eerily quiet. Even the receptionist's chair was empty.

Clarence looked around. "Where is everyone, young man?"

"Um, well, we're down a couple of deputies right now."

Since one of them had been fired last summer because of me, I nudged Clarence before he could say something else. "Let's see what the sheriff wants."

Greg took us down the hall to Rick Fowler's office. He sat behind a desk piled with papers. When we walked in, he pushed himself up with a groan and walked around the desk to greet us.

"Why, Clarence, I'm surprised to see you." He extended his hand.

"Thought I should get out of the house for a little jaunt." He chuckled. "Probably more trouble than it's worth. How are you, Rick? I hear you had back surgery this fall. Are you on the mend?"

"Could be worse."

I was still learning code words and phrases Minnesotans used in their understated way. "Could be worse" meant things were pretty bad. The way he rubbed his lower back and groaned when he moved, told the story.

Once we sat down, Rick opened a folder on his desk and squinted at me through his reading glasses. "You've probably heard we found Brewster Conway over at the old Torgerson house. The one they called Mary's Place. Looks like he might have fallen down and crawled into his van before passing out. Died of hypothermia, we're guessing."

I gasped. "You mean he froze to death?"

"Pretty cold weather. We get these every so often. People pass out and never wake up."

I remembered Kiley telling me they'd met in a twelve-step program. "Sheriff, are you thinking he was drunk? I heard he'd been in rehab." As soon as I spoke, I realized I should have stayed quiet.

Rick peered at me over his reading glasses. "How well did you know him?"

"I talked with him a couple of times when I was visiting the young women at the house."

He sat back in his chair, pain lines obvious around his mouth. "And why were you at the house?"

I glanced at Clarence who sat serenely at my side. He nodded for me to answer the question.

"Well, I got to know the women there a little after one of them had a baby in the backseat of my car."

Rick lifted his glasses and rubbed his eyes. They were red as if he hadn't slept well. "Uh, we think drugs might have been involved."

I was taken aback. "You mean Mary's Place had something to do with drugs?" It hardly made sense to me.

Rick frowned. "No. I mean Conway's fall might have been drug-related."

"Seriously?" Brewster didn't strike me as being high when I was around him, but what did I really know about him except what Kiley had told me.

"We'll have to wait for the coroner and the lab tests, but let's just say we found evidence on him." He studied me as if he expected me to say something.

I stayed quiet. Beside me, Clarence's eyes were closed as if he had dropped off to sleep. Some legal protection. I almost nudged him.

Rick cleared his throat. "Uh...the thing is, we found an empty prescription bottle with your name on it."

Suddenly I was wide awake. "What!?" Clarence stirred beside me, sitting up straighter.

Rick reached down and lifted up a green day pack. He winced as he set it on the desk. Both Clarence and I leaned forward at the same time.

"The tag inside the pack says it belongs to you."

Baffled, I looked at Clarence. "It looks like the go-pack I leave by the back door."

Clarence squinted at the pack and cleared his throat. "Rick, where did you find this?"

"In the van by the body."

I opened my mouth, then shut it again. *Don't say anything. Let Clarence handle this.*

He patted my leg. "Jamie, do you know why Brewster would have it?"

"I think it was a mix-up. Kiley brought a green pack with her when she came during the storm. When she left, she grabbed the wrong one. It was dark."

To my surprise, the sheriff didn't seem interested in the day pack and why Kiley might have had it. He held up a prescription bottle for oxycodone. "What about this?"

I'd been given the prescription last summer after being injured by one of his deputies. Remembering the incident that almost killed Bronte, the muscles in my back clenched so hard, a hot pain shot up the back of my neck. I fought not to cry out. "I..." I couldn't find my voice as I pictured Bronte on her side struggling to breathe.

Clarence came to my rescue. "Are you suggesting that Jamie drugged this Brewster fellow?"

I wanted to put my hands over my ears and block out Rick's voice.

169

"Now, Clarence. I'm only asking."

"Well, perhaps we're done here." Clarence spoke in a measured tone, but I felt the power behind it.

A flush rose onto my cheeks as I raised my hand to stop Clarence. "It's okay. I can tell you about the prescription. If you check with the pharmacy, they only gave me a small supply. I used the empty bottle for Iodine tablets. It's part of my emergency kit. I'm guessing you also found the granola bars, the chemical hand warmers, and a bunch of other things in the pack?"

He set the bottle down. "Uh…given your history…"

I hugged myself as he watched me. What did he mean, given my history? Yes, I was once arrested in Queens for major drug dealing, but it was a case of mistaken identity. Is that what he was referring to?

"What are you getting at, Rick?" Clarence sat on the edge of his chair, leaning on his cane.

Rick took a deep breath. "We're trying to find the source of the drugs."

A chill filled my chest even as my cheeks glowed hot pink. "I…"

Clarence stopped me from sputtering. "Are you suggesting that Jamie was dealing drugs?" He turned to me. "Does he think you'd provide drugs for someone and conveniently leave your backpack with all your identification behind? I've never heard of anything so ridiculous. I think it's time we go."

He made a move to stand while I continued to sit, frozen in place. How could he even infer I had anything to do with drugs or Brewster's death? He *knew* the Queens incident was a mistake on the part of a drug task force. What was he getting at?

Rick reached out his hand. "Now wait, Clarence. I'm not suggesting anything. I'm just trying to put this all together." He gestured to me. "You had contact with Conway at that house. The backpack was found there, near his body. We recovered his phone and found a couple of calls to you." He stopped waiting for an explanation.

If I told him they were from Elena, I might reveal where she was. I stayed silent.

"Kiley grabbed the wrong backpack." I fought to keep the tremble out of my voice.

Rick studied me for a moment. "You think Kiley, his wife, might have brought the backpack to him?"

I nodded. "Yes."

"When you visited the house, did you see anything suspicious—like drug activity?"

Did I see anything suspicious? Was he kidding? A house full of pregnant refugees using tourist visas? And one of them ends up dead after her baby is born. And one of them has a baby while trying to run away. And another is left locked in a closet. Not to mention Kiley traveling to my cabin in a snowstorm with Carmela and the baby. I felt like my head might explode.

Clarence saved me. "Rick, we both know Jamie is not your source. What are you really looking for?"

Rick fingered the report in front of him pursing his lips. "Well, okay then. Let's start over. When did you first meet Mr. Conway?"

I told him about my visits to Mary's Place to see Carmela and the baby. "He claimed to be a minister, but something was off about him."

"Off?"

I struggled to find the words. "He seemed to have rough edges, like he'd spent more time in a bar than a church. The residents appeared to be wary of him."

It occurred to me that the person Rick should be talking with was Kiley. She was the one who had shared her suspicions about him with me. "I think you should talk with Kiley Conway. She must have given Brewster the backpack after she left my place."

Rick nodded. "We haven't been able to locate her. Do you know where she is?"

"Honestly, I know very little about her or where she might be." This would have been a good time to tell him Kiley's suspicions about Brewster, but it would suggest I knew more than I did about the workings of Mary's Place. "She showed up on the night of the snowstorm with Carmela and her baby. She left early the next morning. I'm told she walked to the lodge and was picked up there by a white van. It's all I have."

Rick wrinkled his brow. "Now why would she come to your place?"

I tried to deflect the question. "I certainly couldn't turn them away."

Clarence intervened. "Does that answer your questions, Rick? If you have more, you'll have to wait while I use the facilities. Old geezer bladder, as they say."

The sheriff's expression was not a happy one. "I guess I'm done. If you think of anything else, give the office a call."

After a few more polite words, we walked out into the main area. The receptionist was back at her computer and Rex stood at her desk. Her cheeks were flushed and her eyes were bright. She giggled at something he said.

"Rex," I extended my hand. "I was sorry to hear about Brewster."

He still wore his Ray-Bans. He took my hand in a loose grip before turning to Clarence and introducing himself. "I'm Rex Jordan. I've been doing some pro bono legal work for Viaje Seguro. They sponsored the women and set up Mary's Place."

Clarence shook his hand. "Well, well, a fellow barrister. Jamie tells me you work out of El Paso. I don't hear Texas in your voice."

"Transplant. I grew up in Minnesota but I'm not a fan of winter." He pointed to his face. "A little slip on the ice."

Outside a snowplow drove by, making a scraping noise as it cleared more of the main street.

Rex took off his dark glasses and rubbed one eye. "Uh...this is a bad business about Mr. Conway. Viaje Seguro is quite upset."

"They sponsor other women?" Clarence's brow furrowed as he gazed at Rex. I wondered about his puzzled expression.

"It's a national program. My firm feels they provide a much-needed service for very vulnerable people."

It sounded to me like a prepared sound bite. I felt a sudden desperation to get out of this office. "Rex, maybe we can meet up a little later. I know you wanted to talk with me."

He glanced at his watch. "I'll get hold of you. Right now, I need to talk with the sheriff, and then I need to go back to the motel for a conference call."

Greg walked into the reception area. "Sheriff is ready for you."

Before he followed Greg, I touched his arm. "Just a quick question. Do you know where Kiley is? She left something in my cabin. I'd like to get it back to her."

The startled expression on Rex's face took me aback. "Really? Do you know what it was?"

I knew it was the backpack, but I gave him a non-committal shrug.

"We'll definitely talk."

Once we were in the car, Clarence adjusted his seat belt. "That young man seemed pretty keen on what you have that belongs to Kiley. Do you know what's in her backpack?"

I shook my head. "Never thought to look."

"Hmmm." Clarence scratched his chin. "Something about him is familiar. I've seen him before, but I can't remember where. The old brain, you know, doesn't keep its files in good order anymore."

I knew for a fact that Clarence's files were fine. Maybe a little dusty, but fine.

At Clarence's house, I accompanied him to the door. Joe waited, keeping a close eye on us as we negotiated the sanded, salted steps.

"Lorraine took Elena to the doctor," he greeted us.

"Is she okay?"

"She said it was…uh…a woman thing."

Clarence chuckled, "Too many women around here. Glad Joe hasn't tried to escape."

As I walked back to my car, I noted the dent now covered in a white spray of road salt. I needed to talk with Sheryl Bevins before winter would do more damage to the car. Remembering M.C. and how he had reacted to me, I hoped he would be busy elsewhere and I could negotiate with Sheryl.

My next stop though was the hospital to make sure Carmela and Bonita Amy were okay. If I recalled right, her brother was coming today to pick her up.

Carmela's Brother

The hospital parking lot, now smaller because of the piled-up snow, was nearly full when I pulled in. Norma had told me business picked up after a storm because of heart attacks and broken hips. "People who've been sitting in front of the television watching football all fall suddenly think they can hoist a shovel. Boom! Their poor flabby heart seizes up! And if not that, it's the slip on the ice."

I thought about Rex and his bruised face. He was lucky he hadn't broken anything.

The receptionist's desk and the nurses' station were both empty. I guessed the small staff was busy with patients. I walked down to room 102 where Carmela and Bonita Amy were. The door was closed and inside I heard soft voices speaking Spanish. I hesitated, then knocked.

"Carmela, it's Jamie."

A man opened the door. He looked like an older version of Carmela with the same large brown eyes and dark hair. Carmela called out, "¡Hola! Amy! *Este es mi hermano Alfonso.*"

He held out his hand. "I'm Carmela's big brother Alfonso. Nice to meet you." He spoke with barely an accent. "I'm taking my sister to my home."

I smiled. "I'm so relieved you have found each other."

Carmela beamed and said something in rapid Spanish to Alfonso. He translated. "She wants to thank you for everything you've done."

Carmela spoke again laughing.

"But she says she doesn't want any more sled rides."

Me either.

He invited me to sit down. Bonita Amy slept in a little bassinette, making occasional grunting noises. I pointed at her. "Beautiful baby. *Muy bonita.*"

He nodded. "I am grateful to you. I've worked for a long time to get Carmela to me and now I have her and a niece."

After we chatted a bit about the weather, I asked him how he came to live in Canada.

"It's a long story. Bad things were happening in our village—gangs and militia—always after young men. A friend had an uncle who'd gone to Washington to work in the fields. One night, I took a few possessions and left. Once I reached Washington, I kept going north until I was in Canada. I had a lot of jobs but finally got my college degree. I teach Spanish and coach soccer."

Carmela nodded. *"Sí. Fútbol."*

He told me he tried for several years to bring his family to Vancouver, but something always got in the way. "Our father had an accident and broke his back. When he was better, Mama got sick with cancer and died." He raised his hands in surrender. "Always something."

Outside the room, a cart rattled by followed by the whisper of shoes on the floor. A voice down the hall called, "Nurse! Nurse!"

Carmela shook her head. "Too noisy here."

I agreed. This was no place to have a baby. Turning to Alfonso, I asked the question that was uppermost on my mind. "Can you tell me how Carmela ended up here with Viaje Seguro?"

Alfonso looked over at Carmela who nodded. "The militia. They came one night and took Papa and Juan—Carmela's husband. When they disappeared, Carmela fled north to find me."

I took a deep breath. Too much for such a young woman. "How did you find Viaje Seguro?"

Alfonso and Carmela spoke in Spanish. She gestured, pointing to her belly. He translated. "She was told to cross the border and surrender in the United States. They said the United States would help her get to Canada."

"Oh?" Bad advice.

"Instead they put her in this detention center. When she told them she was pregnant, a man came and offered to help her."

"Was it Brewster?"

Carmela shook her head. "No." She described him in Spanish.

"She says he was tall and skinny and wore a uniform. He spoke good Spanish."

"Carmela, when I found you on the road, were you trying to get to your brother?"

"*Sí. Canadá.*"

"Why run away like that?"

While Carmela explained to Alfonso, someone knocked at the door. A nurse walked in with a clipboard and papers to sign. "Looks like you are ready for discharge. I need these signed and then you can go." She held up a prescription bottle. "You will need to take these antibiotics for another week."

Alfonso translated. "It's okay for you to sign."

I watched her sign, suddenly overcome with sadness about her story. Her parents and husband gone. The journey to the border and everything else made me wonder how someone survived the trauma. Then I looked at the sleeping baby. That's how. She needed to protect her baby.

"Good luck, Carmela and little Bonita." The nurse waved as she left.

Alfonso checked his watch. "We must go. I will drive to Minneapolis where we will catch a plane."

I didn't ask about papers to enter Canada. Alfonso appeared to be quite competent.

In the hallway, footsteps approached and slowed. For a moment, I wondered if someone was outside the door. Maybe the sheriff was finally getting his act together to talk with her before she left.

I turned to Carmela. "Before you go, can you tell me why you were running away the day Bonita was born?" I needed to know if something at Mary's Place scared her.

Carmela spoke with animation. I caught the name Rita a couple of times.

"Carmela says she became scared when Rita had her baby. When she brought him back from the hospital some people came and took him. She didn't want them to have him. My sister worried that they would try to take her baby, too. She thought if she could get to Canada no one would try to take the baby."

"Wow." I thought about Rex trying to work with the women. "Did a lawyer named Rex talk with you?"

Carmela scrunched her face not understanding the question. Alfonso translated. "No. No Rex. She says she saw him at the house, but never spoke to him."

Weird.

I told them I was thinking about writing an article about the delivery and the women. I asked if it would be okay. Carmela's eyes narrowed and her lips trembled.

"It's okay. I won't identify you. I promise. And if you don't want me to write the story, I won't."

She and Alfonso spoke. When they were done, he took a deep breath. "She's afraid someone will send her back. I don't think that will happen in Canada."

I sure hoped he was right.

We exchanged contact information. "Let me know how you are doing. And send pictures." I pointed to the baby.

We hugged and Carmela burst out in tears. "Thank you, Amy."

Alfonso walked me to the door. "My sister has been through so much. Now maybe she will be safe."

Just before we reached the hospital entrance, I saw a man hurrying out the door. I could have sworn it was Rex. When I stepped outside, though, the parking lot was quiet.

Lacey Graham

I felt drained as I waited for my poor dented Subaru to warm up before driving to the Bevins'. Did I really want to try to deal with them today? I almost turned the car in the direction of home and the comfort of my cabin. "Come on, Jamie, you have to get it fixed." With a long sigh, I headed to talk with Sheryl and Lacey.

Smoke curled up through the chimney of the Bevins's house. Two cars were parked in the turnaround. I recognized the one Lacey had been driving when she backed into me. The taillight was still cracked, but otherwise, I could see no other damage. So much had happened since the accident that it felt like old, old history. Still, Toby wanted a down payment before he worked on the car.

I took the estimate out of the glove compartment, remembering the expression of doubt on M.C.'s face when I'd shown it to him before. He'd promised to look into it and had done nothing. I felt anger building inside me as I approached the house. Before I could reach the door, it opened. Lacey stood in the doorway staring at me. She was dressed in black leggings and a long cable knit sweater. She had a teenage slenderness to her. Hardly the look of someone who had recently given birth. I couldn't explain it, but something was off-kilter. She stared at me as if I'd just landed in a UFO.

"Hi, Lacey. I'm here about the dent in my car."

"What?"

"The dent? Remember you hit my car when you backed out of the Christmas tree lot?"

She wrinkled her brow for a moment. "Oh, sorry. Sometimes I forget things."

I held the estimate up. "Your dad and mother were going to talk about this?"

"Oh sure." She sounded uncertain.

"How's the baby?" I hoped I sounded friendly and reassuring. She continued to stare at me.

"Oh, he's cute but he cries a lot."

I noted disappointment in her voice. Perhaps motherhood wasn't all it was cracked up to be.

Lacey made no move to invite me in. This was ridiculous. It was cold standing on the steps, I'd already had a disturbing interview with the sheriff and I'd just bid farewell to Carmela and the baby named after me. I wasn't in the mood to chat at the door.

In my best New York possibly New Jersey mobster accent I stepped close to her. "I need to talk with your mother and get this settled."

"Oh." Her eyes opened wide with a startled expression before motioning me in.

Since my last visit, Sheryl had put up even more Christmas decorations. Garlands of evergreen hung from the stairway railing and the whole house smelled of a combination of vanilla and pine scent. The first thing I did after Lacey closed the door was sneeze.

"Excuse me."

Her mouth opened. "You're not sick, are you? I don't want anyone who's sick around Frankie."

"Allergies," I assured her.

"Mom would get really mad if Frankie got sick."

"Frankie is your baby?" I put on my friendliest smile. "What a fine name."

Lacey stood in the entryway as if she didn't know what else to do with me. Her reactions were so odd I wondered if she was on drugs. Then it occurred to me. Maybe this was residual from a brain injury.

"Could I talk with your mother?"

"I guess. I'll go get her." She left me standing next to all the coats and boots in the entryway.

"Mom, someone is here." Immediately I heard the sound of a baby crying.

From upstairs, Sheryl called down. "Honey, I can't come now. I'm feeding the baby."

"Oh." Lacey stood at the foot of the stairs, rocking back and forth like she had at the door.

At this moment in time, she didn't strike me as someone competent enough to care for a baby. The baby was lucky to have such an involved grandmother.

I slipped off my boots and walked up to her. "Maybe I could go upstairs and talk with your mother. It won't take but a minute."

"Oh, okay." She relaxed her shoulders. "That would be good."

"Sheryl, it's Jamie Forest," I called. "I'm coming up with the estimate on the damage to my car. I left a copy with M.C. the other day, but Toby hasn't gotten the down payment yet."

I was met with silence.

"What room is she in upstairs?"

"Oh, she's in Frankie's room. She likes to sit in there and rock him. You'd think it was *her* baby, not mine." Her lips formed a pout.

"It's nice you have your mother to help you."

Lacey stopped the rocking motion and stared at her feet. Once again, she reminded me of a sullen teenager. "I guess."

"Must be quite a change—with a new baby and all."

She stayed in the round-shouldered posture. When she looked at me, she had a childlike expression. "I expected it to be more fun."

This conversation was making me uncomfortable. "I'll give your mother this estimate and be out of your way."

I heard the baby make its little squawking noises in the first room at the top of the stairs. Sheryl sat in a rocker cooing and talking to Frankie. The nursery was also decorated for Christmas including a little tree with presents under it. The room had the warm, humid smell of new baby along with the piney scent of the tree.

"Excuse me." I stood in the doorway.

Sheryl looked up with a startled expression. "What are you doing here?" She held the baby close as if I might try to snatch it from her.

I took a step forward and detected a slight flinch. "Sorry to bother you. Toby needs a down payment before he'll do the bodywork on my car. I wondered when he will get it."

She squinted at me. "What?"

This was getting old fast. "Lacey ran into my car right after Thanksgiving—remember? When I stopped by last week, I showed the estimate to your husband, but Toby hasn't gotten the money yet."

"Oh?"

What kind of a household was this? Both mother and daughter acted like they'd never seen me before. I felt my cheeks heat up. "Do you know when I can get my door fixed?" I worked to keep my tone neutral despite wanting to yell at her.

The baby made a little gurgling noise. She turned him over on her lap and patted his back. She was stalling. When she finally spoke, she looked beyond me as if someone was standing in the hallway. "I…uh, my husband… uh he didn't think we should pay."

"Excuse me?"

She winced at the sharpness of my tone. "He didn't think we were liable."

I sighed, shaking my head. "This is my punishment, I guess for taking your daughter at her word. I should have called the police."

Sheryl's reaction was immediate. "No! No, don't call the police." She held out her hand for the estimate. "I'll get the money to Toby."

"Thank you." I squatted down to look at Frankie. "He's a beauty." He had light brown coloring like Bonita Amy. I remembered the wedding photo on the mantel. Lacey's husband had this skin tone.

Sheryl gazed back at me with a glow to her cheeks. "He looks like his dad. It's been a rough road for Lacey, though."

"That's what I heard."

Sheryl's eyes widened. "What do you mean? Heard what?"

I took a little step back at the vehemence in her voice. "Uh, I heard she had a hard time getting pregnant."

"Who told you?" Sheryl's eyes narrowed. "Did someone say something about adoption?"

Adoption? Suddenly, I felt very boxed in. I shouldn't have listened to local gossip. "Uh no. No one talked about adoption."

"Because Lacey gets mixed up sometimes." She stroked Frankie's head and talked softly to him. "But you're ours, aren't you?"

Frankie cooed at her.

Sheryl looked up at me with her lips pressed into a thin line. "Lacey's troubles are private."

It was clear she did not want to continue this conversation.

Frankie scrunched up his face and grunted, making an explosive noise. This was my cue to leave. "I'll check with Toby tomorrow to make sure he's got the payment."

As I walked down the stairs Lacey stood at the bottom watching me. "Pretty baby, isn't he?"

"Yes, he's pretty. Lots of hair." Frankie had a full head of dark hair. It didn't match Lacey's light brown.

Lacey nodded like an eager child. "He looks just like Frank, my husband. A baby with lots of hair. That's what I asked for."

I stopped at the foot of the stairs. "You asked for a baby with lots of hair?"

Her expression changed. "But I'm not supposed to talk about that, I guess." She put her hands to her cheeks. "You won't tell that I said something, will you?"

"No, I won't say anything." I smiled at her. "Your husband must be very excited about this, too."

Her face clouded. "I guess. He said he always wanted a little boy. We'll all be together for Christmas—Mom, Dad, Frank, and Frankie."

Sheryl called down from upstairs. "Lacey, honey, why don't you show the lady out and come up here?"

Lacey glanced up the stairs and her expression darkened. "She treats me like a kid. She's not as nice as everybody thinks. Sometimes she's such a bitch. And sometimes she gets real mean. You don't want to be around her when she's in one of her moods."

Hopefully, Sheryl would take care of the estimate and I wouldn't have to be around her—ever. "I'll be going now."

She touched my arm. "You're nice. Not like that woman who came to the house yelling. She really scared me, you know?"

Sheryl called down in an even louder voice. "Lacey get up here!"

"Bitch." She repeated as she tromped up the stairs.

Once I was back in my car, I sat staring at the house. The whole encounter was too odd. Lacey clearly had some mental problems. Was Frankie adopted? But Sheryl said he looked like his dad. Part of me wanted to burst back in the house and ask. The other said it was time to let go.

"Get your car fixed. Make sure the girls from Mary's Place are in safe hands and move on."

Still, it niggled at me enough that I drove downtown to the *Killdeer Times* to talk with Jilly. Maybe she knew more.

Jilly sat at her desk talking loudly to her computer screen when I walked in. "Sounds like you and your PC are having a lover's spat."

She tsked. "Good thing you came in. I was close to clobbering it." She pointed to the screen. "I'm having some software problems. I was hoping to shame the beast into behaving."

I walked over and inspected the screen. The hourglass wasn't filling. "Looks to me like the woofer needs to be backed up before it starts to tweet."

"Thanks. That's helpful." She turned to me. "What can I do for you?"

"I'm after a little gossip. I just came from the Bevins's. The more I have to do with them, the odder they get."

"You mean Sheryl and her Hallmark Christmas decorating?"

"No, I mean her daughter and that new baby."

Jilly stared at the computer screen, biting her lip. "I told Phil we needed to buy new computers. Would he listen?"

Phil Sessions was the publisher. He and I were on somewhat shaky terms these days after he hired me last summer and immediately fired me. I chuckled. "Do you want me to talk to him?"

"Humph!" She turned to me. "So, tell me why you think the Bevinses are odd."

I told her about the puzzling conversation about the baby. "It almost sounded like Lacey thought the baby was adopted and Sheryl didn't want to talk about it."

"It's not like Lacey wouldn't have noticed if she'd given birth, I wager." Jilly poked at the keyboard.

"What adoption agency in its right mind would give that woman a baby? I'm not sure I'd trust her with a Chia pet."

Jilly didn't laugh. "It makes no sense to me either. After the accident, they say Lacey had a hard time." She pointed to her head. "I was older and didn't know her, but my cousin was in high school with her. She told me Lacey changed dramatically after she rolled the car." She sighed, tapping some keys and the computer shut down. "There, take that."

"I sensed she wasn't quite tracking right."

"My cousin said when she came back to school she was quiet, not her old self and every once in a while she'd lose her temper for no reason."

I pictured the look on her face when she called her mother a bitch. I could see it.

"But," Jilly shrugged. "She graduated and went to a little religious college down in Texas. She hasn't been around much since then." Jilly took a deep breath.

"The accident must have been a bad one."

"Her boyfriend died. It ended up in a big lawsuit. I heard the Bevins and the boy's parents sued a liquor store. I heard it was settled quietly. Clarence would know more about it."

The bell over the door jingled. Jilly stood up and greeted the elderly woman who walked in. "Hi, Martha. Good to see you out."

Martha walked up to the counter digging in her purse. "I'm here to pay my subscription. Unlike some of the pikers around here, I want to keep the paper afloat." She glanced at me. "You know, little newspapers like this are folding in the dozens. People think they can get everything free on the internet. Well, someone has to write the stories."

I nodded. "You're right."

Martha handed Jilly cash and walked out the door. Jilly smiled. "Martha comes in once a month to pay for her subscription. She's like clockwork. Used to teach English and used to come in here all the time to show the editor all the copy mistakes. She's slowing down these days."

"I've read the sad state of some of the local papers. I hope the *Times* is doing okay."

"So far."

I left when Jeanine, the editor, walked through from the back. I hurried out the door. Jeanine was not an example of "Minnesota Nice."

The Backpack

I arrived home with a trunk full of groceries and supplies. My plan was to hole up for the next couple of days to finish *Darkening Sand.* The postman had just delivered another manuscript from an author I'd worked with before. If I could get both done before Christmas, I could keep the lights on for a while.

This hand-to-mouth existence exhausted me. I thought about the poor single parents working minimum wage jobs trying to balance the little they made with providing food, shelter, health care, and love to their children. I wondered if that was the life in store for Elena. If she was here on a tourist visa, she wouldn't be able to work—at least not legally. The more I thought about her and what the future might hold, the darker it looked.

"Snap out of it, Jamie." I set the package with the manuscript on the table and hauled in the groceries. Bronte wagged at me, nuzzling against my leg. At least I didn't have to worry about paying for her college.

C.P. Dowling finally wrote the reveal in *Darkening Sand.* Like a replay of *Star Wars* the wise Queen Alusra gathered Levy and her loyal Midgers including Ms. Agather and Golix into the Emerald room and admitted that yes, indeed, Levy was her daughter and the heir to the throne. Moreover, the newly defeated Aga Pumpert was Levy's father who had been overtaken by the evil force of Vachron but now renounced his bad ways. In the dramatic ending, the author left us speculating on whether Aga Pumpert really came back to the forces of good, or would Vachron rise again?

Financially I wanted a sequel. In the depths of my poetic heart, though, I wanted C.P. Dowling to put down her pen and get a day job.

I set the manuscript down with a long sigh. "What am I supposed to do with this?" If I told C.P. her story was hackneyed and predictable, I could destroy her. If I didn't, she wouldn't improve.

"Why did I get into this, girl? I can't make a living doing this." I thought about my life in New York. It wasn't so bad if you didn't count the rotten marriage, the arrest for drug dealing, the noise, the crowds, the smell. "I spent all my inheritance on this place—a cabin by the lake and it's cold three-fourths of the year and full of bugs the rest."

Bronte ambled over to me and put her head on my lap. "What am I going to do?" I needed a little exercise to clear my head. "Want to take a walk down the road?"

She was at the door before I could get up out of the chair. She stood wagging her tail so hard she looked like a hula dancer while I rummaged through the box in the corner of the closet for a suitable hat and a pair of mittens. I found the hat I'd gotten at the second-hand store. It had a fur brim and ear flaps.

When I'd shown it to Jim he'd broken into a wide grin. "Wear that and you'll look just like the sheriff in 'Fargo.'"

As I slipped it on, I spied the backpack Kiley had left behind.

It was almost an exact duplicate of my green pack. Mine had come from Target. No wonder she'd mistaken mine for hers. When I picked Kiley's up, it felt heftier than I expected. "What were you carrying? Gold bricks?" Part of me wanted to open it and find out, the other part told me it was none of my business. Sort of like going through someone's purse. I would drop it off at the sheriff's office the next time I went into town. Maybe he'd give mine back to me.

Thinking about Kiley brought me back to Brewster. Maybe he had a drug habit that he concealed and used his work with Viaje Seguro to pay for it. Or was it something deeper like a connection to the drug cartels?

I laughed out loud. "Jamie, you're working your way up to writing a crime thriller."

Bronte whined impatiently at the door and pulled me from my musings. "Okay. Okay, I'm coming."

187

I set the pack back down and bundled up for the walk. Once again, the fresh crisp air revived me and pulled me out of my gray funk. A slight wind whipped the top layer of snow around like sand in the desert. It reminded me that C.P. had overused the words "twisters of sand" when describing Levy's trek through the dunes.

Back to my bad mood as I started to ruminate about the manuscript.

Bronte didn't care. She loved racing down the plowed drive, picking up sticks, and bringing them back to me. "If only they were one-hundred-dollar bills." I picked one up and threw it for her. By the time we returned to the cabin, it was nearly dark. Overhead, the sky filled with wispy clouds. If I concentrated when I looked up, I could make out a few sparkling stars in the waning night.

"It'll be cold tonight." Bronte dropped a stick at my feet for one last fetch before going in. She didn't care much whether the temperature was in the twenties or the teens. I cared because the lower it went, the more propane I needed to use.

Before going in I gathered an armful of wood for the fireplace. I intended to have a quiet night by the fire figuring out how to fix C.P.'s manuscript.

Jim texted while I stacked wood by the fireplace. **How's life?**

Dumb question. **Cold and dark. Need someone to warm me up.**

He shot back, **Thought you had a dog.**

I was working on a witty comeback when he added, **Oops, gotta catch a bad guy. Maybe back next weekend.**

I sent him a thumbs up emoji. Bronte licked my hand as if she understood how lonely I felt. "Well girl, as usual, it's you and me."

Ignoring the manuscript, I decided I couldn't make appropriate comments to C.P. until my cabin was tidy. The area where I hung my coats and kept winter gear was a mess. After I picked up the scattered gloves, hats, and scarves and stuffed them in the wooden chest, I took the backpack out from the corner. "I wonder if Kiley figured out she grabbed the wrong pack?"

I pictured my pack next to Brewster in the van. He was not a likable man, but no one deserved to die the way he did, passed out in subzero weather.

The buckle on the flap of the backpack slipped open. "No harm in peeking, is there?"

Bronte, busy with her chew toy, didn't answer.

When I opened it, the first thing I saw was a stack of bills about an inch thick and bound with a red strip of paper.

"What?" I stared at the money. Digging deeper into the pack, I pulled out more neatly bound bills. The top bill in each stack was a twenty. Immediately my brain travelled to a crime drama I'd watched a couple of years ago where the ransom money was in a briefcase and looked like this.

"These can't be real." My exclamation sounded like a squeak.

Bronte stopped chewing and raised her head. I stuffed the bills back in the pack, placed it in the corner, and backed away as if it contained a virus.

"This is not good."

My first instinct was to call the sheriff and report it. I had my phone ready when a little voice in my head said, *wait*. I pictured the sheriff talking with me this morning and was filled with distrust. Was this backpack the reason Greg had questioned me about the abandoned car? Was he sent to look for it? If so, what did the sheriff know?

Bronte followed me as I paced back and forth between the living area and the kitchen. I needed to tell someone about this.

"Clarence. I need to call Clarence."

His phone rang six times before it clicked to a voice message. "This is Clarence Engstrom, if you are a client, leave a message. If you are a solicitor, hang up now. Good day."

"Clarence, it's Jamie. Something very peculiar has come up. Please call me as soon as you can."

I hoped Clarence would check his messages.

While I fixed cheese toast and a salad for supper, I kept glancing over at the backpack as if it contained C.P. Dowling's evil power of Vachron. My head spun with possibilities. Would Kiley come back for it? Or worse, would she send someone else? Was this drug money? The more I thought about it, the more I wished I wasn't currently living in the remote woods on the dead end of an old road.

When the phone rang, I grabbed it and answered with a breathless, "Hello."

"Clarence Engstrom here. I'm looking for that New York mob lady."

Usually, I enjoyed Clarence's humor. At this moment, however, the word "mob" sent shivers down my back. "Oh, Clarence. I might be in a little trouble." I told him about the backpack and the money inside.

"Well, that's a conundrum. Did you count it?"

I didn't want to touch it and leave my prints on it. After all, the sheriff still wondered if I had a drug connection. "No, but I'm guessing it's a substantial amount."

"Might fit in with what I learned this afternoon."

"Oh?"

"I was curious about this Rex Jordan so I called his law office in El Paso. I thought I'd reach someone who could tell me more about what he was working on. Elena's description of the paperwork he wanted her to sign didn't sit right with me."

I filled the tea kettle and put it on the burner. My stomach needed a bit of settling.

"To my great surprise, they put me right through to Rex Jordan, principal of Jordan, Sanchez, and Taylor. He was sitting in his office in El Paso looking out the window at the cloudless, toasty Texas day."

"What?" The kettle hissed as I turned up the burner. "He was just in the sheriff's office. That doesn't make sense."

"No, it doesn't. But this Rex knew about our Rex. Turns out his name is Mark Mulvaney. He clerked for a while in their law office. He was let go for reasons Rex didn't want to disclose to me. When he left, he took business cards, stationary, and some computer files."

I pictured his diamond stud and designer clothes. "That's not good. What was he up to?"

"That's a twenty-thousand-dollar question. Or, I guess with inflation a hundred-thousand-dollar question. But I can tell you one more thing, I thought he looked familiar. It took a while to figure it out—had to go deep into that locked vault that's my aging brain. Back when Lacey Bevins had her auto accident, the Bevins along with the family of the boy who was killed sued the liquor store that allegedly sold booze to them. I represented the liquor store."

While I fixed a cup of tea, Clarence told me about the suit and how it ended up in court. Lacey claimed they'd simply walked into the store and bought two bottles of vodka and no one checked their IDs. Gussie Gustafson, who owned the store denied selling liquor to them. Jared Mulvaney was the boyfriend who was killed. His older brother Mark testified that he witnessed the sale. Except they couldn't produce receipts. "It was a 'he said, she said, he said' type of situation. We put several people on the stand who testified that Gussie was meticulous about checking IDs."

"Glad I wasn't on that jury."

"It wasn't pretty. Midway through the trial Gussie had chest pains and ended up in the hospital. Bevins and Mulvaney eventually lost. Rumors circulated later that Mark, who was twenty-one at the time had bought the liquor.

"Oh my god. So, Mark, alias Rex, came back here to supposedly help the pregnant women?"

"Looks that way."

I felt like I had a pile of Legos in front of me and I didn't know how to put them together to build the Lego house. "I'm lost, here. What next?"

"Well, I've had a chat with the sheriff. He's becoming more interested in Rita's death now that the phony minister is dead, too."

I did not feel comforted. "I'll bring the backpack to the sheriff tomorrow, but I'll need you to come with me to convince him it's not my drug money."

He laughed but I didn't find it very funny.

We talked a little longer. He'd found out from Lorraine that Elena was due in two weeks.

"She'll stay with me," Clarence chuckled. "Hope I don't have to be the midwife."

I laughed thinking about dapper Clarence delivering a baby.

"You'll be glad to know Carmela and Bonita Amy were on their way to Canada." He added, "Yoli is still in Duluth. My friends are keeping her safe."

I thought about the women and what they'd been through. "Maybe Viaje Seguro should be renamed 'Viaje Inseguro.'"

Before we ended the call, Clarence warned me, "Keep your doors locked. Call me in the morning. Remember, I'm an old guy so I rise early but don't call before nine."

"You consider that early?"

I felt like I at least had a plan for the evil backpack sitting in the corner of my cabin.

The Visitor

A half hour later, I heard the sound of a snowmobile approaching from the lake. Usually, they'd head to the fish house colony. Instead of disappearing in that direction, the engine noise grew. Bronte's ears pricked up as she trotted to the back door. She emitted a low growl from deep inside her.

Her growl turned into a wild bark as the snowmobile pulled up next to my car. I watched out the window as the driver cut the engine and dismounted. Switching on the outdoor light, I peered through the window to see someone in a dark snowmobile suit, holding a helmet. He waved at me through the window with a grin, his black eye contrasting with his rosy cheeks.

"Rex?" I should have listened to Clarence, kept the door locked, and called the sheriff, but he looked harmless in a snowmobile suit that was obviously too big. Holding tight to Bronte, I opened the door. As soon as he was through the doorway, I noted Bronte's reaction. She didn't bark, but her teeth were bared and the fur on her back stood up like a punk haircut.

I hissed at her. "Sit, girl." She stayed close to me her hackles still raised.

"Sorry to show up unannounced. I was in the neighborhood…and…" His voice trailed off.

I fought to keep my voice calm. "Just happened to be in the neighborhood?"

He smiled in a boyish way. "Well, I guess I'm here for two things."

I said nothing, still holding tight to Bronte's collar.

"First, I'm chilled to the bone and wondered if you might have some hot coffee or tea. I'd forgotten how damn cold it gets here in Minnesota. Been a Texan too long, I guess."

Curious now, I indicated the kitchen chair. "Have a seat. I'll put the kettle on."

I grabbed a chew toy from under the sink and gave it to Bronte whispering, "Stay calm, girl. It's okay." She took it and settled under the table with her hackles still raised.

A voice in my head said, *Jamie, are you crazy? Call 911.*

He unzipped his snowmobile suit and slipped out of the top of it. Underneath he wore a cable knit turtleneck sweater similar to one I'd seen in a *New Yorker* ad. He might have been handsome in that sweater if his face wasn't so banged up.

I fumbled with a couple of teabags. "Sorry, all I have is green. Will that work?"

He gave me a thumbs up. "Anything hot sounds good to me. Thank you."

I put the bowl of sugar on the table and set out a couple of spoons.

He chatted about the weather and how different it was from Texas while the water in the kettle burbled, simmered, and finally grew to a whistle. I handed him a mug and sat across from him. Bronte moved closer to my feet, chewing the toy like an anxious child.

I struggled to come up with small talk and was grateful he didn't see how much my hand shook as I lifted my mug.

"How did you find me?"

He stirred several spoonfuls of sugar into his tea. "Once I was out on the lake, I remembered that you lived somewhere around here." He pointed out the window. "I stopped at the fish houses and asked. They sent me here."

"No secrets in a small community."

He drank his tea in silence, tapping one foot lightly on the floor.

I cleared my throat. "You said you had two reasons for coming."

He nodded, his foot still tapping. I wondered if he was getting ready to spring. *Keep your head, Jamie. He doesn't know that you know.*

"When you said you were writing an article about Viaje Seguro, I put you off." He rubbed his chin as if he were trying to find the right words. "I think you should do it and I'm happy to fill you in on anything you need."

I had to admit, the man had charm. "Tell me what you know about them."

And tell me why you stole an identity and are suddenly concerned about pregnant refugees.

"Viaje Seguro is a small group of lawyers, philanthropists, and concerned people who have seen what happens to pregnant women who are trying to get asylum in this country. It's a mindboggling process and many end up getting deported back to the places where they were endangered. We wanted to stop the deportations, give them good medical care and find ways to keep them safe."

"Sounds like a worthy organization." I willed myself to relax while the thought swirled through my head that the women weren't feeling very safe with Viaje Seguro. "What happens to them after the babies are born?"

"We find safe houses for them while their applications for asylum go through."

"Viaje Seguro provides the financial support for them?"

"We have some wealthy donors."

This was too easy and too pat. "What about the babies? Carmela thought someone was trying to steal Bonita Amy. Where did that idea come from?"

I watched Rex press his lips together in concentration. "Some of the babies are the result of rape. The women have a choice to release them for adoption—but it's a choice they have to make."

The word "release" struck me as unusual. I said nothing.

"We have contacts with adoption agencies with waiting lists of great homes for the babies." He set down his tea. "It's always an option."

I knew he wasn't telling me the whole story—or even half of it. "I'm curious. How did you end up housing the women at Mary's Place? It seems odd to transport them from the warmth of the south to the frostbite of a Minnesota winter."

Rex shrugged. "That wasn't my department. I became involved after Mary's Place was set up because my law firm knew I grew up in Minnesota. I assume one of the donors might have been from around here."

I was tempted to drop all pretense and ask him exactly what law firm he was referring to. Common sense prevailed even though anger grew in me. I *knew* he was exploiting the women. I didn't know exactly how.

"Bevins owns the house. Is he part of Viaje Seguro?"

Rex held up his arms. "Honestly, I don't know. Many of the donors are anonymous."

"What do you know about Brewster and Kiley?"

"Again, not my department. I was sent here to work on the applications for asylum. The Conways were already in place when I came." He took a deep breath. "I thought he was a minister, and she was his wife." His voice trailed off. "I guess I was wrong."

"Was he doing drugs? Selling them?"

Rex slowly shook his head. "I don't know. The sheriff is investigating, and I will leave it to him. My work is done."

Interesting that Rex hadn't mentioned Elena's absence. "I know Yoli is in Duluth and Carmela is with her brother. Do you know what happened to Elena?"

Rex leaned back his hands on the table. While his fingernails were nicely manicured, his knuckles appeared chafed and swollen. He looked down at them and quickly took them off the table. "She was transported to another home in southern Minnesota. She's safe."

"Oh, that's good to know. If you have her contact information, I'd like to speak to her. I understand her English is pretty good." I bit back the urge to spit out, *Liar!*

"Sure. I'll text it to you."

"Does this mean Mary's Place is all done?"

Rex shrugged. "Again, not my department."

The muscles in my stomach tightened as I sat across the table from him. What was he up to? Pieces of the Legos pile rearranged themselves in my head. The Bevins connection, a new baby and a dead mother? A backpack full of cash?

"Rex, tell me the truth. Did Lacey Graham adopt Rita's baby? Is that why they opened Mary's Place?"

For a moment, his expression darkened, and his eyes narrowed. I winced, wondering what he might do next. Almost instantly, though, his expression turned bland. "Now where would you get an idea like that?"

"Coincidence. Suddenly they have a new baby and Rita is dead."

"Trust me. There is no connection. I guarantee it."

Whether he was connected to Bevins and baby Frankie or not, I wanted him out of my cabin, now. He'd lied to me about Elena and probably about Viaje Seguro. I peered at him. "This whole business with the women has left me unsettled. I'm not sure I want to write that article. Too many missing pieces."

He pressed his lips together with a shrug. "I'm sorry. It does seem like a big mix-up."

Mix-up? Two people dead and a pile of money in a pack in my cabin?

I took a deep breath, working hard to maintain my calm. I didn't know whether Rex could be dangerous. Carefully choosing my words, I stood up. "I'm sorry not to be the best hostess, but I'm really tired. If you've warmed up enough, maybe you should be on your way." Under the table, Bronte let out a quiet growl.

He pushed his chair back with a look of apology. "I didn't mean to upset you."

Go away. I bit back the words while Bronte continued to growl.

As he stood, he scanned the room. "By the way, I heard you say Kiley left something behind. If you have it, I can get it back to her."

"Oh, you know where she is?"

"I know how to find her in El Paso if that's where she went."

Without thinking, I glanced quickly at the corner with all the coats. The backpack sat in plain sight.

"Uh, I don't have it. One of the sheriff's men came by this afternoon and took it. You might want to check with him." I was surprised at how easily the lie came to me.

Rex zipped up the snowmobile suit. "Oh, okay. No problem."

As Rex walked to the door, Bronte stood up suddenly and yelped.

"What, girl?" I looked down to see that she had managed to loop the laptop power cord around her leg. I pictured her dashing after Rex and the laptop crashing to the floor. A smashed laptop was yet another bill I couldn't afford.

When I grabbed Bronte to stop her from pulling the power cord, I tipped off balance. Suddenly I was launched into a comedy ballet trying to stay upright, keep Bronte from charging Rex, and saving the laptop.

Rex stood at the doorway staring but made no move to help me. Bronte lurched in his direction with a bark, and I ended up on the floor. So much for grace.

While sitting on the floor working to free Bronte from the cord and keep her from chasing Rex, I grunted, "Sorry Rex, can you let yourself out?"

"Sure. I'll see you later."

I didn't look up as the door closed because the laptop teetered on the edge of the table. I was able to reach up and grab it before disaster struck.

With Rex gone, Bronte untangled and the laptop secure, I sighed with relief. "So, girl, I was able to untangle you. Now can you untangle me from my mess?" Bronte licked my nose in response. "Ugh, dog breath."

As I got up to lock the door, I looked in the corner.

Kiley's backpack was gone.

On Thin Ice

I ripped open the door and yelled. "Rex! What the hell?"

He was halfway to the lake. I watched as the snowmobile crossed onto the snow-covered ice. Bronte tugged at her collar ready to chase him onto the lake. "All he wanted was that backpack. How many lies did he tell me?" I knelt beside her. "You had him figured out, didn't you?"

She licked my hand as a chill seeped through me. What if she hadn't gotten tangled in the cord and given him the opportunity to snatch the backpack. What would he have done? Shivering, I listened to the sound of the snowmobile as it receded onto the lake.

Inside the warmth of the cabin, I called Clarence and told him what had happened.

"The scofflaw absconded with the money, eh? At least you are safe."

"I suppose I should call the sheriff."

"As your lawyer, that's what I could advise. Maybe they can head him off at the pass."

I almost laughed except none of this was funny. "I asked him about Lacey's baby and whether Rita was the mother. He denied it, but his reaction was odd."

"Hmmm. More to think about."

"Rex alias Mark is tied to the Bevins and that baby in some way."

"I'll do a little more sleuthing while you talk to Rick Fowler and tell him about the money."

I ended the call by promising to fill him in tomorrow on what transpired with the sheriff. The conversation with Clarence took less than five minutes and in that time, I still heard the buzz of the snowmobile. Bronte's ears were pricked, but she wasn't growling. Hopefully, it meant he wasn't coming back. Still, the buzz worried me.

"Let's go out for a listen. If it sounds like he's coming back, we're going to hop in the car and head for town."

Bronte wagged her tail in agreement. One thing about having a dog like her, she was generally enthusiastic about everything except taking her heartworm medication.

I pulled on my boots, my down jacket, and my Fargo cap. Outside, the cold brittle air carried the sound of the snowmobile. I peered out over the lake but saw nothing in the shadowy darkness. If he was headed back to town, he would probably go in the opposite direction of the fishing colony and take the Lady Slipper Trail. I followed the track of the snowmobile down the embankment to the lake. I still heard the hum of the machine, but it didn't sound like it was going anywhere.

"That's odd. Is he stopped? Maybe he's lost. Lord, I hope he doesn't come back."

Bronte pointed her nose in the direction of the buzz and barked. I sounded like a "for your information" bark.

"Is he sitting on his machine out there? Why would he do that?" It was time to call the sheriff.

Bronte woofed again and was silent. Above the low drone of the machine, I thought I heard something. Was a human voice calling out? Across the snow and ice, in the calm of the starlit night, I heard a faint, "Help!"

I closed my eyes, straining to hear more. As I did, I pictured the lake and where the sound was coming from. Bronte woofed again.

It hit me, "Oh my god. He headed to the thin ice!"

For a moment I stood paralyzed, my body and my brain fighting. Run out on the lake to rescue or call for help? What if I'd imagined it? I didn't owe Rex anything. He'd come to my house, lied to me, and stolen a backpack full of money. If he was in the water—good riddance.

The argument was moot. I couldn't leave him out there if he was in trouble. I tore back to the cabin. Grabbing my phone, I called 911. "I think a snowmobiler might have gone through the ice on Lake Larissa!"

I gave the best directions I could, considering I wasn't even sure it had happened. The dispatcher told me to stay put because help was on its way. I might have been just a city girl with little wilderness experience, but I knew that if Rex had gone through the ice or was on the edge of it, he didn't have much time.

"Bronte, you stay. I need to get to that snowmobile."

Outside I fumbled with the snowshoes remembering for an instant how I'd last used them to bring Carmela and Bonita Amy to the cabin. I grabbed my ski poles and ran as fast as I could in the clumsy snowshoes following the track Rex had left behind. Inside the cabin, Bronte howled. It sounded like a woman keening.

As soon as I reached the lake, I heard the faint voice again carried across the crystalline air. "Oh god help me!"

I yelled as loudly as I could. "Hold on!"

I cursed the snowshoes and my blundering gait as I followed the snow-mobile track. In my New York job, I'd once fact-checked an article about hypothermia written by an outdoor journalist who had fallen through the ice. I remembered what he'd said about how fast one could succumb. At the time, simply reading about it had sent me shivering to the kitchen for a hot cup of tea.

Thank god for the moonlight. I'd rushed out so quickly I hadn't brought a flashlight. In my pocket, I heard a persistent ringtone. I didn't want to stop and take off my mittens to answer.

How much time had elapsed since I first heard the cry? I figured if he was submerged, he had less than fifteen minutes. Beneath my snowshoes, I felt the hardness of the snow packed against the ice of the lake. In patches, I lost the track for a few moments where the wind had blown the snow away. The ice was smooth and dark and beneath it, frigid water. I stumbled and slid at one point. As I righted myself, I thought I felt a groan as if the lake was waking up. What if it took me? Suddenly, the lake, the air everything was eerily quiet. No more buzz from the snowmobile, no more cries. Perhaps in my craziness, I'd imagined Rex going into the water. Perhaps this was all a bad dream. Except, Bronte knew. Bronte had pointed the way.

In front of me, maybe a hundred yards away, I saw a shadow against the gray white of the snow on the lake. I stopped to catch my breath. In that moment, I heard a faint, "Oh god!" it wasn't the frantic cry for help anymore. It was more like a sound of resignation.

Steeling myself, I pushed on, aware that the feel of the lake was different. The ice was thinning. If Bronte had been with me, she would have barked a warning. But she was back in the cabin, and I was here on this suicide mission to save someone who might have killed a young mother.

The lake groaned again, and I heard a great cracking sound. As I neared the snowmobile, I saw that the lake was sucking it in. The front was already submerged. I pushed back the hysteria that threatened to take over my body. The sane part of my brain repeated, *Back off or you'll go down with it.*

"Rex! Where are you."

A sound came from the side of the snowmobile away from me. "Waah?"

He was sinking into hypothermia like the journalist had described, a drunkenness and confusion.

"I'm coming. Hang on!"

I stumbled around to the other side of the machine. Rex had thrown off his helmet and clung to the snowmobile as it slowly slid into the open water. When it went down, he would go with it. I surveyed the area around him. His legs were submerged in the icy water, but his torso was still out. If I could get close enough, maybe I could pull him out.

I looked down at the snowshoes to see water slowly covering them. The ice around the snowmobile was sinking. For the first time in my life, I truly understood the phrase "skating on thin ice."

"Rex!" I needed to keep him conscious while my brain swirled to come up with a plan. What had the article said? Something about surface area. Then I remembered a section in *Darkening Sand* where Levy was being sucked in by the quicksand. She'd spread her body out like she was doing the back float to distribute the weight.

"I'm going to reach out with my pole. You need to grab it, or you'll sink!"

"Wah?"

"Rex!" I screamed his name so loud my voice rang in my ears. "Listen!"

First, I took off the snowshoes, then as carefully as I could, I spread out on my stomach and extended the pole to him. "Grab it damn it!"

He looked up at me with drowsy eyes. "Huh?"

"I said, grab it."

He still held tightly to the snowmobile. It was tipping further into the water.

"Rex!" Then it occurred to me. He was in a drunken hypothermic state. Rex was not his name. This time I barked, "Mark, damn it. Grab the pole."

"Huh?"

"Mark!"

He reached up and took hold of the pole.

"Hang on." Now what? I didn't think I had the strength to pull him to safety. I inched back a little, aware that water was soaking through my down jacket. "Can you crawl forward?"

"Can't move."

"Yes, you can. Kick like you're swimming." I wasn't sure if this was the right thing to tell him, but I didn't know how else to keep him from being swallowed by the icy waters.

He pulled harder on the pole and I realized that instead of pulling him out, he was pulling me in. "Kick forward!"

Perhaps he would have pulled me in and the lake would have taken both of us. Perhaps Bronte would have been orphaned and C.P. would never have gotten her edits. All of that raced through my head. I could let go and get away. I had no obligation to Rex/Mark. While my brain told me this, my heart held on. It held on to the point where I thought my arm would be pulled out of my shoulder socket. I held on as I realized I was sinking into a stupor as well.

I was about to give up, to either let go or let the lake swallow me when I heard the roar of snowmobiles and the sound of voices. No, the sheriff hadn't arrived, but Matt from the fish house and his fishing buddies had. Matt jumped off his machine, splayed himself behind me, grabbed my legs, and pulled. "Hang on to the pole!"

I felt myself sliding backwards and as soon as he could, he grabbed the pole from me, and like he was fishing, he landed Rex on firm ice. Just as he reeled him in, Rex's snowmobile sank into the water with a gurgling sound.

The sheriff and several deputies arrived while I sat shivering on Matt's snowmobile, the whole front of my body soaked. I tried to ask how Rex was but I was shaking so hard I couldn't talk. At some point someone wrapped a blanket around me and sometime later, I clung to Matt as he took me back to the cabin on his snowmobile.

Bronte nearly knocked me over she was so happy to see her water-logged partially frozen mistress. Matt directed me to the bathroom. "Get those wet clothes off now! I'll make tea and get the fireplace going."

"I'll jump in the shower," I chattered.

"No! Dry clothes and lots of blankets and sit in front of the fire."

I didn't argue with him.

When I walked into the living room wrapped in my comforter, Matt paced by the back door. "Sorry, I can't stay. Just wanted to make sure you were okay. Gotta go..." He didn't finish his sentence.

Ten minutes after Matt left, Rob arrived.

"What are you doing here?"

He grinned. "Poor Matt called me. He figured the wife would have a fit if she knew you two were alone together again."

I collapsed onto the sofa while he brought me a mug of tea. We sat watching the flames lick at the logs, sending glowing sparks up the chimney. He said nothing, letting the tea warm my insides. When I was ready, I told him about Rex/Mark and my crazed rush to save him.

He nodded. "There you are, the typical Eastern tree hugger liberal. Out to save the world. Around here we call you snowflakes."

"Snowflakes, huh?" I leaned my head against his shoulder and fell asleep.

The Lego Structure

I dreamed that night about childbirth, but instead of a baby, I'd delivered a grown man with a diamond stud earring. When I woke up the sun was poking through the window and I was wrapped in my down comforter on the sofa in front of a dead fire. Bronte paced by the back door.

"Want out, girl?"

When I stood up and tried to stretch, a sharp pain shot through my shoulder and down my right arm. For a moment, I saw spots in front of my eyes, the pain was so intense. I slipped back down onto the sofa. "What the hell?"

The sharpness eased but a gnawing ache remained. I must have pulled a muscle hanging on to Rex last night. "Who knew rescuing a criminal could be so painful?" I groaned.

While Bronte romped outside on the sunny 25-degree day, I eased my way into jeans, a turtleneck and a Minnesota Twins hoodie. It was all I could do to not yelp every time I lifted my arm.

Rob had left a scribbled note on the table. "Sorry, have to go. Sheriff wants to talk to you."

"Of course, the sheriff wants to talk to me." I took several ibuprofen and called Clarence.

"Well, well," he answered. "I hear you had an adventure last night."

I closed my eyes and pictured the icy waters of the lake and the way Rex lay after Matt pulled him in. He reminded me of a fresh-caught fish, twitching and gasping for air. I shook my head to clear the image. "I'm told the sheriff wants to talk with me again. He'll have to come here. I'm a little out of commission."

Outside a vehicle approached and Bronte barked and wiggled with delight. Probably not the sheriff.

"If the sheriff shows up and wants to talk with you, put him on speakerphone. That phone of yours can do speaker, can't it?"

A car door shut and Bronte barked louder. I was turned the wrong direction to look out the window and when I twisted to see who might be outside, the pain shot down my back with such force, I squealed.

"My dear, are you alright?" Clarence's voice sounded tinny as he yelled into the phone.

"Pulled a muscle or something. I'll be fine. Gotta go. Someone is here." I groaned, ending the call. The back door opened, and Bronte bounded in followed by Jim.

"Am I glad to see you." I nearly burst into tears. I might have but Bronte was so excited she knocked over her water dish while Jim took off his boots. My first instinct was to rush for the dishrag to wipe it up except when I stood, the pain shot through me again, the spots floated like black inkblots in front of my eyes and everything went dark.

I came to on the sofa with Jim squatting in front of me brushing hair away from my forehead.

"What the hell is going on?"

"Think I pulled some muscles. Hurts to move." I winced, trying to sit up.

"Hey." He gently pushed me back down. "Tell me where it hurts."

"Right shoulder, I think. I get a shooting pain when I try to move my arm."

I moved my legs so he could sit down. "Here?" He pressed on my shoulder. The pain was like a hot bolt of electricity. I yelped. The sound that came out of me reminded me of Bronte when she'd been hurt.

He probed around the shoulder joint while I gritted my teeth and tears welled up in my eyes.

"I think I know the problem."

"Oh?" I was afraid he was about to tell me I needed to go to the clinic. Among other things in my current state of semi-poverty, I'd let my health insurance lapse. One emergency room visit, and I'd have to sell the cabin.

"I want you to sit up and I'm going to give your arm a tug."

"What?" Instinctively I hugged myself.

"Trust me, it's worth a try." He helped me sit up. "This won't hurt a bit. I'm going to count to ten."

On two he gave my arm a sharp jerk. What followed was a long instant of white-hot pain and then a bone-deep ache. The spots roared in front of my eyes, but I remained conscious. I took several deep breaths.

"Now relax."

"How can I when you tried to rip my arm out of its socket?" The ache was rapidly subsiding to a manageable gnaw. After a few moments, I nodded to him. "What did you do?"

He smiled at me. "Your arm was slightly dislocated—not much but enough to wreak havoc. I set it back in place. Now, if you keep your shoulder quiet for a couple of days, you should be fine."

To my shame and embarrassment, I cried. The relief was so palpable, the cure so easy. He held me, careful not to put pressure on the shoulder. When I had finally gathered my wits again, I nestled into his embrace. "How did you know to do that? Do they train you in trooper school?"

"Nah. My mom was resourceful. She didn't like doctors much. If she could fix it, she would. Sewed up my dad on a number of occasions. Fixed my dislocated shoulder after I crashed my bicycle."

"Hmmm." It felt good to simply sit and feel his warmth and his familiar smell.

When I felt a little steadier, we went to the kitchen table. Jim made coffee and fried up eggs and bacon. Bronte followed him around like a puppy. I had to admit that she had good judgment—sometimes.

"What brought you here? I thought you were on all week?" I watched him slowly turn the bacon.

"Rob called me last night. He said you could use some company. I traded a few shifts."

My hopes rose. "You can stay longer than a day?"

He smiled. "At least two and maybe three."

I was happy at that moment to take what I could get.

While he was fixing the eggs, my phone rang. The call was from the sheriff's office. I stared at the ID wishing I'd turned my phone off. Just before the call went to voicemail I answered. "This is Jamie Forest."

"Ah, yes. Rick Fowler here. We have some questions for you."

I hit "speaker" so Jim could listen in. "Rob told me you would be calling. Just so you know, I have Jim Monroe here on speaker."

Rick didn't hesitate. "Hi, Jim. Glad to hear you're back. We miss you in Jackpine County."

Jim sat by me and talked into the phone. The two chatted for a little bit while I worked up a fume. I wanted to have the small talk over. Finally, Rick got back to me. "Ah, that incident last night? I'm going to need you to come in and make a statement."

"Sheriff," I fought back the urge to bark out my words. "That incident was Rex Jordan aka Mark Mulvaney stealing the backpack that belonged to Kiley Conway. I was planning to bring it to you today. It was filled with money."

Rick cleared his throat. "So I'm told. We didn't find a backpack."

I didn't like his tone and neither did Jim. He jumped in before I could respond. "Listen, Rick, Jamie made heroic efforts to save that man. I doubt the backpack was the first thing on her mind as she tried to pull him out of the water."

Rick cleared his throat. "Oh, sorry. I didn't mean to sound like I was accusing her of anything."

"Anyway, she can't come in right now. She's still recovering."

I felt like I was the kid in the corner being talked about.

"Well, can she come in tomorrow?"

I raised my voice. "Tomorrow should be fine. By the way, how is Rex?"

"He's in the ICU at St. Mary's. Can't talk with him yet."

I assured him I would make a statement tomorrow and ended the call. I shuddered, looking at Jim. "He thinks I did something. Why?"

"You're not from around here."

"But…"

Jim pointed to the couch. "Go, sit. Fill me in. I'll bring the coffee."

"Could you put a little whiskey in it?"

He glanced at his watch and shook his head. "It's not noon yet. You'll have to settle for cream and sugar."

Once I sat down on the couch with my aching arm resting on a cushion, he handed me a steaming mug and also a packet of frozen peas. "Ice your shoulder."

The cold penetrated the thickness of my sweatshirt, numbing the ache. I sighed.

Jim sat down beside me. "Speak. What have you been up to?"

It was less of a question and more of a command. I filled him in on everything I could remember from Brewster's death to the visit from Rex who was really Mark Mulvaney.

When I was done, he sat back with his arms folded. "Sheesh. I think you need a full-time guardian."

I thought again about that pile of Legos and how to make it into something recognizable. "I have some theories floating around in my head, but I can't make them into anything solid."

"Sometimes talking out loud brings them into better perspective."

I stared at him. "God, Jim. You sound like my dad. If anyone could walk through a problem, it was him." It was times like this that I missed Dad, his calm presence, and his wisdom.

Bronte sighed, curling up on the floor by our feet. I stroked her back with my toe as I spoke. "Here's what I'm thinking. Tell me how crazy this sounds. I think Rex and whoever is behind Viaje Seguro are involved in a black-market adoption scheme. Find vulnerable women crossing the border who are pregnant and desperate, promise them they will be safe, and then coerce them into giving up their babies."

Jim whistled. "That's pretty out there. Do you have any proof?"

I told him about how Elena and the others had to sign papers. "They thought they were for applying for asylum, but I'm wondering if they were tricked into signing their rights to their babies away. Plus, Carmela was so afraid from the beginning that someone was going to take Bonita Amy." I pictured her in the hospital with the new baby and the fear etched across her face.

"Kiley said Brewster was up to something the day she brought Carmela and the baby to me. She also had the backpack full of money. I wonder if it was a set up for an exchange. 'Give me the money and I will get you a baby.'"

Jim groaned. "It's pretty sketchy."

"I know. Yet…" I thought about Kiley and Brewster. "Maybe Brewster saw that the scam was up and decided to go rogue—sell a baby on his own. Maybe that's why he's dead." I shifted closer to Jim. Despite the pack of frozen peas, an ache radiated down my shoulder and into my back. "Guess I'm not cured," I whimpered.

Jim eased his way off the couch and stood up. "More ibuprofen for you. And more coffee for me. Maybe I'll take you up on the whiskey. This is a little mind-boggling."

While he busied himself with the pain pills and the coffee, I thought once again about the adoption scheme. If that was the case, then I wondered if the Bevins and Lacey fit into it. Did Lacey give birth to little Frankie or was he adopted? Rex had assured me that they didn't have Rita's baby, but Rex was a Class A liar.

When Jim came back, I related my suspicions. "I think the Bevins and their daughter are mixed up in this. That new baby in their household is too much of a coincidence."

Jim shook his head with a concerned frown. "And how would you prove this?"

"Well, we could demand to see the birth certificate. Find out where the baby was born?"

Jim sighed, "People who have enough money can have anything forged." Bronte sat up, her brown eyes staring at the two of us. He reached down and patted her. "This is for the sheriff, not a poet to figure out."

I felt like he'd also patted me on the head. I resolved to look deeper into it—but not today.

Madison's Report

We had a quiet day together. Jim took the opportunity to cross country ski while I napped. Bronte spent the afternoon in a worried pace between the bedroom and the back door. She wanted us all to be in the same room together.

Jim fixed spaghetti for supper. As the smell of the tomato sauce wafted through the cabin I thought about Andrew, my ex who hardly knew how to turn the stove on. How in the world did I get seduced by a narcissistic actor? Maybe it was his boyish charm. Little did I know he was a spoiled only child who expected his wife to be his mother.

I shook the thoughts about him out of my head and concentrated on watching Jim. Tall, trim with an easy gait, he handled the saucepan like he was born to cook. Now I needed to figure out how to convince him to stay permanently instead of running off to specialized law enforcement training.

The supper was delicious. As I ate the spaghetti so delicately seasoned with basil and oregano a deep sadness began to seep into my body. He'd be here tomorrow but then off again. I wished my dad was around to consult. What would he tell me about Jim?

"Penny for your thoughts." Jim watched me.

"Oh, sorry, just thinking." I set my fork down and tried to laugh. "You know, with inflation, my thoughts are worth a lot more than a penny."

"Okay, a fiver for your thoughts. What's on your mind?"

As I sat in the warmth of the cabin and the aroma of good cooking, my dog at my feet, I couldn't tell him. What was wrong with me? Just say, *can't you stay with me?*

Instead, I blurted out, "I'm wondering how to find out if Lacey had anything to do with Rex."

Jim sighed, a deep, troubled sound. "Jamie, could you let it go?"

Hadn't Andrew said the same thing to me many times? I bit back a sarcastic reply and dug into the spaghetti. *Good job screwing up the mood, Jamie.*

"Sorry. I'll try to reboot."

He nodded with a tight smile. "Okay."

After supper, Jim shooed me out of the kitchen and cleared and washed the dishes, something else Andrew had never done. I sat on the couch in front of the crackling fire sipping a brandy he'd found in the cupboard. I didn't remember buying it, but someone must have brought it for me.

I glanced idly at the painting on the wall next to the fireplace. It was a watercolor my mother had done of the cabin and the lake. It had almost a 3-D quality to it I'd never noticed before. The mist rising from the water had a ghostly essence. For a second, I was reminded of the sleeping lady in the park, the one I thought was a snow ghost. Like Rita, she'd had no one to speak for her. It firmed my resolve to get to the bottom of Rita's death.

Jim sat down, swirling his drink, "Okay, time to strategize."

Startled, I asked, "What do you mean?"

"Well, while I was skiing, I was trying to sort through everything you told me. It could all be complete conjecture except for the money. The money makes it real."

"But the money is gone. At least the sheriff didn't find it. It's probably at the bottom of Lake Larissa and the fish are feasting on it as we speak."

"Still worth a look tomorrow."

The thought of going back onto the lake sent shivers all the way to my toes. "I…I don't know if I can do that." I rested my hand on his thigh. "And I'm not sure I want you out there either."

"Hmmm."

"Don't 'hmmm' me." I groused. Jim had his own stubborn streak.

Perhaps we would have had an adult discussion about revisiting the place where Rex had gone through. Perhaps we would have had an argument about it. Instead, my phone rang with a call from Madison.

After the usual greetings and a mention of the weather, she cleared her throat. "I think I have some interesting information for you about Viaje Seguro."

"Hang on. I'm putting you on speaker if you don't mind. My good friend Jim is with me. I'd like him to hear what you have to say."

I turned to Jim. "It's my college roommate Madison. She's had some experience with the adoption business. I asked her to find out about Viaje Seguro."

Madison explained to Jim how she and her now ex-husband tried to adopt and found themselves on chat groups with other people looking for babies. "It's been a while but I contacted a few people I remembered from those days. They referred me to others who referred me to more people. You know how that goes. Anyway, I finally found someone who knew about Viaje Seguro. They only speak to people who have been referred from 'trusted sources.'"

I sipped the brandy. It had a soothing hot feel going down. "Interesting. Their website is filled with dead presidents."

"Dead presidents?"

I explained the listing on the website. "Rex, the supposed lawyer for them said the site was in beta mode and shouldn't have been up."

Jim frowned, "Very odd."

"Well," Madison continued, "the person I finally reached said she and her partner were trying to adopt and talked with one of the counselors from Viaje Seguro. The counselor assured them the adoptions were legal and the babies were born in the United States so were automatic citizens."

"That would explain Mary's Place." I looked at Jim. "Make sure the babies are born here and have birth certificates to prove it."

"The person I talked with also said because these were considered high-risk adoptions—whatever that means—the fee would be around $100,000. For that, you get your baby free and clear."

I whistled, "Wow." That might explain the money in the backpack.

"My contact said she dropped the inquiry at that point. Even though she knew she was treading in murky water, $100,000 was too steep."

Jim asked. "Did she tell you how the adoptions worked? How the exchange came about?"

"Yes. That's why she dropped out of the process. Viaje Seguro wanted the money in cash."

I pictured the stacks of money in Kiley's backpack. "Any idea who is behind this?"

Madison hesitated. "Well, I don't like to jump to conclusions, but she did mention that the counselor sounded like he was from the south—he had kind of a twangy drawl."

I looked at Jim. "What should we do with this information?"

"I'm thinking."

We talked a little longer and ended the call with a promise to try to get together sometime. Madison said she'd love to see my cabin in the woods. I hoped I could hang on to it long enough for her to take a summer vacation.

I set the phone down and took a swallow of the brandy. "Geeze, what was that all about?"

"Human trafficking, I'd say."

I sat watching the sparks fly up the chimney and thinking about how a chance meeting on the road home with a woman in labor had led me to this mess.

The Rotten Smell of Money

We had a gentle love-making that night. Jim didn't want to reinjure my shoulder and I didn't have the energy for any vigorous activity. His kisses were slow and deep and tasted a little like the garlic in his spaghetti sauce. No howling from either the bed or Bronte, just a quiet, "yes, yes."

I fell instantly asleep.

She was under the ice, her eyes wild and her mouth wide open. Her dark hair floated around her face and one hand pressed against the opaqueness of the ice. I reached for her but couldn't penetrate the ice. I tried to call to her, and the words came out in a strangled cry.

Jim's sleep-filled voice woke me as he gently rubbed my back. "Jamie, you're having a dream."

I sat up for a moment panting as I tried to shake the image of the woman under the ice. "Oh, that was a bad one." On the wall above the headboard, the dream catcher waffled in the airflow from the furnace. I pointed to it. "It's not doing a very good job."

Jim pulled me to him. "You know it's to protect children from bad dreams. Adults are supposed to learn from them."

Already the dream was fading. What remained was a feeling of doom for the unknown woman under the ice. It reminded me of Levy in *The Darkening Sand* as she sank into the sandy mire in the book. Except the woman in my dreams would not be rescued.

When I closed my eyes again, sleep wouldn't come. Was this dream about Rita? Someone had killed her and was free to walk the earth. Someone had

215

left her in the icy waters of Black Crow Pond. Where was justice for her, an illegal immigrant, fleeing for safety only to be bashed in the head? The questions went round and round in my brain. I felt like I was on a carnival ride and couldn't get off. Beside me, Jim's breathing was slow and regular like the ticking of a clock. I slipped out of bed and wrapped myself in my quilted robe. The wooden floor was cold on my bare feet. Bronte looked up at me from her mat by the bed and reluctantly followed me.

With a cup of tea, I sat on the couch and opened my laptop. I felt an urgency to find something about Rita. What was her last name? I'd written it down in my little notebook. Sitting on the couch with a blanket over my legs, I couldn't bring myself to get up and dig through my bag for the notebook.

"Rita what?" I whispered. It wasn't a typical Hispanic name—something like Berry. I closed my eyes and pictured the writing in my notebook. "Berah, Rita Berah."

I did a general Google search but came up with nothing useful. Then I tried Facebook. Would a refugee have a Facebook page?"

Rita Berah didn't have a Facebook page, but Sonya Berah did. Sonya only shared with friends but she did have a photo. I stared at it in the glow of the laptop light and what flashed back at me was the pale skin and open unseeing eyes of the body at Black Crow Pond. Sonya looked to be in her forties and listed *Ciudad Juárez* as her location. Could she be a relative? Juarez was just across the border from El Paso.

I hesitated, took a deep breath, and wrote a message. "I am looking for the family of Rita Berah who is in her early twenties. Do you know her?" I hit send.

Two minutes later I had doubts. If she was family, did she know what happened to Rita? Would I be the bearer of bad news?

"Jim is right. I shouldn't be involved." I closed the laptop and finished my tea.

My shoulder still ached especially, with certain movements, but the sharp searing pain was gone. Before going back to bed, I took more pain pills. Snuggling up to Jim, I counted my blessings. I wasn't out on the lake; I wasn't battling the snow and I had a warm body next to me who didn't have dog breath. With that, I fell into a dreamless sleep.

When I woke up, the pillow next to me was empty. In the kitchen, the coffee pot spit and hissed and a male voice whistled softly. This was the way life should be. I stretched carefully noting the stiffness in my shoulder and a barely perceptible ache. I enjoyed being cocooned under the covers while someone else tended to Bronte. I enjoyed the faint scent of Jim's shampoo on the pillow. I enjoyed the rhythmic ticking of the clock on the wall. All that enjoyment disappeared quickly when I remembered I had promised to visit the sheriff today. And I remembered I sent the Facebook message to a stranger in Mexico.

Jim walked in carrying a mug of coffee. Who could possibly dislike this guy? He sat on the edge of the bed and handed it to me. "Bad dreams last night?"

I told him the fragments I could remember of the person under the ice crying to get out. "She wanted me to rescue her and I couldn't." I didn't tell him about my internet search. For some reason, I felt ashamed, like I'd meddled in someone else's life.

With breakfast, I discovered that Jim might be able to fry up eggs and bacon and make a good spaghetti sauce, but pancakes were not one of his skills. He came close to setting off the smoke detector as he burned one after another. It reminded me of my mother when she was still well enough to cook. Every Sunday she made pancakes out of Bisquick and every Sunday the apartment filled with the aroma of burned food.

I picked at the last pancake. "I guess I have to go in and make some kind of a statement about Rex."

Jim smiled sympathetically. "It's the sheriff's case. Your job is to help him out by telling him what you know."

"Are you going to look for the backpack?" I dreaded his answer.

"Just a quick ski out on the lake."

I grabbed his hand. "I wish you wouldn't go." A shudder swept through my upper body as I thought about the sinking snowmobile and Rex flailing in the icy waters.

He squeezed my hand. "I know the lake. You don't have to worry."

I felt dismissed. For all his good traits, Jim had moments when his trooper toughness took over. I slipped my hand out of his and looked away. "Please be careful. Bring your phone."

After Jim put on his ski boots and set off over the snowmobile tracks, Bronte and I watched from the top of the slope. He skied with such grace and ease, moving into the kind of skating rhythm I couldn't manage yet. My shoulder ached as I watched him push off with his poles.

Bronte and I stood together until the chill of the twenty-five-degree temperature penetrated my jacket and I started to shiver. "Guess we'll keep our fingers and paws crossed that he's fine and go in. Okay, girl?"

Bronte, who normally loved the outdoors even in the cold, bounded back to the door. I'd give Jim twenty minutes. If he wasn't back, I'd put on my skis and go after him.

Inside, I booted up the laptop. I had a Facebook message. My heart sped up and again I felt a ping of regret after sending the message last night to a Sonya Berah. The message was from her. "My inglis no good. Can we speek?" She left a phone number.

I stared at the message. She wouldn't have included her phone number if she wasn't curious. I needed to bring this message to someone who spoke Spanish. When Jim returned, we would go to Clarence's and see Elena. Maybe she could help.

For the next fifteen minutes, I stared at *Darkening Sand* trying to block out the thought of Jim on the lake. I told myself that like the manuscript, this would have a happy ending. Except the time ticked by and Jim did not return. He'd been gone almost a half an hour. I had my phone in hand ready to call him when a text came through.

Found it!

I nearly burst into tears. **Are you okay?**

On my way back. Kinda wet and cold.

No kidding, I thought with a grin. **I'll turn up the thermostat.**

Bronte and I waited for him at the shoreline. Watching him ski back to me with his dancer-like ease was one of the best moments of my life. Bronte stood by me wiggling and barking as if he'd been gone for a month.

Inside the cabin, he set the soggy backpack on the floor, stripped off his ski suit, and headed for the shower. I joined him while Bronte whined outside the bathroom door. It was a lovely, erotic experience that ended up in the bedroom. Who cared that our hair was wet or that we dripped on the sheets?

At long last, Jim padded to the bedroom door and let Bronte in. She leapt onto the bed and tried to nestle between us. Jim directed her to the foot of the bed. "No dogs on my soggy pillow, okay?" Bronte settled on the bed with a contented sigh.

"I wonder what she's thinking?" I kissed Jim on his hairless chest.

"I once read that dogs are binary like computer code. Either one or zero—like or don't like."

"I guess she's a one right now and so am I."

He didn't reply as he stroked my hair. Once again, I felt the door to talking about our feelings had closed. This would have been the perfect moment to say, "I love you. I need you. Let's be together forever." Instead, he continued to stroke my hair and I closed my eyes, unable to speak. All these months with the reticent Minnesotans had clearly affected me. Or, maybe I was afraid of what he might say.

We didn't talk much as we ate lunch. I felt like a thin wall divided us. After the dishes were cleared, he picked up the backpack and set it on the table.

"How did you find it?"

"I almost didn't. He must have thrown the backpack out onto the lake when he realized he was on thin ice. With all the snowmobiles and the ambulance during the rescue, I think it got run over. The only reason I found it was because of the green color. A little of it stuck up near where the water started to cover the ice."

I tensed thinking about him going onto the thin ice to retrieve the pack. Jim noticed my reaction. "No, I didn't venture out onto the thin ice. I took off my ski and batted at it until I got it moved to a safer place."

"Still sounds dangerous."

He ignored my remark. "It was pretty wet—like soaked through and damn heavy to bring back."

He unstrapped it and pulled out one of the bundles of bills. "They look new like they just came from the mint."

I didn't want to touch them. They were contaminated in a way I couldn't describe. "Let's get them to the sheriff and be done with it." My voice shook as I stared at the money. Was this somebody's idea of the price of Bonita Amy or Rita's baby?

Jim put the packet back. "Agreed. Whatever this is for, it's got a rotten odor to it."

As I gazed at the backpack, all the lovemaking and sense of well-being slipped away. In real life, bad things happened.

Call from Kiley

The closer the time came to stepping into Jim's truck to take the backpack to the sheriff, the more my mood darkened. Outside, gray clouds threatened more snow. My phone rang as I pulled on my boots. The call was from an unknown name.

As I picked it up, I secretly wished it was someone wanting to sell me a free vacation in Tahiti. "Hello, this is Jamie."

"Jamie, it's...it's Kiley." The voice dropped off. In the background, I heard a dull roar of voices.

"Kiley! Where are you? Are you all right?"

Jim looked up from lacing his boots. My question was followed by silence except for the noises in the background.

"Kiley, are you there?"

Her voice was low and strained. "I heard—I heard about Brewster."

Jim walked over to me and pointed to the phone with a questioning expression. I shook my head and put a finger to my lips. "Kiley, what did you hear?"

She hesitated and finally blurted out. "He's dead. It's my fault."

This was too much for me. Jim needed to hear what she had to say. I put the phone on speaker, beckoned Jim over, and set it down on the kitchen table. "Listen, Kiley," I kept my voice calm. I didn't want to scare her away. "I'm in the middle of doing the dishes. I'm putting you on speaker. Is that okay?"

"I guess."

Choosing my words carefully, I sat next to the phone. "Are you alright?"

I thought I heard a sob. "No. It's such a mess. I just want to go home."

"You called me after you left the cabin. That was good. I appreciated it."

On speaker, I could make out an overhead announcement giving the loading area for the next bus to Kansas City. "Kiley, where are you?"

"I just want to go home. It wasn't supposed to go like this. I should never have taken the backpack."

Jim's expression turned grim. He leaned forward as if he was going to speak. Again, I put my finger to my lips.

"It's okay."

"No. It's not. Don't you see? I took the wrong one from your house and now he's dead."

Bronte sensed the seriousness of the call and settled quietly at my feet. "But, Kiley, at least you tried to give it back to him."

"But I didn't check it. I gave it to him and said I was done."

I pictured her in my jacket handing the backpack to Brewster. "Was this at Mary's Place? Is that where you gave him the pack?"

The overhead speaker announced the final boarding call. "I gotta go now. But, please understand I didn't have anything to do with Brewster dying. I gave him the backpack as soon as we got into Killdeer. He let me out and said we'd meet again in El Paso. I...I took your money and got a bus ticket to Duluth. Now I gotta go. Ask Rex. He'll tell you." The phone clicked dead.

Jim and I stared at each other for a few moments before I picked up the phone. "I've got to call the sheriff."

Sonya Berah

Jim drove us in his pickup truck. I sat with the backpack at my feet. Even though I wore insulated hiking boots, my feet were cold. It was as if the pack emanated a dark chill. In my head, I went over the phone conversation with the sheriff, surprised at how uninterested he was in my call from Kiley.

I turned to Jim as he navigated my rutted drive. "Do you think the sheriff knows something he isn't telling us?"

Jim shrugged.

"But he didn't seem to care much that I'd talked with Kiley." I wondered if Jim had a need to protect Rick Fowler as part of the law enforcement brotherhood. I felt a flush of anger rise up my face.

Looking straight ahead, he replied, "I'm guessing he will put it all together when he has the pieces. Leave it to him."

I sensed the tension in his voice and it occurred to me that he wasn't so much trying to protect the sheriff as trying to keep me out of trouble. "You're right. We'll deliver the soggy money and be done."

Jim glanced at me with a half-smile. "Ya sure, you betcha."

"One other thing." I tapped the laptop sitting beside me. "I want to check out something with Elena before we see the sheriff. It won't take long."

Jim sighed long and hard. "Of course, my little New York tree-hugging mobster."

I didn't find his attempt to lighten the mood very amusing.

As we approached town, big fluffy snowflakes began to fall. I decided to take it as a sign that I could turn all of this over to Rick and go back to my subsistence life as a freelance editor.

Clarence answered the door wearing a grey wool sweater and neatly pressed slacks. He had an old-world stylishness about him that contrasted deeply with Rex. Rex wanted to dazzle. Clarence simply was a gentleman.

We walked back to the kitchen where Joe was making coffee. Elena sat at the table, her face a bit rounder, her eyes aglow. I introduced her to Jim as my *amigo*.

She laughed, looking at Clarence. *"Novio,¿verdad?"*

"Sí."

She studied Jim for a moment. "You are handsome."

Jim and I both blushed.

I sat next to Elena with my laptop. "Do you think you could make a phone call for me?" I explained my Facebook search as I opened the page with the message from Sonya. Elena peered at the photo of Sonya. Her face paled.

"Does she look like Rita?"

Elena's eyes filled with tears. *"Sí."* Something in her expression told me Elena knew more than she was saying. I needed to talk with her alone.

"Maybe Elena and I could go into the living room and talk—just the two of us."

The men agreed, but I could tell they were disappointed.

We sat on the couch facing each other. Elena wiggled around trying to find a comfortable spot. She pointed to her growing belly. "Too big."

"Maybe twins?"

"¡Aye dios! No gracias."

My shoulder ached despite the ibuprofen. I tried to relax as I positioned the laptop.

"What haven't you told us?" I asked once she was settled.

Her eyes filled with tears. "Rita, she tell me some things that I do not tell anyone else."

I nodded.

"Her baby, she have a boyfriend but he is married. He want her to give up the baby."

"And she didn't want to?"

She wiped her eyes with the back of her hand. I reached in my pocket for a tissue and handed it to her. "He tell her if she give up baby he make her a citizen."

I'd pictured this boyfriend as someone from Mexico or Central America. "He was an American?"

"He work at detention center."

"The same place you and Carmela and Yoli were in?"

Elena shivered, hugging herself. "*Sí*. He find us because they keep record of those who are with babies."

I tried to absorb this. Someone was looking for pregnant women. "Was Rita at the center, too?"

"*No se*. I don't think so. He keep her in an apartment in El Paso."

It took a few moments for me to absorb this and figure out why Elena hadn't told Clarence about it. "Elena are you afraid to talk about this because you think they'll send you back there?"

She nodded, her cheeks wet with tears.

I put up both my hands. "Whoa. No one is sending you back there. Clarence will help you. But you need to tell us who these people are."

She shook her head. "*No puedo*. I cannot say. Rita no tell his name. Maybe after baby is born I look at photo."

It was clear to me she wanted her baby to be born here and be a citizen, no matter what.

"Okay, but I'm going to tell Clarence about this man. It sounds like he is preying on pregnant women."

She blinked at me and dabbed her eyes. "They no want us. They want babies."

I took her hand. Through the window, I watched the fluffy snowflakes dropping gently from the sky. In the kitchen, I heard Clarence's muffled laugh as Jim talked.

I squeezed Elena's hand. "Are you ready to make the phone call?"

"*Sí*."

Once I entered the number, I handed the phone to Elena. She greeted the person who answered and quickly moved into a rapid Spanish. Once again,

I cursed my choice to study Italian in college as I made out a few words. They talked for about ten minutes before she ended the call.

I waited, watching the snowflakes make their way to the ground. When she finally spoke, her voice was soft. "Sonya Rita's sister. She know Rita *está muerta*. Is dead."

Maybe the sheriff had reached her. "Someone told her?"

"No. But she say she already know." She held her hand to her heart. "In here."

I wanted to jump in and ask questions. Instead I took Elena's hand again.

"She say Rita have big shot boyfriend in America. Promise to marry her."

Instead, Rita becomes pregnant and he sends her in the winter to northern Minnesota to give up the baby for adoption. Great example of love.

"Can we tell Clarence about what Sonya told you?"

Elena agreed and I called the men in from the kitchen. Elena explained to them what Sonya had told her—everything but the name of the "big shot" man.

"This man has to be connected with Rex and Viaje Seguro." As I thought about Viaje Seguro, I decided Rex was probably another foot soldier. Someone else was in charge. Maybe the man Elena couldn't identify?

I checked my watch. It was time to see the sheriff. "How much of this should we tell him?"

Clarence looked up at the ceiling with a thoughtful expression. "Sooner rather than later Elena is going to be in the hospital delivering a baby, at which time her existence will be public knowledge. Our job right now is to protect Elena and Carmela. If he doesn't ask about them, we won't say anything. You found Sonya on Facebook. You can tell him that. He doesn't need to know we talked with her."

I relaxed a little. Let the sheriff figure out who the "Big Shot" was.

The Sheriff

Jim and I walked into the sheriff's office together. Jim carried the backpack and walked with an easy gait. My legs felt as if they were made of wood. The last place I wanted to be was in Rick Fowler's office again. As we entered the reception area, we met M.C. Bevins.

Jim greeted him. "M.C., I hear you're a new grandad. Congratulations."

M.C. studied him a moment as if trying to remember who he was. I hung back, hoping he didn't recognize me from the day I dropped off the estimate on my car.

"Yup." He headed past Jim and ignored me.

I watched him leave. "He still owes me for the dent in my car."

Jim chuckled. "Good luck getting any money out of him."

Rick sat behind his desk. "I'd stand up, but the back is giving me a little trouble again." He motioned us to pull up chairs.

Jim set the backpack on his desk. "We didn't count the cash, but it appears to be substantial."

Substantial was a good word for it. I stayed quiet watching Rick's expression while Jim explained how he skied back to the place where Rex had gone into the lake and retrieved the money. If he was skeptical about what happened, it didn't register on his face.

"Well," he cleared his throat when Jim was done. "Must be some drug money."

I opened my mouth to say something when Jim lightly squeezed my thigh with a slight shake of his head. He wanted me to stay quiet. My stomach churned and I tensed, pushing back the urge to ask why Rick insisted it was drug money.

"Have you gotten any information from Rex?"

"You mean Mark?" Rick pressed his lips together. "He's still in ICU. They have him heavily sedated. It'll be a while before we can question him."

Rick asked me what I knew about the backpack. I'd already told him about it over the phone but I dutifully retold the story of how Kiley had brought it with her and left it and how I hadn't discovered it until after she left.

"How did Mark know you had it?"

I thought back to the last time I'd been in this office. "I mentioned it to him after I talked with you. I said Kiley had left something at my cabin."

"Did you tell him it was a backpack?"

I didn't like Rick's tone. I felt like he thought I was lying. "No. I just said she'd left something." Jim kept a steady hand on my thigh. He knew I was close to blurting something out.

The sheriff wanted to know what we talked about when Rex/Mark visited the cabin. I told him we talked about Viaje Seguro and adoptions. I did not tell him that I knew at the time Mark was fraudulently posing as Rex the lawyer. I also didn't tell him my question about Lacey's baby.

He studied me before leaning back in his chair with a wince. "Well. I'll count the money and lock it up. Could be someone else is looking for it." He waved at us in dismissal.

I raised my hand. "Wait. Don't you want to know more about my conversation with Kiley Conway?"

Rick raised his eyebrows, "I think we covered it on the phone." I noted the tension lines around his mouth and the way he winced every time he moved. The man was clearly in pain.

Jim spoke. "I heard the conversation. We think she was headed back to El Paso. She said she wanted to go home."

Rick let out a small groan as he reached for a legal pad. He asked us to repeat the phone call while he took notes. I had to restrain myself from asking why he hadn't taken notes when I'd called him. He'd listen to Jim but not me? I pressed my lips together. This was not the time to quibble. At least he was paying attention now.

Jim shifted in his chair. "You might be able to catch her in Kansas City. It sounds like that's where the bus was headed."

After he finished writing down what we'd said, he set the pen down. "I have all I need. We'll take it from here."

I was surprised he didn't want a written statement. But then, what did I know about police investigations? Before we stood to leave, however, I pointed to the backpack. "Do you think this money has anything to do with Rita Berah's death?"

Rick squeezed his eyes shut and opened them with a sigh. "What do you mean?"

"She was murdered, wasn't she? That's what I heard."

Jim pinched my thigh so hard I nearly jumped. I clamped my lips together to avoid yelping.

"That's police business." He glared at Jim. "Who told you it was a homicide?"

I said nothing.

Jim shrugged. "Word gets around. This is a small community."

I couldn't help myself. "Have you talked with her family? Maybe they know something."

Rick's face turned from a winter pale to a summer red. "We haven't located a family."

I bit back a sarcastic remark and tried to keep my voice steady. "I found a sister on Facebook. Maybe you should contact her. She lives in Mexico." Reaching for my bag, I brought out my phone and wrote down Sonya's name and phone number. By the look on Rick's face when I handed him the information, he was close to having a stroke. It was time to leave.

Once we were back in Jim's truck and he had the heater going full blast he turned to me. "Rick's not your enemy."

The anger over everything from Viaje Seguro to women being exploited bubbled over. My voice came out in a too-loud sputter. "Jim, something very evil has happened and he's sitting on it. Why was Bevins there? Is he directing the sheriff? This is so wrong!"

And again, the tears.

The Link

J im put an arm around me and held me close. "My little Mafia moll, you get too involved. Let's go home, leave Rick to his job and play in the snow."

The flakes were coming down harder. Already they had covered the dirty crusted snow with a layer of glistening white. Time to enjoy a Minnesota winter.

Except, I wanted to make sure Toby had gotten the money so he could order the part he needed for the door on my car. "Can we make a quick stop at Toby's?"

When I walked in the door, Toby's shop had the hot wire odor of an electric heater behind the counter.

"Nope," he shook his head. "Haven't heard a thing from Bevins. Better try her again." His expression told me he didn't expect he'd ever hear from her.

Back in Jim's truck, I grumbled, "Damn that woman! Let's head over there. I'll tell her you're my mob hitman and if she doesn't pay up, she'll find a horse head in her bed."

Jim patted my arm. "Settle down. We can deal with it tomorrow. Today we make a snowman."

A snowman? In the midst of all this drama, he suggested a snowman? Peering out at the pure white flakes falling from the sky, it suddenly seemed like a wonderful idea. I laughed. "I'm not sure I have any carrots and I know I don't have any coal."

"We'll improvise."

I let go of all the worry and tension as we rolled snow to make Frosty.

Bronte thought it was great fun, especially when Jim found sticks for the arms. She jumped up and grabbed Frosty's right arm and ran down the driveway with it, Jim in hot pursuit.

Oh, if life could only be one big playdate. I watched them feeling a moment of euphoria before the thoughts of the women and their babies crept back into my head.

After a breathless, gasping and intense lovemaking, I lay in the cinnamon scent of the candles burning on the bedside table and wished I'd been a little bit more careful with my shoulder. It ached down to my fingertips, but I didn't tell Jim.

In the bathroom, I took a double dose of ibuprofen and the image of Rita crept back to me. My life, my editing, my meager existence couldn't go on until something was resolved. Who was the "Big Shot?"

Later, we sat wrapped in a blanket on the floor in front of the couch watching the flames licking at the chimney. I approached it again.

"Help me think this through, Jim."

He knew immediately what I was talking about. "You aren't going to relax until you have this figured out, are you?"

"Probably not."

He sighed. "In my experience, sometimes the answers never come."

"I feel like I could make that Lego thingy if I had the right pieces."

With an expression of resignation, Jim set down his glass of wine. "All right, let's set out all the pieces and see what we can put together."

I ticked off what I knew: pregnant women identified at a detention facility and brought to Mary's Place. Told they would be given asylum after babies born. Encouraged to sign papers to give babies up for adoption. Rita's baby given up and Rita murdered. Mark impersonating Rex. Viaje Seguro philanthropic or human trafficking? Backpack full of money. Brewster dead and Kiley on the run.

Jim shook his head. "That's quite a list."

"It seems so big to me. Like organized crime or something. What's the glue that holds all of this together?" I reached over and poked the fire. I stared at the sparks as if they would spell out an answer.

Jim stretched his arms over his head. "What if we're looking at it wrong? What if it isn't some grand conspiracy but something simpler?"

"Like what?"

He took the poker from me and jabbed at one of the burning logs. "What if it's what it looks like. Viaje Seguro is legitimate. They're trying to help the women. Rita had something like post-partum depression and fell. And the money and Rex..." His voice dropped off. He shook his head. "That part doesn't fit."

I finished my wine, feeling warm and drowsy. Leaning against Jim, I closed my eyes intending to think through his idea of simplicity.

The cabin dimmed and I was plodding through the sand trying to make my way to Watersmeade. Queen Alusra whispered in my ear, "Family. Remember it's always family."

I tried to ask her what she meant, but someone was shaking me.

"Hey, Jamie. Wake up. You're drooling on my sweater."

I opened my eyes to the glow of the fire and Jim's embrace. "Sorry. Fell asleep."

"Noticed."

I pulled away from him and yawned. "Perhaps we should go to bed."

"Perhaps."

In bed, under the warmth of the comforter, I snuggled up to Jim. The words from the dream came back to me. *Family.* What about family? I drifted off to sleep.

While we slept in the cozy little cabin, the gentle snow of the day changed from fluffy dry flakes to brittle icy pellets slamming against the wall and roof as the wind rose. I woke in the darkness to the wind rattling the windows.

Bronte, sleeping at the foot of the bed, stood up and wandered over to me. I put my hand out and she licked it. Two words, *simple* and *family* cycled through my brain. What did family mean? I thought about Madison and how important having a family was to her marriage. I thought about Sheryl Bevins and the importance to her of having a grandchild. And I thought about simple rather than complex.

What if? My thoughts were interrupted as Jim shifted in bed pulling me to him. Problem solving would have to wait.

By morning the snowstorm had blown itself out, but not before it dumped a half-foot of snow in my plowed driveway. I looked out the window with dismay. It would cost me another twenty dollars to get it plowed. Winter was getting old, fast. At least in New York, somebody else had to deal with the snow removal.

Jim slept late and when he finally showered and walked into the kitchen, I pointed outside. "I think you should get shoveling."

"Good morning to you, too."

I fixed the last of the eggs and bacon. Food supplies seemed to disappear quickly these days.

Jim's phone rang while I was washing up the dishes. "Hello?" His expression turned somber. Holding the phone up he looked at me. "Excuse me."

He took it into the bedroom. I noted the way he raised his voice and decided this would be a good time to slip on my going outside clothes and let him have more privacy.

Bronte plunged through the snow as I shoveled a path from the back door to the parking area and another path to the woodpile. I hardly noticed any soreness in my shoulder. Never in my wildest dreams growing up did I see myself as an outdoorsy kind of person. As I scooped up the snow and threw it aside, I thought again about family and simplicity.

"Bevins." I said it loud enough that Bronte came running. She had Frosty's left arm in her mouth and expected me to throw it for her. "Don't you see? They are the glue. Bevins owned Mary's Place. Bevins runs a transport business and could get the women here. But, girl, the biggest piece of it is that the Bevinses have a new grandson."

I nearly dropped the shovel in my enthusiasm to tell Jim my theory. On the back step, I stomped the snow off my boots and opened the door. Jim stood with the phone in his hand and a grim set to his mouth.

"What?" I pulled off my boots and ran to him. "What's happened? Is it Jake?"

He sat down with a deep sigh. "Marie, his mother. She overdosed on something. They have her in the ICU." His shoulders sagged. "I have to get back for Jake. The neighbor is watching him right now. Marie's boyfriend that she met in AA seems to have flown the coop."

"Oh god. I'm sorry. What do you want me to do?"

He raked his hand through his hair and let out a long sigh. "I'm so tired of this."

I helped him pack up his things. When he was ready to leave, I hugged him hard and whispered. "Uh...You can always bring Jake here, I guess."

I was trying to be supportive and do the right thing, but my reluctance was too obvious. What would I do with a sick five-year-old secluded away in this cabin? And did I want a family right now or ever, for that matter.

He kissed me goodbye at the door. "I'll let you know what's going to happen."

I watched his truck slue down the unplowed driveway and felt like the worst human being in the world.

I might have continued castigating myself, but Clarence called.

"I hear you had a little tiff with the sheriff."

"You know, Clarence, sometimes I wish I still lived anonymously in the big city. Who told you?"

He chuckled. "The sheriff. Called me after you left and wanted to know where you got your information on Rita Berah. He thinks you are a community jinx."

"What did you tell him?" Bronte put her paw up on my lap and looked at her empty food dish. I'd forgotten to fill it and now my pants were wet from the snow melt on her. I held the phone to my ear as I scooped dry food into her dish.

"I commiserated with him about the foreigners coming to town and ruining our sleepy little community."

For a moment he had me. "You did not!"

"I told him you were working on an article for a big magazine and you'd been asking questions. People like to talk even if it's to spread rumors."

"Am I in trouble?"

"In my legal opinion—no. Did you make a friend of local law enforcement—no."

I sat at the table weighed by all the bad things I'd accomplished today. The worst was my weak attempt to help Jim. "So, what can I do for you?"

Clarence hesitated before talking. "I have to admit, I divulged Elena's whereabouts to the sheriff."

"You what?" Bronte trotted over to me with a concerned expression.

"I offered Elena's help to talk with Rita's sister."

"Clarence…" I found I was sputtering. We were trying so hard to keep her whereabouts secret.

When he answered he used a gentle tone, "Don't worry. I extracted a promise from Rick to not tell ICE or anyone else about her. He might be a bit thick, but I think he's trustworthy."

"Okay." I was less trusting.

"But that's not totally why I called. Rick said something else that got me to thinking. He said M.C. Bevins has been asking him a lot of questions about Mary's Place. Bevins told him it was because Sheryl had rented the house to make Mary's Place and he felt he should know what was going on."

"Sounds questionable to me."

"My thoughts exactly. Too many connections. I'm wondering if we should make a little visit to see Sheryl and the new baby."

I thought about it for a moment. "Why would we do that?"

"You haven't gotten your money yet for the dent in the car, right? Wouldn't hurt to show up with your lawyer."

On a scale of zero to ten with ten being the highest form of meddling, this looked like about a ten and a half. I weighed it for a moment. "Sure. How about tomorrow morning? I should be plowed out by then. Besides, I need to come into town and get groceries. Jim is expensive to feed."

"Ah yes."

I didn't tell him about Jim's abrupt departure. It still hurt.

Frank Graham

In the afternoon, as I paged mindlessly through *The Darkening Sand*, Lars rumbled in with the snowplow. While he scraped the snow around the car, I felt a sense of loss. Somehow having a snowed-in driveway had given me comfort. I didn't have to go anywhere because I couldn't. Now the road was open. It reminded me of the chapter in *Sand* when a turncoat Midger named Bil-Bar ordered the bridges let down for Aga Pumpert's forces to invade.

"Don't be so silly." I dug in my bag for my wallet and pulled out the last of my $20 bills to hand over to Lars. Snowplowing was another expense I'd never considered when I packed up to move here.

After Lars left, I put the manuscript aside and opened the laptop. "See girl, the answer is "simple" and "family." What do you suppose that means?"

I went back to Sonya Berah's Facebook page but it yielded nothing new. Next I looked up Lacey Graham but found nothing. She was not on Facebook, but Sheryl Bevins had a page. Her photo showed her with a wide smile holding the new baby with the heading "Grandma, at Last!" Without friending her, I wasn't able to see any other photos.

I studied the baby who wore a green and red elf hat. Could this be Rita's child? Hard to tell. The coloring was right, but Frank Graham also had light brown skin.

Bronte rubbed against my leg before walking to the door. "You want to go out? Maybe a walk would be good."

In the snow-covered yard, the chickadees frolicked. Rob told me he always knew when spring was on its way because the birds went from calling chickadee-dee-dee to "Hi, sweetie." I wasn't sure if he was pulling my leg, but I'd keep that in mind if I was still here when spring came.

While Bronte chased a stick, I walked down the driveway thinking about the Bevins. M.C. held the purse strings and had an air about him of authority. Watching him in county board meetings I knew he was not one to cross. Would he pay for a grandchild? Maybe. Lacey had been his princess according to Jilly. I pictured the conversation. "Daddy, can I have $100,000 to adopt a baby?" "Sure, honey. Whatever you want."

Family. Which caused me to wonder about Lacey's husband. What had Jilly said about him? He worked for the government somewhere near El Paso. El Paso certainly came up often.

Bronte brought the stick back and set it by my feet. "One more chase and we're going in." I threw it and turned back to the cabin. It struck me as I reached to open the door. Jim's word, simple. What if the whole thing was simple? Find a pregnant woman, make an offer she can't refuse, and voila! A baby.

Is that what happened? Rita's boyfriend sees an opportunity to make a little money and get rid of a baby he doesn't want? Then he gets rid of her. The whole mess cleaned up and he's back to his wife.

With a cup of tea steaming by the laptop, I tried Facebook again. Lacey had said something about Frank. I searched for Frank Graham and first came up with the page for Franklin Graham, an evangelist who was once banned from Facebook for hate speech. Maybe I was going down a bunny trail. I tried again by typing in Frank Graham and Texas. I found two. One looked to be a twenty-year-old coed complete with a cheerleader suit who went by the name Frankie. The other was a man in his thirties, with Hispanic features and a crew cut. Lacey's husband.

"Girl, I think I've found something." Frank worked for Intl-Care Services. When I looked them up, an article on the NPR website said they were one of the largest private contractors for detention services.

I called Clarence and told him I was sending a link to a Facebook page. Would he ask Elena to look at it and tell him whether she knew this man?

Fifteen minutes later he called back. "Now I know why I use you as my investigator. She recognized him but didn't want to talk about it."

Clarence and I talked back and forth plotting out our visit to the Bevins tomorrow. By the time we were done conspiring, the sun had gone down along with the temperature. Clarence promised he'd have Elena call Sonya one more time before we went to the Bevins'.

Jim phoned just after I'd crawled under the covers. I decided not to tell him about the plan for tomorrow. I was afraid if he heard what we'd plotted out he would tell us to simply call the sheriff. Instead, I asked him about Jake and Marie.

"Jake's fine. I have him with me for the time being. Marie's mother is going to watch him when I'm working."

"Good." I tried to show enthusiasm, but my voice came out too flat. "I'm glad he'll be with you."

"I'm afraid it might get messy when Marie is better. She and her mother do not get along." He filled me in that she'd gotten into heroin thanks to her AA boyfriend who apparently wasn't drinking but was using. She would be sent to outpatient treatment. Jim sounded resigned. "I've seen too many relapses in my work to think she'll make it through treatment. I might have to go for custody."

The little voice in the back of my head said, *buck up and give him the support he needs.* I stayed silent a little too long. "Jim, you need to do the right thing." My words were not said with comfort in mind. We ended on a strained note. He didn't know when he'd be back.

When I set the phone down, I wished someone would walk in and slap me. "Jamie, what's wrong with you?" Oh, how I missed my dad who could have given me wise and reasonable advice.

I scratched Bronte behind her ears. "The trouble is, I don't want to share Jim with anyone."

I slept badly that night.

The Plan

The next morning, Joe accompanied Clarence to my car while Elena stood in the doorway looking worried. In the past couple of days, her pregnant belly had grown.

Joe leaned in the door after Clarence had buckled himself up. "No broken hips, please."

Clarence brushed him off. "If I break one, I can get a shiny new one. It'll keep the health care industry in business."

We sat for a few minutes to strategize. "I think there's a good chance Rita was the mother and the Bevins paid a lot of money to make sure the baby was born here. I don't think Rita really wanted to give him up for adoption." I didn't say what was swirling in my head—M.C. killed Rita to protect the adoption.

Clarence's eyes sparkled with mischief. "Let's prove it."

The plan was simple. Clarence had talked with Sonya and agreed to represent the family in claiming the adoption was coerced. He would ask for the adoption paperwork to assure that the Grahams's baby was not Rita's. He'd tell them he brought me along as the driver and also to verify the paperwork.

As I sat in the car with Clarence, I realized how incredibly dangerous this plan could be. What if we were going down the wrong road altogether? Lacey might have given birth to Frankie after all. Except, he looked to be only a couple of weeks old and I'd checked with Norma. Lacey hadn't had a baby in Killdeer. Who would risk travelling from Texas to Minnesota in the winter with a newborn? Plus, Lacey's thin figure didn't look like what I'd

239

expect from a postpartum mother.

If the Bevins wanted a baby badly enough to kill the baby's mother, they certainly weren't going to confess to a lawyer and his freelance editor about their sins.

"Well, let's go. My waterworks won't hold up if we sit here too long."

"Clarence." I turned to him. "This is really a bad plan. Bevins isn't going to confess to anything and we might be at risk."

He sat up straighter. "Nonsense. We don't need a confession. We need to see the birth certificate and adoption papers. If they have them, they might be forged. You can be my eagle eye to check for that."

I don't know what made Clarence think I knew anything about forgery. Plagiarizing, yes. I'd even taken a workshop on it as part of becoming a fact-checker.

With a sense of being sent to the front lines without protection, I drove to the Bevins's. Several cars were parked in the drive including Sheryl's offending SUV. I pulled up behind it. Even in the brightness of the sunny, freezing day, the outdoor holiday lights were on framing the house in reds and blues. The snow beneath us was brittle and squeaked with our footsteps.

I held on to Clarence's arm as he walked up the steps to the front door. He wobbled a little on the first step. "We can leave now," I whispered.

"Nonsense." He rang the bell.

After a few moments, M.C opened the door and stared at us with a startled expression. He held a cup of coffee in his hand. "Clarence. This is a surprise." His tone was hardly friendly.

"Can we come in? I have a conundrum and I'm hoping you can help me out."

M.C. stepped back to let us in. From upstairs Sheryl called down. "Is that UPS? Tell them to put the packages in the entry."

I noticed M.C. shot a glance at the stairway but didn't answer. The tension in his body was almost palpable as he pointed to the living room.

Once again, I felt like I'd just walked into a set for a holiday special. The tree was lit up and surrounded by brightly wrapped packages. The room smelled of hot chocolate. All we needed was the handsome couple to kiss under the mistletoe. I gazed up and sure enough—mistletoe.

"Clarence, what's this all about?" M.C. pointed to the couch.

Clarence eased onto the couch with a benign expression. "I've been retained by the family of Rita Berah regarding the baby boy she gave birth to here in Killdeer. It appears the baby is missing."

M.C.'s hand spasmed enough that a bit of coffee spilled over the rim of the cup. Otherwise, his expression of puzzlement remained the same. "What do you think that has to do with us?"

Clarence smiled as he shrugged. "M.C. it probably has nothing to do with you and I truly apologize. I know this is an intrusion at a time of great joy for you. I simply need to be able to tell the Berah family that Rita is not the mother of your daughter's new baby."

M.C. who was standing scowled. "Are you questioning our grandson's adoption?"

At least now the question of whether Frankie was adopted was answered.

Clarence continued his diffident smile. "I simply wanted to clear this up before it needed to get tangled into the court system. I only ask because of the coincidence of the baby arriving shortly after Rita gave birth and that Rita was staying in a house owned by you."

I had to admire the way Clarence was hooking M.C. into having to explain the timeline of the adoption. Would he take the bait and defend his daughter?

M.C. stiffened and a flush rose up his neck to his cheeks. If Clarence noticed, he didn't show it. I felt like the room with all its glitter was closing in as M.C. struggled to keep his composure. This was a man who didn't like to be challenged.

"Engstrom," M.C. clenched his jaw. "I think it's time for you and your young lady to leave." He pointed at me. "This is an unwarranted intrusion."

"Now, M.C. we haven't always seen eye-to-eye, but you have to admit we could clear everything up in about five minutes. Let me look at the adoption papers and we'll be out of here so you can enjoy being a grandpa."

I could picture Clarence in a courtroom charming a judge or jury. I wouldn't want to go up against him.

M.C. growled, "When hell freezes over. This is none of your business."

Behind me, I heard a little gasp. When I turned Lacey stood in the doorway looking pale. "Daddy, don't tell them about Frank, please."

She rushed in and burst into tears. "I knew this was bad."

Family

"Honey, don't say anything. These people are leaving." M.C. pointed to the door. I saw him as the lion protecting his pride.

"Clarence." I kept my voice steady. "I think we should leave." I extended my hand to him. Lacey stood weeping as she clung to her father.

"He didn't mean it." She looked up at her dad. "It's just she was making so much noise."

What was she talking about? Clarence sat with his hands folded and a benign expression. He made no move to ask her.

M.C. spoke to her as if she was a child. "Lacey, sweetheart, now is a good time to be quiet and let me handle this." He pushed her away while glaring at us. "See, now you've gotten her all upset. It's hard enough to adjust to a new baby without your accusations."

I waited, hoping Lacey would say more. She watched her father with the same worried expression I often saw on Bronte when she wasn't sure what was happening.

When she didn't say anything more, I spoke to her gently, the way I would to calm Bronte. "Lacey, did you adopt Rita's baby?"

"Don't answer that!" M.C. barked and Lacey jumped.

"If you did, we can work something out with her family." I wasn't sure about adoption law, but I didn't think Rita's family had any legal claim on the baby if she'd signed papers.

Clarence helped me out. "That's right. I'm sure we could work something out."

I thought M.C. was about to grab Clarence and rip him off the couch. His hand curled into a fist and he took a menacing step. I moved between the two men holding my hand up in a "stop" gesture. "Can we talk about this?"

I don't know how the scene might have played out if my phone hadn't pinged at the same time Frank Graham hurried into the room. I glanced down at the phone in my hand and saw the words in all caps **EMERGENCY!** It was from Joe.

Graham father of baby!!!!

Puzzled, I looked at Frank. He was skinny, actually not so skinny as wiry. The scrawny beard I'd noted on Facebook had been shaved revealing a weak chin.

"What…what's happening here?"

"We're talking about Rita's baby."

The color drained from his face. "What do you mean?"

I pointed to my phone. "I'm told you are the father."

Lacey's mouth dropped open. "No, that's not true." She peered at Frank. "Tell them, Honey. It's not true. Frankie came from an agency."

Both M.C. and Clarence gaped at him. Frank was breathing hard. An expression of uncertainty crossed his face when he looked at his father-in-law.

M.C. was the first to say anything. "They're lying to us. Clarence, you old fool. What are you up to?"

"Daddy, what are they talking about?"

"Shut up!"

He *knew*. M.C. knew his son-in-law was the father of Rita's baby. The word "family" came rushing back to me. This whole scheme went back to Frank and getting his girlfriend pregnant.

I held my hand up. "It's okay. I get it now. Rita wanted to keep the baby, but you couldn't abandon Lacey, could you?"

M.C. shouted at me. "This is enough!"

I spoke directly to Clarence. "I think M.C. and Sheryl knew where the baby came from, but I don't think they wanted to hurt Rita." I turned to M.C. "Am I right? Frank told you about the mess he was in?"

Lacey shrieked. "What? What are you talking about? That woman who came to the door yelling in Spanish? Frank, you said she was a homeless crazy person who was trying to steal our baby. You said you'd take care of it."

As we stood in the perfect Christmas setting with the tree adorned in bright lights and the packages waiting to be opened, the Lego pieces finally started to build a crazy fragmented house.

M.C. grabbed Frank by the upper arm. "What is Lacey talking about?"

Lacey's voice rose in panic. "She came to the door, Daddy. This woman with dark hair. She spoke Spanish and I didn't know what they were saying."

While everyone's attention was on Lacey, I set my phone to record.

Upstairs the baby started to cry, and Sheryl called down. "What's all the fuss about? Lacey, why don't you come up here?"

Lacey looked at her father who pushed her in the direction of the stairs. "Go tend to the baby."

"Can we all sit down? My old legs don't hold me like they used to." Without waiting for a reply Clarence sank back on the couch.

M.C. continued to grip Frank, his face suffused with anger. "What have you done?"

Frank tried to pull away. "I didn't do anything. I told her to stay away or else. She'd signed the papers. It was too late to change her mind."

I doubted that was true. Adoptions weren't finalized so soon. All the more reason to get rid of Rita.

Clarence coughed. "Well, this really is a fine mess, isn't it? If I have it right in my muddled head, Rita was your girlfriend. She was pregnant and you convinced her to give up her baby to you. You didn't want your wife to know so you cooked up the whole adoption scheme." He pressed his lips together in a grim expression, shaking his head. "Then when she came by demanding the baby back...well, did you bash her in the head or something?"

"Well?" M.C.'s bicep bulged as he gripped his son-in-law harder.

Frank shook his head jerking out of M.C.'s grip. "No. No. I didn't hurt her. I told her to go away."

Really? He didn't look like someone who would kill the mother of his child. I studied his expression. He looked weak and scared. If not Frank, then who?

Footsteps pounded down the stairs and Sheryl burst into the room. "What is going on here? Lacey is sobbing upstairs." She cast an evil eye at me. "Who are you to stick your nose in our business? The baby belongs to me." She hesitated. "I mean us. Ah, Lacey and Frank."

And the last Lego of the malevolent house snapped into place. I kept my voice calm even though my heart pounded. "Sheryl, did you kill Rita?"

The room turned dead silent. Upstairs both the baby and Lacey wailed in unison. M.C. stared at his wife as if she were a rabid dog.

"Sheryl?"

She appeared to be caught between the cries from upstairs and the people in the room. Pointing a finger at Frank, she growled, "You weak-minded idiot. What else could I do?" With that, she stomped out of the room and up the stairs.

Stunned, all four of us watched her leave. I found I was holding my breath. Finally, Clarence spoke up. "Excuse me, all this excitement is too much for an old man. Would you mind if I used the facilities? The prostate isn't what it used to be."

In the midst of this drama, Clarence had to pee? If I ever wrote an article about being an accidental midwife, no one would believe the scene in the perfectly decorated living room.

I watched Clarence walking stiffly down the hall before I turned to M.C. "Did you know this?"

By the look of anguish on M.C.'s face, it was clear he had no idea what his wife had done. He shoved Frank into a chair and commanded, "Stay!"

I blocked him when he tried to walk past me. "Wait, were you involved in Viaje Seguro?"

"What? What are you talking about?"

"Mark Mulvaney?"

He knit his brow as he looked up the empty staircase. "She handled it—the adoption."

The expression on his face said it all. M.C. might have known about Rita's baby, but the rest was news to him.

Another Lego piece snapped into place. "Oh my god, they used you too."

Clarence stepped out of the bathroom holding a cell phone. "Ah, these devices are handy. Glad Joe talked me into getting one." He showed it to M.C. "Called the sheriff and he's on his way. I'm sure we'll get this all sorted out."

Who knew Clarence could be so conniving?

The Last of the Subaru

The next hour was chaos with Lacey sobbing hysterically, M.C. demanding to talk to a lawyer other than Clarence, and the sheriff shooting me the evil eye. When I tried to explain my theory of Viaje Seguro and its adoption scheme, M.C. lost his temper and accused everyone in the room of a mass conspiracy. He even used the word "deep state."

While everyone's attention was on his rant, no one saw Sheryl slipping out of the room. No one noticed her absence until we heard the sound of a car door opening.

I ran to the door first to see Sheryl strapping Frankie into the car seat. How she maneuvered him so quickly I'll never know. Before I could get outside, she was in the car set to make her escape.

Maybe she would have succeeded, except we all heard the crash and the sound of metal rammed into metal. Sheryl rammed my car over and over with her SUV, trying to move it out of the way. In her fury and her panic, she kept at it until the sheriff finally stopped her.

In my head, I saw more estimates and more dollar signs. The damage looked substantial.

Fortunately, the baby was safely buckled into an infant car seat. Sheryl, on the other hand, suffered quite a whiplash.

Since my car was non-functional, Joe had to pick us up in Clarence's ancient Cadillac.

Two days later I sat in Clarence's kitchen with Joe, Elena, and Clarence.

Lorraine had left us a newly baked loaf of banana bread. She'd gone home to wrap packages to send to Carmela and Bonita Amy.

"I still can't put it all together." The banana bread had a hint of vanilla and something else pleasing to the palate. "Rex, the Bevins, Lacey, Frank, and Viaje Seguro. I get that Sheryl wanted Rita out of the way—she was determined to be a grandmother or more realistically the mother of the baby. But all the other things."

Clarence wiped a crumb off his sweater. "There's an old saying, 'follow the money.'"

I set up my laptop on the table in front of Clarence. "After the fiasco at the Bevins, where, incidentally, Sheryl managed to total my car, I spent some time looking at Frank Graham's Facebook page. Here's what I found."

Joe and Elena gathered behind Clarence to look at a distorted selfie of Frank and his two pals from the detention center. Mark aka Rex Jordan and Brewster Conway. "They all worked together. I'm guessing when Frank told them about his girlfriend Rita's pregnancy, they came up with the idea of Viaje Seguro."

I showed them an article I'd found about a lawyer running an adoption scheme where he brought women in from another country so the babies could be born here and be citizens. He made a lot of money until he was finally caught.

"Note the date of the article. I'm guessing that's where they got the idea."

"Hmmm. That Frank fellow doesn't strike me as any kind of mastermind."

"He no genius," Elena scowled at the photo. "Brewster no smarty either."

I nodded. "That's where I got hung up. Who was really in charge of this operation? Could it be Rex who wasn't even smart enough to pass the bar? It seemed doubtful."

"M.C.?" Clarence sat back. "I never liked the man, but I thought he was honest."

Flipping down the lid of the laptop, I motioned for everyone to sit down. "I have to agree with Clarence. So that leaves us with either an unknown mystery person, Kiley or Sheryl. When they picked Kiley up at the bus depot in Kansas City, I'm told she claimed to know nothing about who was behind the baby-selling scheme."

"Can you believe her?" Joe sliced another piece of banana bread.

I shrugged. "She rescued Carmela and Bonita Amy. I think Viaje Seguro had a family lined up to take the baby when Kiley put a stop to it. The money we found was probably a down payment—half now and half when the baby is delivered."

Joe grimaced, "Sounds more like a used car sale."

Clarence shook his head. "If that's the case, I doubt the couple hoping for a baby will file a report on the lost money. They probably knew this was illegal."

I shivered, thinking about the green backpack and all the sorrow it had brought.

"Follow the money." Joe's tone was thoughtful.

I agreed. "One of the first things Jilly told me about Sheryl was how she was always looking for ways to make money. What a golden opportunity to get a grandbaby and make a fortune 'adopting out' the other babies to desperate people who could afford the price. She already had experience setting up websites for her various enterprises. Why not set up a phony charity? M.C. let her handle rentals of the houses he owned in town. And I'm sure she could figure out how to use his transport business to get the women here."

"They want our babies to sell? ¡*Puta!*"

"That would be my guess, but it's up to the sheriff and his crack crew of investigators to figure it out."

Clarence took another piece of banana bread. "By the way, my sources tell me Rex or Mark or whatever he's going by now is awake and talking. He got linked into this quite by accident. He was working as a manager for the detention site when he happened to talk with Frank and found they had the Bevins in common. Such a coincidence. He also said Frank helped Sheryl with the body after she hit her with a shovel."

We sat silent for a few moments until Clarence spoke again. "So sad all around. Sonya says the family will take Rita's baby back to Mexico."

Elena looked at me with a puzzled expression. "Why Brewster die? He use drugs? He want money for drugs?"

Brewster was the one Lego piece I couldn't place.

I shrugged. "The drug tests won't be back for several weeks. I don't know what they will find." The more I thought about Rex's bruised face and his claim he'd fallen on the ice, the more I wondered if he'd fought with Brewster over the money. "It's possible he and Brewster got into a fight when they discovered Kiley had brought back the wrong backpack. Brewster either crawled back into his van and passed out or Rex shoved him in and left."

We sat in silence for a few minutes, the only sound the hissing of the coffee in the coffee maker.

Finally, I pushed my chair back and stood up. "Unfortunately, I have to figure out what to do about a car. My insurance hardly covers enough to buy a ten-speed bicycle," I sighed. "I'm not sure Bronte will want to ride on the back of one. Meanwhile, Toby is renting me a wreck that gets eight miles to the gallon."

I started for the hallway when Clarence beckoned me back. "Ah, well it turns out I happen to have an extra car that I might consider selling cheap. It was my wife's car. I've been paying Toby to maintain it all these years. It's time to let it go."

At this point, if Clarence's late wife drove a broken down, rusted-out station wagon, I'd take it.

Later that afternoon, I bid farewell to the wonderful old Subaru and slid into a Ford Escape that was the same age as my old car. I was now the owner of an SUV with 1200 miles on it and a gas tank I could hardly afford to fill.

First Christmas in the Cabin

I t took me until Christmas Eve to finish my comments and edits on *The Darkening Sand.* By my third read through I was growing to like the idea of Midgers and young Levy with a magic amulet. If C.P. Dowling could clean it up, address some big holes in the story and delete about 25,000 words, she might be able to find an agent.

In town, the streets were busy with people doing last-minute errands. After I mailed the manuscript, I stopped at the *Times* to wish Jilly a happy holiday.

She assured me things would quiet to nothing by mid-afternoon. "A lot of people around here celebrate on Christmas Eve. My mother, good Norwegian that she was, used to make lutefisk, white sauce, and boiled potatoes for Christmas Eve. You can't imagine how badly the house smelled of dead fish."

I'd already been warned about this dried cod that was reconstituted by soaking it in lye. "Maybe I should try it."

"Not if you value your life. I started a new tradition once my mother was gone. We have pizza."

Driving away from the festive lights of downtown Killdeer into the grayness of the afternoon, I was overtaken by a wave of melancholy. Unlike Thanksgiving with a cabin filled with friends, I had no plans for Christmas. I couldn't afford to fix a big meal and after everything that had happened, I didn't feel particularly festive.

When Mother was still well enough, we always went to Rockefeller Center, rented skates, and wobbled our way around the rink. Mother loved to skate and would tell us about being out on the lake in the winter. As I thought about it now, I shivered, picturing the gaping hole in the lake that nearly swallowed Rex.

At home, Bronte wagged her tail as she greeted me but even she seemed subdued. "Not very jolly, are we?" Despite having my dog by my side, I was lonely.

The pine tree I'd dragged in a couple days ago drooped in a stand in the corner of the living room. I found a string of lights and a few dusty ornaments in a box in the loft. With Bronte watching I put up the lights and topped the tree with an angel who was missing one of her wings. The angel slumped forward. When I tried to fix her, she slumped to the side.

"It figures," I sighed.

After I finished the tree, I flipped through a pile of mail I'd been ignoring, afraid of the bills. Wedged in between the local advertiser and a Lands End catalog was a thick, creamy envelope. The return address was the law firm that was supposedly working on the year-old lawsuit with the NYPD over my false arrest. I set it aside but didn't open it because I knew they would tell me they'd dropped the suit. I hoped it didn't mean I owed them money.

Bronte and I spent Christmas Eve in front of the fireplace. I didn't even bother to plug the lights in the tree. "Costs money, girl, and the lights are so old they'd probably set the tree on fire."

I gazed again at Mother's painting of the lake with the ghostly mist rising to the dawn. Thinking about her and what an artist she could have been, I retrieved her sketch pad from under the pile of mail. In the undulating light of the fireplace, I flipped through the pages. Her sketches had both a haunting beauty and a darkness to them. In several it was almost as if she was trying to reach for the light. When I turned to the last page, I stopped, stunned.

It was a drawing in black and white of an empty park bench—the bench where we'd seen the sleeping woman all those years ago. Above it, rising in a faint cloud, was the woman, the snow ghost, translucent against the background of the trees. What captured me was the expression of calm and peace on the face of the ghost. Perhaps, as the disease in her brain was taking over, Mother was trying to capture a needed peace. I closed the book and hugged it tight.

The outside was quiet—not even a distant hum of the snowmobile. Jim did not call or text. I'd hardly heard from him since he took over the care of his son. I crawled into bed that night filled with sadness. Bronte settled beside me resting her head on Jim's pillow. "Maybe tonight I'll be visited by some ghosts who will cheer me up." She yawned at me and nestled into the pillow.

Christmas Day dawned clear, sunny, and nearly thirty degrees outside. I fixed coffee and glanced over at my pathetic tree. An empty wine glass sat on the floor by the fireplace. I had a gnawing headache. How much wine had I drunk in my Christmas Eve melancholy? During the night the tree had sagged even more. The one-winged angel tilted to the right like she wanted to lie down. "Sad."

I opened my laptop to check my finances and closed it before loading the page. Maybe I'd go for a ski and try to shed this dark cloud. As I finished my coffee trying to work up the energy to take a shower, I spied the cream-colored envelope.

"Might as well get the bad news over." I opened it slowly my head filled with all the bad information it probably held.

I had to read it twice to take it in. "Oh my god!" No, the lawyers hadn't totally settled with the city, but they had gotten a preliminary reimbursement for my expenses. The money was being electronically transferred to my checking account. Quickly I logged into the bank account and there it was! "Bronte! It's enough to keep us here until spring! Hallelujah!"

Bronte woofed with excitement. Her woofing turned to a genuine bark, her tail wagging so hard I thought she might fall over. "Hey, I'm glad you're happy. But aren't you overreacting?"

She was now at the door barking. I glanced out the window to see the red of Jim's pickup truck. He was opening the passenger door and as I watched, a little boy wearing a bright orange stocking cap jumped down.

He giggled, pointing at a squirrel.

When I let Bronte out, she nearly toppled little Jake in her enthusiasm.

They took to each other immediately. Perhaps it was her maternal instinct, but she followed him around the rest of the day. I had to admit that Jake was pretty cute with eyes that sparkled with delight at the sad looking Christmas tree.

An hour later another car pulled up and Clarence, Joe, and Elena stepped out. Next came Rob and Brad and finally Travis. The only guest from Thanksgiving who couldn't make it was Norma. She was spending the holiday on shift at the hospital.

By midafternoon the cabin filled with my friends for an impromptu Christmas celebration. Jim confessed to putting it together after he received a "pathetic" text from me about my pathetic Christmas. I'd sent it last night after going through my mother's sketch pad and finishing a bottle of wine.

Everyone brought something to eat including a small sampling of lutefisk. They stood staring at me as I tried it.

"Well?" Brad pressed. "What do you think?"

I made a show of savoring it before swallowing. "Not bad. I think I'll have some more...next year."

The little tree, now lit up by the bedraggled lights, looked as festive to me as Sheryl's glittering living room.

Midway through our thrown-ogether potluck, Elena stood up and announced. "I think I have baby."

I stared at her. "Here? Now?"

She laughed. "I go to hospital, okay?"

Joe and Travis helped her out to Clarence's car. Travis took charge. "Joe, you drive. I'll count contractions."

The Christmas baby was born before midnight with Joe by Elena's side. While Jake slept soundly on the couch with Bronte at his feet Jim and I settled in for a long winter's nap—and a few Midger moves.

Acknowledgements

Thank you to Gabriel Valjan who went above and beyond to help me with the Spanish in this book. He also advised on treatment for hypothermia. Mark Roberts was an extraordinary reader who was refreshingly honest in pointing out mistakes in grammar and inconsistencies in the story. Terry and Kathy Dunklee helped me with details on ice fishing, ice depth and cross country skiing. Jerome Norlander, of course, put the commas in the right place. Thank you to my agent Dawn Dowdle and my editor Shawn Reilly Simmons. Last but not least, thank you to Nadia Swift and Gus Norlander who were invaluable in helping me with the storyline.

About the Author

Linda Norlander is the author of A Cabin by the Lake mystery series set in Northern Minnesota. Previous books in the series include *Death of an Editor* and *Death of a Starling*. Norlander has published award-winning short stories, op-ed pieces and short humor featured in regional and national publications. Before taking up the pen to write murder mysteries, she worked in public health and end-of-life care. Norlander resides in Tacoma, Washington, with her spouse.

SOCIAL MEDIA HANDLES:
https://www.facebook.com/authorlindanorlander
https://twitter.com/LindaNorlander

AUTHOR WEBSITE:
https://www.lindanorlander.com/

Also by Linda Norlander

The Cabin by the Lake Mysteries
  Death of an Editor
  Death of a Starling

CPSIA information can be obtained
at www.ICGtesting.com
Printed in the USA
BVHW042237200523
664579BV00005B/117